Readers love *Who Knows the Storm* by TERE MICHAELS

"*Who Knows the Storm* is a great, fast-paced action/thriller with a strong focus on family."
—Boys in Our Books

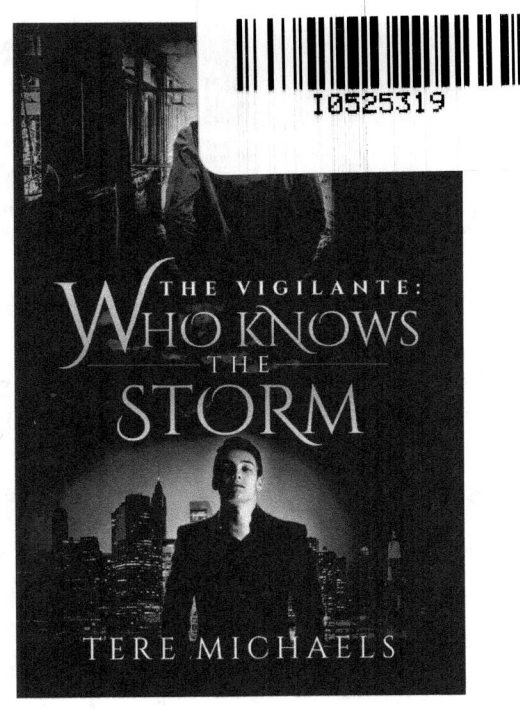

"A whole lot of suspense, an element of danger and a well woven storyline made this book a must read…"
—MM Good Book Reviews

"…this book IS sexy! *Who Knows the Storm* IS definitely worth checking out!!"
—The Blogger Girls

"This is a story that I will enjoy reading again and again."
—Prism Book Alliance

"This was the appetizer round… I am ready and waiting for the next course."
—It's About The Book

By TERE MICHAELS

Groomzilla
One Holiday Ever After (Multiple Author Anthology)
One Night Ever After (Multiple Author Anthology)

FAITH, LOVE, AND DEVOTION
Faith & Fidelity
Love & Loyalty
Duty & Devotion
Cherish & Blessed
Truth & Tenderness

THE VIGILANTE
Who Knows the Storm
Who Knows the Dark

Published by DREAMSPINNER PRESS
http://www.dreamspinnerpress.com

WHO KNOWS THE DARK

TERE MICHAELS

DREAMSPINNER
PRESS

Published by
DREAMSPINNER PRESS

5032 Capital Circle SW, Suite 2, PMB# 279, Tallahassee, FL 32305-7886 USA
www.dreamspinnerpress.com/

Who Knows the Dark
© 2015 Tere Michaels.

Cover Art
© 2015 AngstyG.
www.angstyg.com
Cover content is for illustrative purposes only and any person depicted on the cover is a model.

ISBN: 978-1-63216-708-8
Digital ISBN: 978-1-63216-709-5
Library of Congress Control Number: 2015944003
First Edition October 2015

Printed in the United States of America
∞
This paper meets the requirements of
ANSI/NISO Z39.48-1992 (Permanence of Paper).

No one saves us but ourselves. No one can and no one may. We ourselves must walk the path.

—Gautama Buddha

True love is selfless. It is prepared to sacrifice.

—Sadhu Vaswani

There is only one day left, always starting over: it is given to us at dawn and taken away from us at dusk.

—Jean-Paul Sartre

BEFORE

THE YACHT sailed under the skeleton of the Verrazano Bridge, around the rusted pylons, and headed south. The captain and crew moved in perfect tandem, all armed, with two of the men patrolling the dock with eagle-eyed attention. Nox leaned against the port railing, welcoming the sun on his face and shoulders after being in that dark restaurant for so long. He watched the horizon, not the disappearing skyline behind him. He would rather think about the future.

Except....

A noise alerted him to the presence of someone else on the deck. He turned his head to find Rachel, a blanket wrapped around her shoulders, coming to stand next to him. They hadn't seen her for dinner, or the quick head count Nox insisted on.

His back stiffened; despite her seeming change of heart, Nox still couldn't relax around Jenny.

Rachel.

"I meant what I said." Nox let his gaze briefly rest on the choppy water below.

Rachel turned slowly to face him; in the scant light, he saw one eyebrow raised and a smirk of amusement on her face. "My word wasn't good enough the first time?"

"I don't trust you," he murmured, low and urgent. Sam slept belowdecks, with Mason keeping watch. The crew, sleeping in shifts, was nowhere near. Cade had been in the shower when Nox had said he needed some air.

"You should learn to let go of the past, Nox. It was a long time ago, and we're all different people," she said, steely and calm.

"You're still a murderer."

Rachel laughed. "So are you, my darling."

They stood in silence as the boat streamed through the water and out to sea.

"I'm curious—is Mr. White dead?" Rachel asked, breaking the quiet as the sun set completely in the distance.

Nox tightened his grip on the railing. "Yes."

"You know, then?"

"Yes."

"Mmm." Rachel pulled the blanket around her shoulders to shield her neck and jaw. "Another thing to keep from young Sam."

"He's never going to know," he responded calmly, finality in every syllable.

"About Mr. White? About your shared lineage?" Rachel tipped her head to one side, that smirk still dancing around her mouth. Behind them, a light went on, bathing them both.

"None of it." He reached out, grabbed her upper arm, and squeezed it. "They're all dead—my mother and father, that piece-of-shit rapist." Nox paused. "Jenny."

Rachel stared at him long and hard, then smiled. "True," she said softly. "And Rachel is just some nice woman who helped you and Sam in your time of need. A friend of Cade's. You're his devoted father, who would do anything to protect him. All is right in his world."

Nox's stomach knotted. Every instinct reminded him Rachel could not be trusted. He didn't answer her, just kept their gazes locked until she looked away, and then he dropped his hand from her arm.

"Change of subject?" Rachel asked.

He was just about to turn away, eager to check on Sam. Eager to crawl into bed with Cade. He paused a moment, though, his muscles tense as he waited. "What?"

"We got away pretty easily," she said, head tilted to one side. "No one's after us so far."

Nox frowned. "I made sure...."

"Someone knew you were at the restaurant. They sent Damian and I there, but not the cops," she mused. "Damian got a boat, found the only trustworthy crew in the city, apparently. Got an injured teenager, a cop, and several people with warrants out for their arrest all the way here without even a tail. For suspect number one, you sure didn't attract attention." At the end of her little speech, she paused. "Ever wonder—why didn't they just kill you?"

Her words took him aback, moving him a literal step back; then he turned on his heel and let his conflict over Rachel's question fuel him down belowdecks. His emotions focused his physical movement, even as his mind bounced around.

Sam being let out of jail.

The warning when they could have easily put a bullet in his head. Getting out of the Iron Butterfly in enough time to save their lives.

In the master stateroom, Sam lay curled up under the blankets, Mason's upper body spooned around him, one leg on the floor, his sidearm visible. Protecting Sam.

Nox felt gratitude and a pang of sadness at the same time, anger whooshing out of him like a pricked balloon. He'd done his best, getting them away from the city, away from the people trying to hurt them. Wanting answers took a backseat—at least for a moment.

He closed the door quietly and made his way to the smaller bedroom on the opposite side of the deck.

Nox moved in the darkness, making his way around the tiny stateroom. Their gear was stashed on top of a dresser in the corner, moonlight creating patterns as it shone through the round window over the bed. He stripped down to his underwear, silent and stealthy, his gun tucked under the mattress for the best access.

Clad only in boxers, Cade slept on, flat on his back, arms akimbo.

A spike of relief shot through Nox as he settled next to Cade. The mattress dipping roused Cade; he turned his head with a quiet sound of confusion.

"Shhh, go back to sleep," Nox whispered, but Cade struggled to open his eyes even as he pulled Nox closer.

"Everything okay?"

"Fine." Nox pressed a kiss against Cade's ear. "Everything's fine."

Cade sighed, winding around him until Nox was a prisoner in the bed, trapped by the bulk of his lover's body. Cade used him like a mattress, pressing him down as he got comfortable.

"Go to sleep," Cade murmured into Nox's chest. "We're safe. Go to sleep."

Nox didn't argue, didn't share the turmoil burning through his brain. They weren't yet safe—they'd gotten away. Nox's main concern was elevating their circumstances so Sam would be all right. So Cade was safe. They were going to South Carolina, and maybe everything would be okay.

Even as Nox's heart steadied, with Cade in his arms, his brain refused to quiet.

Why didn't they just kill you? Why?

Interlude

NOX BOYET is tired.

No—no, he's exhausted.

He's depleted of everything—hope and energy and the ability to raise his head off the pillow.

And the only reason he hasn't gotten the gun hidden in the top of his closet and blown his brains out is the child sleeping next to him on the bed. Killing himself would mean killing his brother—his flesh and blood, his everything.

His son.

The snow is piled up outside, higher than the first floor windowsills. What little progress has been made repairing the neighborhood—the backhoes in the distance, the delivery of building materials to the store on the corner—was obliterated by the nor'easter dumping wet snow amid lightning and wind for the past three days.

There isn't even the hope the National Guard will come by and offer to rescue them, because the Guard are long gone, like most of the people who used to live here.

Nox feels the weight of living push him down into the mattress. He's moved most of their supplies up here to his bedroom. Canned food and bottles of water, the lanterns and flashlights—remnants of his mother's paranoia—are all stacked around the bed in easy reach. Wadded-up towels block every window and door in a futile attempt to keep out the cold air.

He doesn't want to get out of bed, out from under every blanket in the house.

The townhouse shakes and shudders under the assault. He vaguely wonders if it wouldn't be a blessing if it crashed down on top of them—while Sam is asleep, and while Nox just doesn't give a damn.

For five years he's been pushing through. He's protected his brother and raised him as best he can. Sam is a good kid with a friendly smile; he has more patience under the circumstances and hardship than Nox could have imagined having at that age. In his limited capacity of "fatherhood," Nox thinks Sam is actually the strongest person in their fractured little family. So many days when things don't go right—when the neighborhood violence feels like it's going to come through the walls, or more mundane things like electricity fluctuations or water shortages that mean he can't wash clothes or flush the toilets, or Sam is scared or sick or mad—Nox wants to cry with the helplessness.

His biggest accomplishment since that terrible day five years ago is keeping himself and Sam alive.

Sometimes it's not enough.

The realization that he's almost twenty-one, that they are alone—utterly and completely alone—has infected his bones like a vicious virus lately. The lack of adult human contact cuts into him in a way he didn't imagine possible. He wants his confused mother and his distant father with a hunger that brings him to his knees.

He just wants more.

Sometimes he thinks of joining those people on the streets, the ones who live in the burned-out and abandoned houses that surround them. They take what they want and join together in gangs and packs to survive. There's no honor, he knows that—how many of them beg him before he destroys their weapons and drugs? How many of them offer to give up other dealers?—but it tempts him. They wouldn't care who he really is; they would help him hide from...

The drug dealers who had killed his father.

The tangled web wraps around his neck and squeezes. In the end he just has Sam and his own cracked moral compass.

Sam startles in his sleep, whimpering a little as he tightens his grip around the stuffed cat in his arms. It is an old toy from Nox's childhood, a memento found in his mother's closets a few years ago, and a reminder that Natalie—for all her difficulties and delusions—had loved him.

He cried for a day, clutching the stupid orange tabby while Sam gurgled clueless in his makeshift bassinet.

That cat stays in Sam's arms while he sleeps, as they both hope to ward off the night terrors that seized Sam recently. Another thing that makes Nox feel so helpless.

So, so helpless.

"Shhh, it's okay, Sam," Nox murmurs, brushing his hand over Sam's too-long curly black locks. They both need baths and clean clothes and clean sheets and something fresher than the endless cans of beans and soggy vegetables they've been consuming.

Or maybe the house will fall down on top of them, and it will all be blessedly over.

Now

SLEEP ELUDED Nox.

Cade's gentle puffs of breath, his nearness and warmth as he lay with his back to Nox, the gentle rocking of the boat—they were so alien, so triggering to Nox's insomnia that even the act of closing his eyes felt impossible. The questions hanging over his head gave way to the spiraling paranoia that had plagued him for so long; he felt like he was in the guillotine, awaiting execution.

Any second the blade could drop.

Were they really safe?

Was the ship being followed?

Where was his gun?

His body jerked, provoking a disruption in Cade's gentle breaths. Nox held perfectly still until Cade's rhythmic breathing settled, then zeroed in on the shadowed spot where the gun was.

The Sig, even hidden within his reach under the mattress, felt too far away.

If he were home, he would still be on patrol—circling the blocks of his territory, knocking off dealers and wandering users.

He'd still be performing an exercise in futility.

Nox blinked up at the shadows, his body humming with unspent energy and anger. All those nights, all those years, sacrificing his sanity and his body, protecting his corner of the city—they meant nothing in the end. The bigger picture spoke of something far uglier than people a few hits and bad decisions away from death wandering into his neighborhood.

He needed to find out more about the man in the warehouse, the one behind the death and disaster raining down on the city.

He wanted to know where Mr. White got his messages. He needed the names of the people who killed his father, the ones who gave the orders to kill everyone at the sanitarium. Every last person who had contributed to the destruction of his family—Nox thirsted for their identities.

And then what?

Maybe he'd storm back into the city and kill them all, a bloody-handed avenger to punish them for all the destruction they'd brought to his family.

Maybe he'd bring their wrongdoings to light—and in this fantasy someone cared, someone took the weight of retribution from his hands and let him go free.

When Nox thought about his life, when he traveled the extremes—wealth to poverty, normalcy to chaos—he felt keenly aware of his lack of power. He saw the manipulation, the decisions made by people he'd never met, turning his reality into a nightmare.

But in the end, it was the knowledge that Sam would have died with his mother that shook Nox to his very marrow and fed his anger. Maybe he could walk away from all of it, but not from Natalie, and not from Sam.

He gasped in the dark, the weight of knowledge pressing down on his heart. The pounding thud of its beat filled his ears until it was the only thing he heard.

One choice he'd made, one decision.

That was all it took to change the course of his world.

The decision to leave the city made perfect sense—Sam needed a safe place, and Cade didn't belong in that mess. Sailing down the coast was logical.

And none of that very sensible thinking stopped the clanging alarm in his head.

Nox wanted safety. Almost as much as he wanted revenge.

If he didn't have Sam, he wouldn't rest until every last one of them paid for their crimes. But because of his son, he had changed his course.

Logic and vengeance battled each other for his commitment, for his allegiance. And now, panting and gasping in the dark, Nox had another decision to make.

TIME PASSED with Nox's body fighting his brain to peace. He needed to sleep, to relax—his mind wasn't even forming coherent thoughts. He had a sliver of moonlight and the rock of the boat to keep him company, along with Cade's heavy weight against him.

With a sharp intake of breath, Cade began to move, rolling back against Nox with a shiver. Instinctively Nox reached around to pull him close, and their bodies shifted together like matching puzzle pieces. Cade made a sound of contentment as they touched, then deepened the contact as he ground his hips back—against Nox's suddenly interested dick.

Distraction beckoned. For a moment he could shove aside his incessant circular thinking, push aside the exhaustion and inability to rest that were wearing at him. He trailed his hand down Cade's arm, following the curve of muscles and warm skin, then circled his wrist for a moment before retracing his path back to his shoulder.

"Mmm," Cade murmured, twining his legs between Nox's as he arched sleepily, opening his body—curve of neck, open knees—like an offering that Nox couldn't refuse.

Nox didn't hesitate. He let his hands wander over Cade's chest, teasing pecs through the thin material of his shirt. Cade twisted in response, reaching back to grasp Nox's hip.

The request was now quite clear.

Even the diversion of a tempting Cade in his arms—the press of his dick against the firm tease of Cade's ass, the wordless insistence of satisfaction—couldn't shut down Nox's brain. As much as he wanted to sink into Cade's body....

Nox slid his arm underneath Cade's shoulder and pulled him closer against his chest; he pressed his free hand against the inside of his thigh, urging his legs open wider. Cade made a sleepy sound of confusion that morphed into a guttural purr as Nox tucked his hand up through the leg opening of Cade's boxers.

The sweat-damp warmth of Cade's cock teased under his fingers; Nox let himself play for a moment at the crease of his inner thigh. He manipulated the soft furred sac until Cade started to move his hips. He clasped Cade's dick with a smooth hand and stroked slowly, root to tip, until Cade rocked and moaned, chasing his own pleasure against Nox's hand.

It felt surreal, almost confusing in the silent intimacy of actually knowing a lover, knowing how he sounded when he was close, knowing the jerk and twitch of his body and letting that sound, that scent ignore your own desire.

Like Cade used his hand, Nox used Cade's body to get off, everything damp and rough and speeding up as they fed off each other's need. Nox's breath stuttered as Cade ground roughly against his dick, caught in the trap of Nox's hand and the cradle of his hips.

His hand slick and his orgasm close, Nox rolled them both over, pressing Cade into the mattress. The eager groan, muffled by the pillow, spurred Nox on—he locked his knees on either side of Cade's hips, bracing himself with his free hand.

The sharp sting of rubbing against his shorts, rutting against Cade, kept everything in focus. He rocked with abandon, slotting his covered dick in the valley of Cade's ass, feeling the stiffening of Cade's body as he spilled over Nox's palm.

It hurt as he pulled his hand free, and somehow that fed more movement, faster until the combination squeezed his balls and he came in his shorts somewhere around the small of Cade's back.

He collapsed next to Cade, breathing frantically. The sway of the boat caught up with him for a moment, knocking the ground out from under him until he felt like the bed was floating.

Cade didn't turn over or say anything. His quiet gasps didn't morph into anything else.

They lay there in silence, Nox closing his eyes until the room regained gravity.

Exhaustion snuck up on him, his body overwhelming his mind as he finally dropped off to sleep.

CHAPTER ONE

SOMETIME BEFORE dawn, Cade gave up trying not to be so damn awake.

Lying facedown on a bed next to a sleeping lover with come drying in his shorts was in no way a new experience, but something about the circumstances—and this particular man—kept his eyes stretched open to the point of pain.

The past few days left him weary and bruised, inside and out. The memory of Billy's dead, bloody body followed him through dreams and moments of stillness; he wanted to move and run and distract himself until he couldn't feel the slick on his hands. The violence he wanted to outrun was currently breathing beside him, of course, leaving him with a fluttering anxiety in his chest.

He gathered up the scattered clothes, strangely unnerved by the fact that he could sneak out of the bed and putter around the room without Nox waking up. Shouldn't he be jumping up like a crazy person, gun in hand and trigger finger itchy, not lying there, still as a stone and breathing shallowly?

It was just a flicker of movement when Cade stepped close to the bed to get his boot; he realized Nox hadn't been asleep at all. An act, pretending so he could... what? Watch Cade?

A knot formed in Cade's stomach; he moved faster after that, eager to remove himself from scrutiny. He disappeared into the bathroom with his clothes and a tiny grooming kit, raced through a whore's bath—enough water to clean off the come and layer of sweat permeating his skin—and dressed before he headed out to the main space.

For somewhere quiet and safe to freak the fuck out.

The galley of the yacht wasn't huge, but it was sufficient and reasonably stocked with a few perishables and a great many cans; the first mate had showed Cade where everything was and how to operate the cooktop the night before, when they'd all wearily eaten lukewarm soup before tumbling into bed.

"It started with a letter," he muttered to himself, as he made too much bacon and turned every slice of bread into overbuttered toast. "A stupid letter, because I couldn't say no."

He could regret it—saying yes to Mr. White's request, going back again to confirm his suspicions about his mysterious client "Patrick Mullens"—but something about his involvement in this hot mess felt like…

Predestination.

It was a word he would never say aloud to anyone, but in his bones, he felt it. Whatever the outcome of this crazy ride—which would most likely end with him in an early grave—it felt meant to be.

A fucked-up fairy tale.

"Morning."

Cade turned to find Rachel in the doorway, dressed uncharacteristically casual in black jeans, boots, and a long-sleeved gray T-shirt, her long red hair in a braid over one shoulder. She was familiar—comforting in a way, even if Nox bristled and growled every time she breathed. Whatever her sins of the past, it was because of her they had been able to save Sam and get out of the Iron Butterfly alive.

"Hey. Please tell me you like bacon and carbs."

"If there's coffee, I'll like anything."

Cade gestured toward the oversized coffee machine currently chugging its way through the last stages of brewing.

"Far be it from me to minimize our current dire situation, but I already miss room service," Rachel said lightly as she leaned against the counter to watch Cade put the last of the greasy bacon on the platter.

He snorted in response. "Room service, heat, my closet at the Butterfly." His heart squeezed a little as he thought about Killian, his friend and dresser, and the other people he'd worked with for the past few years. How many of them were dead in the rubble of the casino back in the District?

Rachel seemed to recognize his frown, her own face softening in response. "Maybe we can ask Damian to access a list of who…."

Cade was already shaking his head. He didn't want to know names, connect them to the faces of friends and coworkers. He could barely keep it together as it was.

"I just wish I knew where Alec disappeared to," he murmured.

Rachel turned to unhook the pot from the coffee machine. "He left," she said, her voice back to its usual cool take-no-prisoners tone. "He took off before everything went down."

Cade picked up the platter and exhaled. "We both know that's not true, Rachel."

Resolutely Cade walked to the table to place their makeshift breakfast in the center. There was already a stack of small plates and napkins, and the small container of jam from the yacht's refrigerator. It would have to do until they arrived in South Carolina.

Another thing he didn't want to think about.

"What do you think happened, then?" Rachel asked from behind him. She came to the table, coffee mug in hand.

"You lied and said he was working when he wasn't...."

"Trying to keep Zed off his back."

Cade shook his head. "No one had seen him for over a week, he didn't answer his phone, his apartment was cleared out."

"Right. He left. I tried to cover for him, to see if he'd come back, but he didn't. Not even a call." Rachel sat down on one of the two padded benches flanking the table. If Cade closed his eyes, they were back in her office, Rachel strong and in control and Cade hoping to stay on her good side.

But his eyes were open, and gratitude didn't mean obedience, not now.

"That's not really your style, Rachel," Cade murmured, looking her right in the eye.

She tilted her chin, defiant and poised, even as a fugitive, even plunked down in the middle of the ocean, sans makeup and security guards.

"I covered for you, my love, many times." She exaggerated cocking her head to one side, as if examining him. "Alec had a big mouth, which tended to get him in trouble. He asked the wrong questions of the wrong people."

Cade's breath wavered.

"I told him he might reconsider his working and living arrangements and not leave a forwarding address."

"He wouldn't leave without saying good-bye to me," Cade said softly. "We were too good friends."

Rachel dropped her gaze to her coffee mug and gripped the white porcelain sides. "Cade, you have a great deal to learn about loyalty."

Before Cade could respond, he heard shuffled footsteps behind him.

"God, is that coffee?" Damian moaned.

Once upon a time, Cade would have been dodging Damian and his angry scowl, afraid of the consequences of a bad night or complaining customer. Now, he poured a cup of coffee for a middle-aged, round-shouldered Korean man who was just as homeless as he was.

They sat around the little table, picking at the bacon and toast in between cups of coffee. It felt like old times—if old times didn't include Damian existing three feet away from Zed, or Rachel in one of her sexy get-ups, slinking all over the floor like the administrative siren of hell.

"What happened at the Butterfly?" Cade finally asked when he couldn't manage one more piece of greasy, singed meat. He threw a crust of bread on his used napkin, then looked at his two former supervisors in turn.

Neither would meet his gaze.

"Alec *left*." Cade emphasized the second word sarcastically. "Those men showed up with Sam…. I'm not so naive to think there wasn't organized crime in the District, but at the Butterfly—that wasn't how we operated, at least not out in the open." He exhaled loudly even as he dropped his voice. "They killed Zed. Why? We all knew he had less than savory connections—did he suddenly change his opinions on working with fellow criminals?"

Rachel and Damian had a wordless conversation, one that left Damian ruthlessly shredding his napkin onto the tabletop.

"About a year ago, some men showed up to talk to Zed. He wasn't very happy to see them," Damian muttered. "They wanted a larger cut, for protection and…." He darted a brown-eyed gaze to Rachel, then Cade. "They wanted him to start distributing from the casino."

Cade frowned. "Distributing what?"

"Drugs, darling. More specifically Dead Bolt. Make it available to the guests." Rachel lifted and dropped her shoulders. "Add it to the menu, as it were."

"Are you kidding me?" Cade tried to imagine their clients high on that crap, euphoric, and then the ugly fallout—well, at the very least he'd heard the stories and seen the results, usually under a tarp in the alleys around the less stringently controlled casinos. "And he said no?"

"He said maybe—and show me my cut of the money," Rachel repeated the man's quip. "They balked, he refused, and then all of a sudden...."

"Bomb threats," Cade said suddenly, as things clicked into place.

"Bomb threats. A lack of the police protection we previously enjoyed. Zed agreed to a smaller cut to get his security back, but he didn't want the drugs *in* his casino. Not around his people." Rachel leaned back, then ran her fingers through the ends of her pale red braid, and twisted the hairs almost absentmindedly. "He knew where it would lead and, well, I don't think he wanted the temptation for himself."

With a sharp sound of frustration, Cade finished the dregs of his cold coffee. "So they killed him, took over the Butterfly, and blew it up? Why bother? They could have just kept it. Done what they wanted after he was dead."

"It's the—was also the—smallest casino on the strip." Damian stroked his temple as if to soothe a headache. "Maybe they made it an example. This is what happens when you don't do what we say. We aren't afraid to do what we want." He shrugged. "That's my guess at least."

"I still wonder...," Rachel began, then stopped, lips pursed.

"What?" Cade eyed her shrewdly. Rachel didn't wonder anything—she knew, and if you were lucky she shared the information.

"The text I got, to send us to the restaurant. We wouldn't have found you otherwise."

Damian piped up immediately. "I've been thinking about that. Maybe it was one of the employees—you know there had to be spies. Someone afforded us the same courtesy you gave Alec." He gestured toward Cade. "And him."

"Hmmm" was all Rachel contributed to that scenario.

"Convenient," Cade muttered. The information flooded his already overwhelmed brain as he tried in vain to make the right connections.

His nerve endings jangled with too much everything—stress and adrenaline and memories and threats yet to come. He stood up abruptly, plates clattering.

"I'm going to… uh… I'm going to talk to the captain. See what's happening," he said.

"Shouldn't our great protector be doing that?" Rachel asked, all big eyes and faux frown.

"He's sleeping," Cade said. "And he earned it."

Desperate for some fresh air, he left them sitting at the table.

CADE SAT on the cold deck, regretting wearing only a sweater as the wind whipped by. The captain assured him everything was fine. There might be an edge of a storm to get through farther out to sea, but they were on point to arrive sometime after midnight.

And no, no one seemed to be following them.

Instead of going back downstairs, Cade settled in and watched the increasingly choppy gray water.

"Hey, Cade?"

He turned to find Mason Todd standing behind him, smartly dressed for the weather in a heavy jacket and knit cap, hands shoved in his pockets, pale and looking like a frightened teenager.

"Yeah. Hi." Cade shaded his eyes as the sun burned behind Mason's broad-shouldered form. "What do you need?"

"I talked to the captain…."

Cade smirked. "Me too. He must be really enjoying all the paranoid cops and nosy hookers on board."

Mason shrugged. "I'm sure he doesn't care so long as the cash is in his pocket."

Cade's neck was starting to hurt, so he patted the deck next to him. "Have a seat."

Mason settled down beside him, folding his long body next to Cade's. They sat in silence until Mason coughed awkwardly.

"So—quite a ride," Mason said while Cade leaned back on his elbows. It was a yacht; maybe he'd just pretend he was on a vacation and not fleeing from prosecution and people trying to kill him.

"You could say that."

Mason wrapped his arms around his knees; sometimes Cade forgot the rookie was barely twenty years old and clearly fueled by White Knight Syndrome.

"Regrets?" Cade asked, because he was curious. And because he didn't assume everyone was as crazy as he was.

When Mason didn't speak for a few long moments, Cade worried that the answer would be yes, and while Nox would be delighted, Sam would be heartbroken. And frankly Cade didn't want that kid any sadder or more disappointed.

"No," Mason murmured finally. "I took a solemn oath to uphold the law and I... I don't think that's what I was doing in the city. I was just allowing the wrong people to stay in power."

Cade felt the motion of the boat under his body; it was strangely relaxing. He watched the squalls on the water and felt the bite of the wind against his skin, stinging from the cold water, the briny smell of the ocean. "And now? What do you think you're going to do?"

A tiny shrug was all he got.

I feel ya, kid, Cade thought.

CHAPTER TWO

NOX WOKE up with a start.

He remembered falling asleep for what felt like a moment after the distraction of Cade's body and his own orgasm, but it hadn't lasted long.

Now he lay awake with his eyes shut, trying to find a place to rest his mind. When Cade woke up, Nox hid behind the illusion of sleeping, hoping to avoid conversation.

Whatever Cade wanted to know, it was fairly certain Nox didn't have an answer for him.

Blankets tangled around his waist, Nox pulled himself upright, blinking in the light streaming through the high round window of the cabin wall.

The moment of hazy respite ended as his panic spiked back into action. How long had he slept? Gripping the sheets, Nox listened. The boat continued to move, albeit a bit rougher than last night, and there was neither silence nor chaos above deck. The smell of coffee and slightly burned bacon wafted in from under the door, and voices were heard moving close and then far away. A wash of something—shame? Embarrassment?—drove him to move quickly. Sleeping so late and so soundly was at complete odds with his usual habits.

Nox tumbled out of bed, skin pebbling from the coolness. He found a stack of clothes that weren't his—jeans, a black turtleneck, socks—on top of his boots, and everything else he'd been wearing before bed gone. His other weapons were tucked into his shoes, his gun unmoved from the mattress.

Cade had apparently done some housekeeping.

Cade.

The young man's presence in his life had been necessary these past few weeks. He couldn't have ever imagined needing help, but Cade was there—getting Sam out of jail and then helping Nox rescue him from the Iron Butterfly.

And the rest….

He didn't have any excuse for how far he had dropped his guard since he first laid eyes on Cade Creel.

Dressed after a quick washup in the adjoining bathroom, where a tiny men's grooming kit had awaited him, Nox breathed in and settled his jangling nerves as he opened the door.

The scent of breakfast drew him down the narrow corridor and past the staterooms. Even Sam's room was empty—and therefore devoid of the hovering Mason Todd—and Nox walked a bit quicker.

The part of his life that was "Nox and Sam" had suddenly expanded in ways he didn't know how to navigate.

In the main space, where the kitchen was, Nox stepped into a crowded gaggle of passengers tightly squeezed onto two benches around a square table. Plates of bacon and toast and full mugs of coffee crowded the space, as conversation swelled then died off when Nox's presence registered.

A band of felons and escapees turned to face him and flinched, as if a black cloud had just stepped in front of the sun.

His spine stiffened.

"Dad!" Sam, of course, was the first to greet him, his voice hoarse but cheerful. His glasses long gone, he blinked myopically from under a knit cap, wisps of hair poking out around his face. Swimming in an oversized navy sweater, he was tucked between Mason and Rachel—much to Nox's jaw-clenching displeasure. "There's real coffee!" Sam added and followed that up with a ragged cough.

"Sounds good," Nox murmured, sliding his hands into his pockets, where he felt comforted as his fingers touched the handle of his knife like it was a talisman. "How are you feeling?"

The tiny smile on his son's face gave him the smallest measure of peace. "Better," Sam croaked, then shrugged when his voice seemed to fail him. "Upright at least," he mouthed.

Nox couldn't muster a smile, but he felt his expression soften. "Don't push yourself."

"Mason and Rachel…," Sam started again, but the wheeze-cough of his lungs stopped him in his tracks. The wet sound had Nox moving toward the table out of instinct.

"Mason and Rachel are taking excellent care of you," Rachel interjected, patting Sam on the back as Mason held him by his shoulders. She flicked her gaze to Nox, a charming smile on her face—which stopped him in his tracks. "Some things you don't forget, right? Like riding a bike."

Nox felt the telltale signs of anger return—a flash of red, a throb in his temples, the squeezing of his fists against the fabric of his pants—and tried briefly to decide between shooting her or tossing her overboard. Before he could open his mouth, something else filled his sight.

A smiling Cade.

"Have something to eat before you murder anyone," he said dryly, pressing a mug to Nox's chest. The heat refocused him; the burn reminded him of all the worried eyes pointed in his direction.

"Rachel?"

"Yes, Cade?"

"Behave yourself."

"I have no idea what you're talking about."

Nox wrapped his hand around the mug and nodded at Cade, hopefully letting him know that violence was momentarily off the menu.

"There's bacon. I managed to wrestle enough onto a plate for you," Cade said, his cheerful voice never wavering. "Want to eat up on deck? Blink once for yes, two for no, and three for they'll never find her body."

"We can eat here, that's fine." Nox finally broke eye contact with Cade as he stepped around him to refocus on Sam.

"I did a walk of the ship when I woke up," Mason said, a trickle of nervous chatter in his tone as he refused to make full eye contact with Nox. "Cade and I talked to the captain. He said we should reach Charleston by midnight."

Nox waited for a salute after his report; Mason's hand twitched on the seat back just a few inches from Sam's shoulder, and Nox knew it was right there, under the surface.

"Thanks," Nox mumbled as he slid into the space Cade had vacated. Damian, to his left, shifted over as much as the wall would allow him, a haze of trapped animal coating his eyes. A plate heaped with bacon and four slices of overly buttered cold toast dropped in front of Nox.

Nox looked up to find Cade hovering over him, steaming cup in hand.

"That's the extent of my culinary attributes, but I find everything else I can do makes up for it," Cade said airily as one shoulder rose and fell in a graceful move. "When Sam's feeling better, I'm putting him in charge of this chuck wagon. I've seen him cook chicken—the young man has skills."

Sam and Cade shared a fond smile.

Up close Sam was clearly still suffering the ill effects of his kidnapping and the subsequent destruction of the Iron Butterfly. They could pretend things were better, enjoy breakfast after an actual night's sleep, but Sam's pale complexion and bruised, scratched face, not to mention his labored breathing, told the story that was their reality.

They were fugitives and this was an escape attempt.

"Deal," Sam croaked, as cheerfully as he could muster. He was resting against Mason, as if Mason were the only thing keeping him upright—not that Mason minded, judging by the expression on his face. "I think a little more sleep and I'll be up and around."

A coughing fit followed, and everyone seemed to pretend it didn't sound like Sam's lungs were trying to crawl out through his throat.

"What did I tell you about talking too much?" Rachel murmured, rubbing circles against Sam's back. "Let's give your lungs a break, okay?"

Sam nodded as he wiped his mouth with a napkin. "Sorry," he mouthed, but Nox shook his head.

"We'll get you some paper and a pencil so you don't have to talk," Nox said, shooting daggers at Rachel. How could he hate someone so much and yet feel dependent on her? It turned his stomach violently. He kept seeing her with baby Sam in her arms at the National Guard tent all those years ago, cooing and clutching him so Nox would do whatever she said.

She's Rachel now, not Jenny was a mantra that just didn't cut it.

"What a great idea." Rachel slid out of her seat carefully, a tiny smirk just for Nox. "C'mon, honey, let's get you back to bed. I'll bring you some tea."

The whole thing took less than a minute—Rachel on one side, a nervous-looking Mason on the other, leading Sam back to the stateroom. Father and son shared a tender smile, but then Sam was gone, and Nox's appetite in his wake.

Cade slipped into the seat across from him.

"Eat. We have a ton of shit to deal with, and I need you at your ten thousand percent badass alphaness. We can discuss your issues about your son and his hunky boyfriend later," Cade said lightly, but Nox felt the steel undertones. When he looked up from his plate, Cade's smile was thin.

"I don't like her around him," Nox muttered, reaching for his coffee mug. Beside him, Damian twitched.

"Well aware. But right now Sam needs a caretaker, and the boys need a chaperone, as their puppy eyes are starting to make me nauseous," Cade deadpanned. "She's depending on us to keep her alive. If she wanted to sell us out, we wouldn't have made it out of the harbor."

Nox grunted, because he didn't want to tell Cade he might be right.

He turned his attention to the plate of cold food.

Every mouthful was fuel for his body and a few minutes to clear his mind. The discombobulated feeling of waking up dissipated, along with his automatic reaction of anger every time Rachel opened her mouth. He focused on every peppery burned bite of bacon and every dry scrape of toast. At the bottom of the cup of coffee, Nox found a surge of energy.

"I'm going to talk to the captain," Nox said after wiping his mouth. Cade's attention had drifted during the silent meal, and at Nox's words, he snapped back to earth.

"I already did that."

"I know."

"So did Mason." Cade's grin was fighting to escape his lips.

"Well aware."

"But you're still going to."

Nox gave him a pointed look. "Moving on, we need to find a way for you to reach out to your parents."

Cade sighed, clasping one palm over his eyes. "Not looking forward to that phone call."

"Is this going to be a problem?" Nox asked sharply. Because if there wasn't a farm to hide on at the end of this bullshit, he would have to pull an alternate plan out of thin air. Which was why he didn't bother to depend on other people.

Cade shook his head. "No, it's going to be fine. My father is filled with disapproval about my—well, previous—occupation, but he wouldn't turn me away. My mother will make you all eat a lot of food and sit through a couple of Bible studies. And, well, if there's one person I am sure'll have my back, it's LJ." He blinked at Nox as if registering something new. "Question is—am I telling them the whole story or making up something to ease our way in?"

Nox pushed the plate away, leaning back against the vinyl seat. "You can't lie to them."

"Seriously? Given your cast of alternative identities, I would think you'd be creating a fabrication right off." Cade shot him an annoyed glance.

"The first place the feds are going to look is where you'd most likely show up—home."

"My parents can tell them they haven't seen us."

"And if they're being watched?"

Cade looked irritated, posture straightening as he twisted in his seat. "Then why did you agree to this?"

"We didn't have any other options." Nox ran his fingers through the tangled mess of his beard. "You need to contact them and see if anyone's been asking about us. Then we need a way to get to the farm, where we won't be seen."

"So you're going to the place they'll be looking for us?" an astonished voice asked. Nox and Cade turned in unison as Damian spoke.

"Hide in plain sight," Nox answered. He'd been doing it for years. He flicked his gaze back to Cade. "Can you do that?"

Cade blew out a breath but nodded. "Yeah. I can do that."

NOX HEADED above deck to speak to the captain.

The blast of cold air took him aback; he'd wrongly assumed that heading south meant some relief from the winter up north, but the air was icy and the water churned violently, leaving the deck covered in puddles of water. In the distance, through the growing fog, he could see the faint outline of land.

The damages of the devastating weather patterns that had destroyed his city still littered the Eastern Seaboard. Nox was aware of it—he wasn't entirely a recluse, and while his concerns lay in his immediate vicinity, there was no denying how much wreckage still existed almost twenty years later.

After laying waste to New York City, the superstorms had continued their destructive pounding both up and down the Eastern Seaboard. Some states were spared the full power by a stroke of luck— a timely wind, a lucky turn of the storm—but others felt the assault of Mother Nature like she had a personal vendetta.

Rhode Island to Maryland saw miles and miles of destruction, cities and businesses reduced to kindling. Massachusetts and Maine were a roll of the dice—seaports wiped out when ten miles up the road there were still docks intact. The Carolinas, Georgia, and Florida fared a little better, but some cities never fully recovered from the losses. With so much destruction and so little federal money to spread around, most just accepted the mess and rebuilt farther inland.

Decaying docks and abandoned seaports slipped by mile after mile; in the distant cities, people still went about their daily lives, but everything close to the coast—from New Orleans to Boston—had taken several giant steps back from the waterfront.

Trucking firms cashed in as they carried goods from the docks to warehouses, now relocated miles inland. International shipping became a costly enterprise—it was dangerous work, as even rebuilt structures sat on unstable ground—and everyone paid for it.

And so it went. Some people got richer when the game changed, but many others suffered the ill effects, never to recover their money or stability.

"There's a private dock in Charleston where I have a connection," the captain said as he joined Nox starboard. His inflection on "private" suggested it wasn't luxurious as much as it was controlled by underworld elements. They stood at the railing, watching the boat cut through the angry waves. "You can disembark there."

"What are your plans after the drop-off?" Nox asked casually, resting his hands on the railing. "Back to New York?"

The man at his side barked a laugh. "No. Not a good move in my opinion. My crew and I are relocating to better climes."

Nox didn't bother to ask where.

"Once we're in Charleston, can you recommend anyone for a truck? I'll want to buy it."

"If you have enough money, you can get anything you want."

CHAPTER THREE

NOX WENT back to the stateroom, forcing himself to walk past the closed door where Sam and Mason were staying. The young couple's adoring devotion to each other prickled nervously under his skin. He couldn't help but wonder what would happen when their little band of refugees went their separate ways.

As much as he wanted to be done with Rachel....

When he entered the cabin, all of his and Cade's belongings were spread over the room. Clothes on the bed, shoes on the floor, open bags in the corner. And in the middle, Cade—hands on his hips—surveyed the mess.

The extreme frown on his face didn't quite match the far-flung clothing and general sense of disorder.

Standing in the doorway, Nox coughed to get Cade's attention.

"Oh, hi." Cade didn't even look up. "I'm just... repacking everything."

The fashionable young man slowly disappeared over the past few weeks; Cade wore jeans and a heavy black sweater, far removed from his slim-cut suits and artfully sculpted hair. His dark blond hair fell forward—free of product—absently pushed away now and again as he surveyed the room. No more smooth moves and sensual smiles, no slinking boy with a smart mouth—the frown lines on Cade's face were starting to look permanent.

Nox thought of Sam down the hall, sick and injured, of Mason, whose career was gone in a heartbeat, and here was Cade, so far removed from the world he'd once called home. They were all just literally drifting toward the unknown, untethered from almost everything they'd had before.

He rubbed his eyes, digging in until he replaced the ache with a sharper sting. For so long he'd wondered what it would be like to be free from the prison of the city, and it turned out freedom felt just as confusing.

Nox stepped fully into the room and then shut the door firmly behind him. "You okay? I thought you'd be more excited about going home."

"Mmmm. I have a complicated relationship with home." Cade kicked the base of the bed lightly. "Weird shit with my brother. He's the shining star. He stayed behind while I went off to suck dick professionally, so he could take over the family farm. Doesn't matter that they've been spending my paychecks for the past few years to supplement their income—I'm still the black sheep. Showing up with this ragtag bunch of losers and a warrant hanging over my head? I can't wait for my dad's stern talking-to," he said dryly.

Nox didn't know what to say to that. His own family dynamic, pre- and poststorm, was nothing but an exercise in insanity with very little reference to the real world. Although, the distant father—Nox got that one all too well.

"Maybe we should skip the farm and see what we can figure out at the docks," Nox offered. "Or you could head home yourself without the... baggage."

"That you are," Cade said, dry and vaguely amused, flashing tired blue eyes in his direction. "But Sam—he needs medical attention and a mom to fatten him up. You can't drag him all over the place without a destination in mind. At least not yet."

And that was the bottom line. Nox couldn't come up with a long-term plan until Sam was better. Or until he knew what he was up against.

You know the plan, a small voice muttered in the back of his head. *Hide Sam, then go off and get yourself killed.*

"You're right," Nox said, almost absentmindedly.

Cade responded with raised eyebrows. "I am, aren't I?"

"Even a broken clock is right twice a day." Nox picked up a rolled pair of gym socks and threw them at Cade's head.

"So what do I introduce you as?" Cade's curious gaze roamed over Nox. "To my family?"

Nox shrugged, leaning back against the wall, arms crossed over his chest. "Nox Mullens, your... friend." They certainly weren't just that, but Nox's vocabulary didn't have a word for what they were.

"Right," Cade answered, his tone a bit frostier. He turned his attention back to the stack of clothing. "My friend Nox and his kid and a baby-faced ex-cop and two people I used to work with, one of whom might have been a hit woman of some kind."

"If the authorities have already gotten there, it really depends on what they've been told. I mean, I'm hoping they don't think you capable of bombing a building. That's a good start." Nox pushed off from the wall. He tried not to sink into the spiral of being in a place without his usual contacts or cover. Everything was new and uncertain, and the only person he could trust was Cade.

"Yeah, I know." Cade picked up a black sweater, then threw it back down. He sounded defeated. "I keep pretending things are better, that there's some sort of light at the end of the tunnel and it's not an oncoming train."

Feeling awkward, Nox extended his hand and his fingertips just brushed across Cade's shoulder. It wasn't like he could disagree.

Cade stiffened under the touch. He stepped out of range of Nox's hand, giving him a tight smile. "I'm going to finish packing up, then find something for lunch. Why don't you... uh... check on Sam?"

Nox shoved his hands in his pockets, stepping back toward the door. "Okay."

Cade didn't respond. He went back to the clothes as Nox left the cabin.

SAM WOKE up from his third nap of the day, annoyed as soon as he opened his eyes.

Everything hurt—his chest, his ribs, and his stomach. The coughing irritated every ache and pain, like he'd swallowed broken glass. Every once in a while he'd get a fever, and the slick of sweat over his skin felt like it weighed ten pounds.

He'd never felt this bad. He'd never been this frightened—because his dad looked unsure, and that was something Sam didn't have a lot of experience with. Even the flush of excitement he once dreamed of feeling—off the island, out on the ocean, going someplace else for the first time in his life—he couldn't enjoy a second of it. Things were too up in the air to celebrate freedom.

The only good part of this entire experience was Mason.

With his serious blue eyes and gentle demeanor, Mason made it all easier. He never left Sam alone, he played nurse and bodyguard—even if Sam drew the line at having him play bathroom escort—and his every touch and word was so tender.

In the midst of an unknown future, Sam was in love.

They hadn't kissed or anything, but that was fine. Sam didn't have a clue what he was doing, and their precarious current scenario wasn't exactly conducive to dating.

Understandable if Mason didn't make a move; Sam sure as hell wasn't looking his best these days.

It was fine.

"I got you some water from the galley," Mason was saying as Sam blinked awake. "Do you need anything else?"

Mason stood next to the bed, wearing jeans and a button-down dress shirt, untucked, his blond hair damp. He'd showered while Sam was asleep—and Sam blushed at the thought of Mason in the next room. Naked and….

Yeah.

"Thanks," Sam whispered, suddenly reminded of the pain he was in. He coughed into his hand as he struggled to sit up. Mason, of course, leaned over to help him, his big warm hands on Sam's body, and Sam tried to keep his composure.

Thank God his body was too tired and broken to pop a boner.

Sam sat up and relaxed into the headboard, then watched Mason putter around the room—he straightened the blankets, collected used tissues and empty cups of tea, and readjusted the exact location of the water bottle on the nightstand. Checked his gun.

Sam sighed with absolute adoration.

"You're a great nurse," he murmured, ducking his eyes to the hills and valleys of the blanket over his legs. "You're really good at taking care of people."

"Oh well, thanks. I guess that's my backup option now that I'm not a cop," Mason said lightly.

Sam winced. This was his fault—and his family's fault—that Mason was caught up in all this drama. "I'm—"

"No, it's fine. I made my decisions."

The floorboards creaked a little as Mason walked around the room.

"And hey, if I do decide to be a nurse, my high school girlfriend is an RN in Cambridge. I'll give her a call," Mason said lightheartedly—as Sam's heart sank like a stone in the river.

"Girlfriend," Sam said. At least he thought he did. His mouth was moving, he knew that. Air was being expelled from his lungs. Maybe there was sound, but he couldn't tell over the roaring in his ears.

Wait—had he been wrong this entire time?

"Ex-girlfriend, I should say. We broke up before I moved to New York."

Sam's breath hitched. "Wow, pretty recent." He prayed for a coughing fit, one that would destroy his voice forever so he'd never have to speak again.

"Yeah. It worked out for the best, though." Mason's voice got closer; Sam felt the mattress sink down next to his knees.

He didn't look up.

"I mean, I'd hate to have to call her and tell her that I... I met someone else," Mason said softly.

Sam's breath caught in his throat—and a fit of coughing erupted at the least opportune moment. He slammed his hands down into the mattress as he doubled over. Not even Mason's soothing hand on his back could help; he choked and gasped as his lungs burned and felt like they were twisting in his chest.

It took a few moments to catch his breath; he panted out the precious chokes of air until he could inhale without reacting badly.

Mason murmured comforting words and pushed tissues into Sam's shaking hands. He wiped his mouth and eyes, pretending the tears weren't shameful or emotional but were from the force of his coughs.

"Okay?" Mason whispered, pulling Sam into his arms.

Sam didn't know how to answer that question, so he said nothing, laying his damp forehead against Mason's shoulder, reveling in the warmth of having someone hold him so tenderly.

"I wish I could help you," Mason said, his voice gentle against Sam's ear. "I hate seeing you so sick."

He wanted to say *I'll be fine*, but those words were stuck in his wrecked throat and his terrified heart. He shook his head, an all-purpose answer and the only one he could think of.

"I wish we'd met under better circumstances" were the next words, and Sam jerked in Mason's arms. He leaned back so he could look Mason in the eye.

"I wish…." Mason swallowed; his gaze was locked onto Sam's face, earnest and emotional. "I've never… I mean. I guess I've found some guys attractive, but I uh… I've never…." He looked at Sam pleadingly.

Sam nodded, a tiny smile tugging at the corners of his mouth. "Me neither," he mouthed.

Relief illuminated Mason's expression. "I like you so much," he whispered, leaning closer. "I just don't know what to do."

Feverish and overwhelmed, Sam pressed their foreheads together, shaking as they touched. He wanted to tell Mason they had time, but the truth was, they really didn't know.

"We'll… figure… it… out…," Sam mouthed, his voice just puffs of air. But Mason heard him, because he pulled Sam closer and closer until their bodies were curled around each other.

It felt like heaven, and if this was the worst Sam's body had ever experienced, the simple pleasure of Mason's embrace made everything worth it. His heart pounded, and the warm scent of Mason's body filled his senses. Nothing else mattered.

An aggressive knock on the door drove them apart; Sam whimpered as the sudden move sent his body into another ripple of pain. Mason caught him and then lowered him down onto the pillows.

"Sam?" The knock came again. Mason was already standing up, looking flustered as he pulled at his clothes, as if they had been doing something other than hugging. Sam forced himself not to squeal with joy.

"Yes, sir, you can come in," Mason called, his voice cracking a little.

Sam wanted to point out that Mason didn't have to be afraid of his father—but that was a lie.

Nox opened the door, his face already set in an expression of annoyance, with the protective flush that Sam knew all too well. He imagined the closed door was about to become a thing of the past— even if his father had to remove the thing from its hinges.

He waved weakly, but Nox's face didn't move out of its annoyed rictus.

"Mason, I'm going to spend a little time with my son now," Nox said, measured and cool.

Mason gave Sam a weak smile, then turned to Nox. "Yes, sir, of course. I'll be on the deck."

Nox didn't say another word; he barely moved out of the way so Mason could walk out the door.

Sam wanted to roll his eyes, but even that hurt.

When Mason cleared the doorway, Nox slammed the door shut.

"I brought a pen and paper so you don't have to strain your voice," he said brusquely and walked over to sit on the bed. He produced a small steno pad with a pen clipped onto the side.

"Thanks," Sam mouthed, taking the offered items. Maybe he'd write a letter to Mason, tell him how he felt, what he wanted.

Doodle a few hearts.

Maybe explain how if his father decided to split off from the group, Mason could come with them.

"Use the paper. I want you to get well as soon as possible," Nox said, resting his hands on his thighs.

He wasn't looking at Sam.

That was never a good sign.

Sam flipped the pad open, then uncapped the pen.

"Doing my best," he wrote.

He showed the page to Nox, who nodded, his gaze still aimed toward the headboard, over Sam's shoulder. "I know. I don't mean to rush you. I'm just concerned that we won't be able to stay long with Cade's family. We might have to move again, quickly. But hopefully first, we'll have time to get you well."

"Where can we go? After the farm?" Sam scribbled.

Nox sighed, rubbing Sam's knee over the blanket. "I don't know yet. I'm sorry that I can't give you a better answer, but we'll figure it out."

Sam's stomach plunged. He knew how seriously his father took their safety. He still felt the heat of guilt for his part—even if he didn't quite understand it—in the men who were after them, the ones who had targeted him with the letter.

He wanted to ask if this meant his dream of finding his biological parents was over.

He wanted to ask why these people were after them; was it just because of his father's nocturnal activities?

So many questions, but the defeated look on Nox's face directed his hand to write only one thing.

"I trust you, Dad."

Interlude

SAM IS eight.

In the morning, if the power and Wi-Fi are working, he logs in to his virtual school. He loves all his classes, honestly, especially the ones with teachers who do video chats. There are people from all over the world in his class, kids whose families live in remote locations or in places without enough spots in school. Most have stories about being displaced by the storm, and most remember it because they're all older than he is.

Sam is super smart.

After lunch, he sits back down at the tablet and does his homework. His science teacher, Ms. Begget, gives him extra work and more reading than anyone else. It's not even extra credit. His English teacher does the same, sending him e-books not on their reading list.

Sam is lonely, and this is a good way to fill his time.

His father comes home at five, before curfew, usually tired and distracted. Sam's gotten good at making dinner, though most of the time there isn't much to it. Open some cans, toast some bread. Set their places on the kitchen island, fill two glasses with iced tea he makes himself.

Sometimes Sam eats alone, because his father is in a mood.

On those nights his father changes into his other uniform, straps on his gun, then heads out into the night. Sam hears the beeps on the alarm and knows his job.

Lights out.

Stay in your room.

Keep the door locked.

Cell phone at his side.

Windows covered in heavy drapes.

Some of his schoolmates mention siblings and mothers or other fathers; his Spanish teacher had them discuss grandparents, aunts, uncles, and cousins for two days last week. Sam pretended to be sick so he didn't have to say, "What are those?"

CHAPTER FOUR

THE WEATHER became progressively worse as the day wore on. The captain sent everyone belowdecks while the crew scurried about above them, boots slamming over their heads, as if to add echo and weight to the sense of emergency. Cade's stomach had years of experience on fishing boats with his family on vacations, but the others weren't faring so well; Rachel was the worst, pale and shaking as she lay on the bottom bunk of the tiny bedroom she'd chosen. Damian volunteered to babysit her—Cade assumed that was less out of the pureness of his heart and more that he didn't want to be in the same room as Nox.

Not that he blamed him.

Cade left a few bottles of water and extra towels with Damian, then walked carefully down the hallway to the kitchen. Even steady sea legs couldn't keep him from being tossed from wall to wall as the ocean raged around them.

Sam and Mason were tucked in for the night; he'd checked on them first. They'd given up the pretense of Mason as bodyguard, and now they slept with Sam curled up on Mason's chest, the blankets tucked around them tightly.

Cade felt a weird pang under his ribs when he saw them, their faces utterly content in the thin light from the hallway. If he had to put a name to it, it was probably jealousy moving over his mood in waves.

Back in the galley, at the kitchen table, sat Nox, cleaning his knife and looking slightly green around the edges. Cade observed the tightly coiled body under the mismatched clothing and felt his own growing realization. Nothing about his feelings made sense; quiet and safety were not possible with this man. There would always be danger and stress if he stayed on this ride. He wouldn't get rich or even find that sweet spot where you didn't have to struggle or scrape.

There was no way back, and the future was a hazy shade of confusion. The smart move was to walk away.

"Been a while since you were yachting?" Cade asked, startling Nox.

Nox gave him a strange look. "A few times on the Staten Island ferry when I was a kid. We took a class trip I think," he said absently, running the cloth around the heavy blade and curved handle, half worshipful and half ritual.

"You want something to eat?" Cade fidgeted, braced against the countertop.

Nox shook his head, gaze back to his knife. "Not a good idea."

"I shall write a strongly worded e-mail to the cruise director when we disembark," Cade quipped before he carefully made his way to take a seat opposite Nox.

They sat in silence, or rather just not talking, because nothing was quiet in the wake of the storm. Moans and squeals, the crash of waves, shouts from above deck as they rocked and shook, rising and falling at the mercy of the water.

There was a metaphor in there, but Cade's brain refused to let him poke at it. He laid his head on his folded arms, watching Nox—in need of a shave, a haircut, and possibly twenty years of therapy—and tried to come up with words to explain this man to his family.

Deliver an impassioned speech on his feelings; share exactly why this man was the first he'd brought home to meet them, this man so difficult to explain. What were they to each other, exactly?

Good question.

The yacht gave up a mighty groan, listing to the right suddenly and violently, throwing Cade across the floor.

"Shit," Nox said above him. Dazed, Cade felt a strong hand grip his jeans at the waistband, then was yanked to his feet. "Go to Sam's room."

Cade didn't hesitate or argue. Bruised hands in front of him, he grabbed on to bolted-down furniture, then the walls in the hallway, falling twice before he reached Sam's door.

NOX HAD just enough time to pocket the knife before the boat reversed its dramatic lean. He slipped and hit the wall violently, bruising his shoulder as he tried to grab something, anything to keep from falling. Something in the distance crashed to the floor—he heard everything behind the cabinet doors straining to get out.

It felt like one more wave would rip the yacht apart.

Above deck he could do nothing, but the almost animalistic desire to get out drove him to desperation. Trapped—they were going to die when the hull cracked open and the water rushed in....

Nox gulped back the terror, swamped by the sense memory of cold, dank water and his baby brother tucked into his jacket.

"Nox! Nox!" He heard his name screamed, his eyes opening when he didn't remember closing them.

Cade's terrified face greeted him from across the room; he clung to the doorframe, white-knuckled. The lights flickered then died, and Nox made his decision—he pushed up, then threw himself toward where Cade stood precariously, one hand reaching for him.

Nox grabbed Cade's hand as the emergency lights lit up the darkness.

Interlude

JENNY'S HANDS don't shake because she is a professional and she's going to live through this nightmare.

Period.

She knows Nox is just looking to make a break for it, and part of her wants to say "fine, fuck you, good luck with that" before sailing away on the ferry. But he's insurance if things don't go as she planned.

The papers, tucked into a sealed plastic bag, press against her back.

There's also the fact that he's a teenager and that new little baby isn't going to last long with just him.

Jenny wishes she didn't give a shit about that baby.

A phantom ache makes her momentarily sick to her stomach; she refocuses on the next step. Get onto the ferry, get them the fuck out of this hellhole.

She pays the conductor a wad of bills, flashes her big eyes in his direction until he directs her to the little huddle of people off to the side of the loading entrance. His own personal moneymaking collective.

"Let me get my brother," she yells over the din of hysterical, and nonpaying, New Yorkers, all scrambling to fit on the ferry. The man—distracted by some pushing and shoving—nods.

Jenny turns to where she left Nox; when their eyes meet, she sees he's going to bolt. It's written across his stupid, determined face, the way he clutches the baby close to his chest. She takes a step in his direction, the entire moment freezing down to their locked gazes.

You idiot, she thinks. *You fucking idiot, you have no idea.*

Nox's chin goes up as he begins to step backward, bumping into the throngs of terrified sheep.

It's more ego than anything else that moves her feet, but she only makes it a few steps before things go crazy.

The National Guard—who have been not so patiently herding people into a line—suddenly spring into action. Floodlights drown the area, blinding everyone. People shout and shove as someone comes over the loudspeaker and directs them to move quickly.

Everything escalates. Jenny gets picked up by the swelling crowd and tossed among the crying and screaming New Yorkers as they struggle to move. Furious, she throws elbows, trying to get free.

She ends up on the boat.

Nox is out of sight, lost in the sea of humanity. Jenny falls to the deck, her will to live and quick reflexes the only reasons she doesn't get trampled.

They aren't even fully loaded as the ferry begins to move away. Shrieks accompany the roar of the engines, the lurch of the boat on the violent waves. Jenny scrambles to the edge of the deck, pressing against the handrail in a desperate attempt to stand up. The boat lifts and then crashes, throwing passengers every which way. She hears bodies hitting the water.

Holding on for dear life, she hears a violent crash and gunshots before everything lurches *one last time*.

RACHEL HUDDLED on the floor of the largest stateroom, a blanket wrapped around her as she shivered in fear. Cade had come to get her after the lights went out and had brought her into the large cabin where Sam was recuperating. And now they were all braced in the room, waiting to ride out the storm or drown—whichever came first.

She couldn't begin to give a shit about anything but her own bitter irony that she was going to die at the hands of the ocean after all.

"I didn't pull myself out of the fucking water to have this happen," she muttered, forehead to her knees as another groan of the yacht sounded like the closest to a death knell that they'd heard so far. "I didn't survive for... this."

"Rachel?" Cade's voice cut through the darkness, the weak beam of a flashlight reaching her corner.

"What?" she snapped, irritated by the heavy wetness of her voice and the very real desire to have him come over and put his arms around her.

"I'm coming over there."

Murmurs and thumps followed, and the little light came closer until Cade collapsed next to her in a graceless heap.

Shaking, Rachel pretended she wasn't about to cry when he wound an arm around her shoulders and pulled her tight against his side.

"Shouldn't you be with your boyfriend?" Rachel murmured, tucking in close against him.

"He's not a cuddler, even in the face of death," Cade said lightly. She could feel his tremors, far deeper than just the teeth-rattling movements of the boat. "Damian's praying in the other room—I didn't want to interrupt, and a threesome with Sam and Mason on the bed seemed a bit excessive as a last hurrah." He had a death-grip hold on her. "So this is shitty."

"I fucking hate boats," she whispered. "I hate the ocean. I hate this entire fucking life."

"Agreed."

Rachel grasped a fistful of Cade's shirt; the dark made it easier to reach out for a human touch, to be vulnerable. And since they were probably going to die in the next hour or so, why the fuck not?

Something crashed outside the door, causing them both to jump. There was a bit of commotion on the other side of the room; Cade shone his flashlight in its direction.

Nox, gun drawn, was up, Mason a few steps behind.

"You can't shoot a storm," Cade yelled, but they ignored him. "What the hell?"

"Someone's down here," Nox said, then snapped his fingers at Cade. "Shut off the light."

Sam's ragged cough began as Cade turned off the flashlight. Drowning suddenly felt secondary to whatever Nox and Mason were reacting to on the other side of the door.

The sudden blast of gunshots made Rachel dive for the floor, unhanding Cade as she fell onto her stomach, shielded by the bed. But there were no flashes in the bedroom, no smell of a discharge.

The sound was coming from outside.

CHAPTER FIVE

CADE MOVED on instinct as Rachel hit the floor. He crawled to the bed and felt around frantically until he grabbed Sam's leg. Sam slid over the side and into his arms just as the sound of the door being wrenched open filled the room.

Shouts. More gunfire, this time closer but still outside the room. Sam was heaving for breath next to him. Cade tamped down his own surge of fear and wrapped an arm around Sam's middle to hold him close.

"Clear!" Mason yelled as the gunfire stopped abruptly.

"Cade!" That was Nox.

He raised his head enough to call back. "We're fine. I got Sam."

No response came. Cade heard men's voices, the thump of something hitting the floor, and then another thump—bodies, probably dead bodies, because, oh God, he knew what that sounded like. A wave of nausea overwhelmed him.

"What should we do?" Sam whispered nervously, snapping Cade back to the moment and away from the specter of Billy, dead on the floor.

"Just stay here till your dad comes back," Cade answered, pushing up onto his hands and knees. "Stay down, okay?"

"Take your own advice," Rachel bitched, still flat on the floor on the other side of Sam.

"It's fine. They yelled clear."

You're an idiot, his brain said.

He didn't dare turn on the flashlight, unsure that the danger had passed. More thumps and crashes sounded, farther away from the stateroom. Cade peeked over the top of the bed, but in the darkness he couldn't make out anything clearly. Mason and Nox were presumably in the main living area of the yacht; Rachel and Sam were curled up next to him—

Damian.

"Damian!" Cade whispered loudly, crawling around the foot of the bed. "Damian?"

"Here" came a weak whisper from somewhere outside the stateroom.

"Are you okay?" Cade got as close as he dared, the smell of gun discharge strong—and the stink of blood familiar. Swallowing, he ducked his head around just enough to catch the outline of Damian tucked up against the wall.

"Yeah, yeah." His shaky voice hitched and squeaked. He sounded like Cade's insides felt. "I'm fine."

"Come in here. Go stay with Sam and Rachel, okay?"

The scent of fear was ripe, as was the metallic tang to the air; Damian inched over him, then crawled back around the bed. Cade waited a moment until he heard Rachel's and Sam's whispers and Damian responding. He took a second to ground himself in courage before he followed the sounds of men's voices down the hallway.

Nox and Mason, and the captain. The boat continued to rock and shake, but Cade realized—beyond his own nervous shiver—the violence of the storm had started to subside.

He crept to the end of the hall, steadfastly ignoring the blood draining from the body on the floor. At the doorway he paused and made out dim figures thanks to the emergency lights.

"How many?" Nox's fury couldn't be contained.

"Just the one. Must've stowed away," said the captain, sounding choked and winded.

Nox made a sound of disgust. "Your crew—"

"Two of my guys are dead," the captain snapped. "You want to interrogate the rest of them? You'll have to wait—they're busy trying to steer the boat back on course at the moment."

Silence reigned as the boat shifted again, another dramatic wrench to the side, but moments later the rocking slowed down.

"I'm going topside."

No one said another word as the captain stomped away.

Murmurs, then Mason and Nox talking quietly; Cade couldn't stand another second.

"What the hell happened?" he asked, revealing himself. The chatter stopped as both figures turned in his direction.

"A stowaway with a gun, from what they could put together. Hiding in the engine room. Shot the first mate and another crewman before taking control of the ship's steering, aiming us for the heart of the storm. No ID, just a nondescript guy in black clothes carrying a cheap gun."

"One guy?" Cade asked after Nox finished his story. They were huddled under the emergency light near the stairs. "To kill everyone?"

"He was redirecting the ship—maybe a rendezvous point?" Mason interjected. "Move us to where the others could...."

"An awful lot of trouble to kill us now on the open water. Why not just do it at the docks?" Nox muttered.

"Great, now we're criticizing people who wanted to kill us because they didn't do the job correctly." Cade shook his head, his scathing look wasted in the darkness of the ship.

"I'm just saying, it's sloppy and half-assed."

Mason hummed a little, then offered, "Maybe it was just a random looking to rob us. Not to mention a free trip off the island."

"Maybe." Cade tried to read Nox's angry silence as him having an opinion as to who it was. Or why they would. Given the firepower and precision at the Iron Butterfly, he refused to believe the grand plan for killing them consisted of one guy and a gun with a single clip.

"We bring down the remaining crew members to look at the body, see if they can identify him."

Cade heard Nox's words and gave a shudder. "And if not?"

"Either way, we're getting the hell off this boat as soon as possible."

Quiet agreement, then Nox pulled out his gun, nodding to Mason. "Get everyone packed and ready to go."

"HIS NAME'S Wick. He's a small-time Dead Bolt dealer," one of the crew said; he was the last one brought down to observe the body they'd dragged into the small stateroom. "I've seen him around for years."

"Who does he work for?" Nox asked, carefully watching the man's lined and weary face.

The man shrugged. "Nobody. Wasn't big-time or nothing, just making enough to live, you know."

Nox felt Mason's eyes on him as Mason stepped forward and touched his foot against the dead man's leg. "So someone might hire him to do a job? And he'd say yes?"

"Yeah, maybe." Something about the man's tone made Nox look up.

The captain bristled from the doorway. "Did you know about this? Did you tell him who was on board?"

A twitch in the man's left check was the only thing Nox needed.

He moved swiftly, one second resting calmly against the wall, the next pinning the crewman to the ground and twisting his arm in a painful wrench.

"You told him what?" Nox hissed.

The man whimpered, fighting for only a moment before sagging under the weight of Nox's anger. "Just... just some rich people who were on the run. That's it."

"So a robbery," Mason said slowly. "So take whatever we had, then how was he getting off the boat?"

Another cry as Nox gave the man incentive to answer. "I... I was gonna move the boat off course, bust up the radar so we'd have to dock, and then... then he'd get off and... and split the take with me."

"You fucking piece of shit," the captain hissed. Nox didn't look up, just twisted and twisted until the guy cried out in agony. "You killed Harris and Niemen!"

"No... no. Wick did, I swear!"

Nox looked up at Mason; the lights were back on, and the full extent of the damage done to the ship by one—possibly two—men was clear. Two crewmen shot execution-style. Half the operating systems damaged or destroyed. The body of one Mr. Wick lying on the floor.

It didn't add up to anything that made sense, and frankly it was pissing him off.

"I don't give a shit who killed who. Get us to land, and then you can do whatever you want to him," Nox murmured to the captain, giving one last jerk before letting the coconspirator go. The man fell to the floor, weeping and shaking and muttering his innocence.

"Fine." The captain gave one last harsh and unforgiving look, then turned on his heel.

Nox waited until the captain was gone, then nodded to Mason.

"You were right. Just a robbery," he said evenly.

Mason's eyebrows disappeared into his hairline. "Seriously? You believe him?"

Nox kicked the man at his feet. "Yeah, why shouldn't I?"

The man whimpered.

With a frown, Mason put his gun away, sliding it into the back of his waistband. "So we'll get off the boat and head for the farm?"

Jaw set, Nox stepped over the doomed crewman and around Mr. Wick's body. While he knew the people behind the bombing of the Iron Butterfly and the production of Dead Bolt had to be smarter than this—wise enough not to put their trust in a dock rat and a small-time criminal—his options and their resources were limited.

"Yeah. That's always been the plan, right?" He walked out into the hallway, claustrophobia beginning to eat away at his brain. The boat rocked under his feet as he made his way to the stateroom where everyone was camped out.

"Well?" Cade asked instantly, rising. Behind him, Sam and Rachel sat on the bed, both looking like shit. Damian hid in the corner, hands nervously playing against his thighs.

Nox looked at them, one after the other. No, resources were low and their prospects were basically prison or death. Changing course right now would lead them into another proverbial storm of the unknown—and Nox was tired of not knowing.

"Ill-advised robbery attempt," Nox said, avoiding Cade's heated stare. "It's taken care of. But we're docking a little early. Everyone needs to be ready to go."

"Are you sure?" Cade asked, walking into Nox's personal space without hesitation.

Nox blinked, then nodded slowly. "Positive. Be ready in a half hour, and dress warm."

THE OLD waterfront, destroyed by weather and neglect, creaked and rocked against the side of the yacht as they pulled into a collection of junked debris forming something resembling a slip, most likely for private yachts a very long time ago. The floodlights on the deck were extinguished; the entire maneuver was done with flashlights from the remaining crew and a few scattered lights on the dock.

Nox—armed and tense—stood in the shadows, watching the entire thing unfold. Everyone else was belowdecks, armed with their luggage and orders to be on their toes. He had high hopes for finding transportation, but if not, they were about to set off on a very long walk.

The unease of their little run-in with Mr. Wick and his crewman accomplice sat ugly and cold in his stomach. The rest of his group accepted the explanations, but Nox couldn't put aside his paranoia. If the past seventeen years had taught him anything, it was not to ignore the voice inside himself. His gut said they were being maneuvered, and staying alert was the only thing that would save them.

And a small, ugly whisper reminded Nox of the thought underlying it all—he was using them as bait to draw out the threat, instead of truly trying to escape it.

The captain whistled a complicated series of chirps. There was silence, then a returning salvo of the same. The yacht lurched as it slammed into the shadows sticking out of the water.

They came to a halt, everything quiet save for the water lapping against the side of the boat.

"Mr. Mullens," the captain said as he approached Nox. "Welcome to South Carolina."

NOX RAPPED on the door to belowdecks.

Mason emerged a second later, followed by Cade, with Rachel and Damian helping Sam up the stairs behind them. Each of them held a bag, Cade with two and Mason pointing a gun at the remaining crewmen on the deck. As soon as he hit the cold air, Sam began to cough, and Nox's shoulders ratcheted up around his ears.

Working alone had its benefits. Working to keep a group of people alive strained every nerve in his body.

He had to find them transportation.

"We'll get you on land. Carlos will meet you on the other side— he knows some people who can help you," the captain said, herding them across the deck, then to the small gap between the yacht and the dock. Professionalism took over as his personal anger seemed to simmer and bank; Nox had no doubt that the betrayal of his employee was going to end in the poor jackass being fed to the fishes sometime very soon.

That is, if Nox decided the crew would walk away from this endeavor.

A crewman flashed his light to illuminate their path to actual land. It looked like an obstacle course, full of holes and gaps in the decaying dock, much to Nox's dismay. He heard the rumbling of concerns behind him.

"I'll go first. Watch the way I walk," Nox said, bravado keeping his voice on an even keel. "It'll be fine."

Over the side of the yacht, Nox took the wide step onto the closest piece of dock. He couldn't see the water, but he could hear every slap and slip under the damaged pylons. The wide shine of the flashlight from the deck gave him his next objective. His boots slipped on the metal under his feet, and after a pause to catch his breath, he steadied himself, then moved again. Ahead he could see the folded metal; it would be a razor's edge from the center of the damaged dock to the concrete slab that would provide safety.

A buzz sounded between his ears. Nox approached each jagged hole, each uneven patch, like stones across a river. Step, balance, step, balance. Jump, balance with arms straight out, lungs straining with effort. He held his breath with the last leap and landed on both feet on the solid ground.

Slowly he turned around and looked back at the yacht.

Cade was already halfway, nimbly navigating the dock like it was second nature.

"Seriously?" Nox muttered, and Cade made the last jump and bumped into him as he landed.

"Gymnastics for eight years. Your lumber wasn't that difficult to beat," Cade said, throwing two backpacks into the shadows. "Let's get everyone else over."

Nox smothered a faint burn of amusement as he signaled for Damian to go next.

Sam was next to last. They decided to wrap a rope around his waist—one end on the yacht with Mason, one end in Nox's hands—with Cade meeting him halfway as a guide. The wind started to pick up, as the storm they'd escaped was fast approaching, and it made Nox more anxious.

"Come on, let's go. I'm not dressed for the weather," Cade joked, darting over the holes in the dock to the middle. "Pretty, yes—practical, nooo."

Nox couldn't see Sam's expression, but judging by the way the rope trembled and Cade's cheerful patter, he assumed his son was terrified.

Because *he* was terrified.

"Here we go," Cade said as he moved toward the yacht again. The flashlights from the boat and the ones behind Nox—wielded by Rachel and Damian—shone a clear path. Nox began to pull the rope gently as Sam moved.

Everything dissolved to slow motion—Sam's shaky steps, Cade guiding him over each hole and around each jagged edge. Nox held his breath, fingers tight on the rope.

"Little bit more," Cade said, clear as a bell, reaching out to take Sam's hand to lead him over and around the fold of the dock. "Just put your foot—"

The jerk of the rope pulled Nox forward. Thrown off-balance, he began to slide off the concrete dock onto the damaged planks. A flashlight went flying as someone grabbed the back of his jacket.

CHAPTER SIX

NOX WRAPPED the rope around his wrists, skidding on his knees. The sharp burn of the steel cut through his jeans, and the rope jerked as he tried to stop the free fall.

He could hear shouts—"Hold on, hold on, keep the rope tight!"—and he concentrated on that. *Hold the rope, hold it tight.* The hand on his back suddenly strengthened, even as the light from their side of the dock wavered.

"Cade!" Rachel yelled. "Do you have him?"

The rope tightened, and Nox started to slide again. His jacket slid upward as Damian—he assumed—kept him from going down into the divide of the crumpled steel.

"Got him!" Cade suddenly shouted back. The sound was lower than before, echoing from somewhere under the dock.

Oh God. Sam had fallen into the water.

"Pull me up!" Cade was screaming. Nox threw his body backward, pushing with his legs in an attempt to get back up on the concrete dock. Hands scrabbled at him. Damian grunted and Rachel cursed as he inched up, the rope jerking in his hands, cutting deep into his wrists.

More shouts followed, then the sudden reappearance of the lights. One last grunt and Nox found himself on his back on the concrete, breath whistling as the pain hit him all at once.

"Well shit," Rachel bitched from somewhere over him. She sounded as winded as he felt. "He's hurt!"

"What?" Someone—maybe Mason—was yelling back.

The rope unwound from Nox's wrists, and he panicked, struggling to get up.

"Stay down, you idiot. You're bleeding," Rachel said. He felt pressure against his knees and shins, the starless sky above him blinking as the pain erupted. "We got Sam—and Cade—everyone's fine, and you're a bleeding moron." She leaned harder against him until Nox closed his eyes, teeth digging into his bottom lip.

A few seconds later, the clattering noise of everyone joining them on the concrete dock roused Nox. Sam was coughing, and that more than anything propelled Nox to move again. He struggled to sit up—and this time someone helped him.

Their little group huddled together—Nox on the ground, bleeding and woozy, and a dripping wet Cade, with Sam—unbelievably, of them all—standing up and looking concerned.

"What the hell happened?" Nox asked weakly.

"Sam slipped, I went into the water. What the hell did you do?" Cade chattered.

"Hold this," Rachel said to Cade, indicating the coat on Nox's legs, which Nox realized she was using to stop the bleeding. "I'll see what I can find."

Nox, weak as he was, snapped his fingers at Mason, who had his gun out. "Go with her," he said, looking up into Cade's irritated face. "I'm fine," he added, even as a wave of nausea roiled through his stomach.

"Whatever." Dripping—and smelling fairly disgusting from the water—Cade pressed against Nox's legs. "We're like a fucking disaster movie. Who'd you piss off in another life?" His teeth were chattering, and Nox—instinct over thought—put his arms around Cade's shoulders.

"My legs aren't going to fall off. C'mere." Nox grunted as Cade fell onto his legs and into his arms.

"Ugh. I hate you," Cade mumbled, burrowing against Nox's chest.

Blood and dirty water—Nox's head spun.

SAM SAT on the edge of the concrete, slumped over the bags they'd brought with them. Sliding down through that hole in the dock, he'd been sure it was the end. Cats had nine lives, and if he were lucky, so did he—because God, swinging on that rope, waiting to be pulled up, the sharp edges and the pull of the water....

"Hey, let's get you into the truck," someone said, and Sam jumped.

"Sorry." It was Damian, flashlight in hand, looking about as exhausted as Sam felt. "They got a truck. Rachel and the cop."

"Mason," Sam mumbled as he rolled onto his knees and slowly got to his feet. "His name is Mason."

An arm caught him, someone smaller than him, so it was Rachel, still cursing and grumbling.

"He stood there and glowered. I did all the talking," she sniped, leading Sam toward the large panel truck idling in the distance. "Damian! Get the bags."

It used to be a delivery truck, Sam imagined, now basically just rust painted over in industrial white, with several obscene words tagged on the side; it reminded him of the ones used to move Dead Bolt in the city. Rachel brought him around to the cab and hefted him into the passenger side.

"You're so strong." Sam laughed deliriously, grabbing the stick shift to pull himself up.

"I'm a badass, darling." She shoved his butt into the seat.

Sam slumped, still laughing. "Is my dad okay?"

Rachel leaned against the door, looking up at Sam with a smirk. "He's bloody and grouchy, but I think that's just a regular Saturday night for him."

"Pretty much." Sam sighed. He heard thuds and shouts from behind the truck. "Um… is it…."

Rachel shook her head. "Too much testosterone in one place. That's why I'm hanging with you."

"Should I be insulted?" Sam coughed in his hand. Dammit. He'd been doing so well.

"No, sweetheart. I'm sure when your balls drop I'll find you more annoying than not."

Sam didn't quite understand his father's dislike of Rachel. She seemed cool and could be funny when she wanted to be—plus it was kind of nice to have a lady fussing over him. Some women at his old job and a few online teachers had, but Rachel was…

Kind of nurturing.

And if he wasn't already entirely sure he was gay, he might have a crush.

While the arguments and arrangements raged behind them, Rachel sat on the floor of the truck, tiny and tough at once, patting Sam's leg whenever the coughing overwhelmed him.

"Mason's got a nice ass. I hope you have plans when you feel better," she teased, leaving him sputtering in ways that had nothing to do with his traitorous lungs.

"We... I...."

Rachel waved her hands. "Stop, don't hurt yourself. I'm just teasing. You both are a little sickening, but it's the only thing that isn't entirely made of shit at the moment, so...."

Sam dropped off. He woke with a start as the back of the truck rattled; someone had slammed the door. A second later the driver's side door opened, and then Cade—drier and dressed in clean clothes—jumped into the truck.

"Rachel's in the back, which she isn't happy about, but she said to make sure you keep the blanket on yourself, okay?"

"Hey," Sam said. "Sorry about...."

Cade put one hand up as he stuck the key in the ignition with the other. "I'm sorry I slipped and went into the water and nearly knocked your ass down. Saving you was the least I could do."

"Thanks. I owe you—twice."

Cade snapped his fingers. "Good point. I'm marking that down."

The truck rumbled to life.

"Everyone else is in the back?"

"Yeah. I got into a slap fight with your father about who got to drive, but guys with ripped-up knees can't manage a clutch, therefore I won." Cade looked delightedly evil before the cab light flickered out. "And now we ride, my young friend. The Creel Farm awaits."

SAM FELL asleep again as Cade navigated the truck onto the highway. A cheap, disposable cell sat ominously in Cade's pocket; he would drive for two hours, then stop to place the mother of all calls.

His mom would be his main defender; she desperately wanted him home anyway, and so he was arriving with a warrant out for his arrest and a host of ragtag freaks in his back pocket? He'd distract her with big puppy eyes—that had worked for most of his life—and then throw sickly and sweet Sam into her arms.

Ammo against his father's dislike of his lifestyle—the dirty laundry of which he was depositing on their doorstep. A bit of leverage to at least give them enough time to make a plan. Feverishly, Cade focused on the potential scenarios.

Arrest.

Cast out into the night.

Sticking around and having his father be an endless source of frustration and judgment.

How hard he prayed for number three.

"Lord, it's me again, your favorite hooker. I would just like to ask that you shine a bit of luck in our direction, because God knows... well, you know. You know we need a break right about now." Cade gripped the steering wheel, barely able to keep the shitty truck on the road. "We could also use a transmission miracle, if you're not too busy."

He'd spent most of his life without a plan, playing fast and loose with the idea of having goals. He had fallen into his life at the Iron Butterfly, and just as quickly he'd been cast out, with little more than the clothes on his back. Every time Cade's brain darted to the idea of his money—if it was still in his accounts, if he'd have anything since the Butterfly was smoking ruins—it made him physically ill. Empty pockets, no prospects.

He was his father's every snide comment come true.

Depressing.

"And oh hey, this is the guy I'm sleeping with—boyfriend? Yeah, no clue," he muttered to himself. "First I'm going to avoid prison, then we'll talk."

"Hmmm?" Sam coughed from across the cab.

"Shhh, go back to sleep." Cade tightened his fingers on the wheel, concentrating on the road and not his current laundry list of dramas.

CADE KNEW this drive well enough—highways to byways to increasingly smaller and less cared-for roads. The Creel Farm sat two hours southwest of Charleston, a tiny oasis in the center of a massive housing development, paved roads, and strip malls. With so many displaced by the superstorms, life in the South became more appealing—so much farmland ripe for the picking for developers with big insurance settlements and a desire to increase their bottom line.

Once upon a time, the Creels had been rich on tobacco money, generations of the men making a fortune through the lungs of other people. Bless addiction, they'd laugh. But increasingly radical weather and economic downturns kept carving out pieces of the farm. A cousin got hooked on the ponies and sold his corner. Two uncles got caught in messy divorces and lost their shares to bankruptcy. A few generations got morals and Jesus and didn't want to become rich on the backs of other people's misery.

The empire became a square getting smaller and smaller every year.

Now the last Creel—Lee Sr.—farmed a modest plot of land braced up against some protected forest. He was the last holdout, more stubborn than all those before him. Despite the McMansions dotting his view and the super Walmart down the road, he was determined to keep the family tradition alive.

And he only needed one son to do that.

Cade saw a small turnoff ahead, one he knew led to an abandoned quarry. He slowed the rattling beast of a truck, pulled over, then stopped once he was entirely off the main road.

Time to face the music.

Sam mumbled in his sleep but quickly fell back under. Cade opened the door quietly and then slid down onto the road.

In the light from the truck, he dialed the familiar numbers to the landline his mother insisted on.

One ring, two.

"Creel Farm." His brother, LJ. Cade had a second to decide if he wanted to disguise his voice and ask for his mother before that was decided for him. "Cade?"

"How the hell did you know it was me?"

"No one calls this number 'cept bill collectors and you." LJ's drawl registered more welcoming than he might have imagined. "You okay?"

Surprised, Cade opened his mouth to speak, but his tongue stuck to the roof of his mouth. Was he okay?

Probably not.

"I'm alive. How's that?" Cade said finally. "Have people been around there asking questions?"

"Oh yeah. Sheriff Vance brought some suits over. They said they needed to ask you some questions about a bombing."

Cade's breath caught. "Did they say why?"

"Well, something about a material witness warrant. I took a picture of it with my phone while they were arguing with Daddy."

Interesting tactic—claiming that Cade was just a witness despite what the official word was back in New York. At the mention of his father, Cade winced. Better rip that bandage off.

"How's he taking it?"

LJ laughed. "He went all out—waving his shotgun, ten-minute screaming fit about the government taking away the land of real Jesus-loving Americans, then he threatened to call the media and the militia. It was ugly. Those suits ran out of here as quick as they could." LJ paused for a dramatic moment. "I'm pretty sure at least ten percent of it was how he really felt, and the rest he just made the hell up."

"Do you think they're watching the place?" Cade's stomach dropped. What if they bugged the phone lines?

"Nah. I got cameras set up around the perimeter, and Daddy's been takin' walks with his gun lately. If he spotted anything, we'd be bailing him out of jail right about now. Plus I made sure they can't get into the phone lines."

A weird relief rattled Cade's knees. "I don't know what that means, but good. Great."

"You coming to see us?"

"How'd you guess?"

"I don't hear no noise or anything, so I'm guessing you're out of the city." LJ paused. "Plus I just traced this call, and you're over by Devil's Quarry."

Cade almost dropped the phone. "This is a disposable cell—you shouldn't be able to do that."

LJ laughed again. "Yeah. You shouldn't be able to."

Before Cade could ask, there was a shuffling at the other end, and a feminine voice said his name.

"Caden Lee!"

"Oh hey, Momma."

His mother cried through most of their conversation; Cade's main contribution was about eight hundred "yes ma'ams" and a few dozen "I'm okay, reallys." He managed to work in the part about a sick teenager and swore to her on the Lord and every dead ancestor in the family tree that he was innocent and so were his friends.

She trusted him.

Lee Creel Sr., however—that was a different story.

Nothing surprising about him slamming into the house so loudly Cade heard it through the phone. Nothing shocking about his insistence he didn't want to speak to his son at this time.

Then more slamming and his mother's quiet sigh.

"So I'm going to get back on the road. We should be there in about forty minutes," Cade said finally. "Tell LJ to open the back barn up—I'll come in through the fire road and put the truck in there."

"All right." His mother sounded reluctant to let him off the line. "Be careful, okay?"

"Yes, ma'am."

She told him she loved him and then hung up. Cade leaned against the door, sagging with the effort of dealing with his family. The sound of crunching gravel made him jump as a shadow came around the side of the truck, startling him further.

"Everyone okay?" Nox asked, limping toward him, dark and hidden in the shadows.

Cade waved the phone at him. "Called my mom. We're a go for hiding in plain sight," he said, joking weakly. "Glad to see no one killed you. What's your body count in the back there?"

Stepping into the circle of light from the truck, Nox looked as tired as Cade felt. "Mason wouldn't let me strangle Rachel."

"I knew I liked that kid." Cade pushed off the door, his body protesting movement with various creaks and snaps. "We're about forty minutes out. I'm going to drive in round back—there's this road no one really knows about—and then we'll be in the barn. We can sneak into the house from there pretty easy."

Nodding, Nox leaned in to check on Sam, who was still snoring peacefully in the front seat. "Good job."

Cade shrugged. "To the surprise of even myself, I am extremely competent in emergencies."

"I'm not really surprised," Nox said softly, and Cade felt a sizzle over his skin at the words, the affectionate tone of Nox's voice. A walking trouble magnet with a planeload of baggage, and of course Cade's butterflies seemed to respond to only him.

"My stubbornness comes in handy—go ahead, admit it." Cade tried to play it off, fluttering his eyelashes.

"You're good to have around." Nox touched him then, like he had back in the stateroom. Just his fingertips against Cade's body—his chest this time, somewhere in the vicinity of his heart. "Never going to be able to thank you."

They'd fucked more than once, but the quiet intimacy of this moment stripped Cade bare. He pushed off the truck and into Nox's arms, crushing their mouths together before Nox had time to react.

Cade kissed him soft and sweet and slow, tasting him with a darting tongue. Not too deep, nothing to escalate—just a moment in the middle of the craziness to say *yeah, I don't get it either*.

"Yeah, I don't get it either," Cade said as he drew their mouths apart. He licked at the taste of them mingled together and laughed when Nox grunted. "Maybe I'll let you fuck me in my childhood bedroom," he murmured as Nox ran his hands down Cade's back.

"Ugh" came a voice from inside the cab.

Sam was awake.

CHAPTER SEVEN

ONCE CADE had secured Nox in the back of the truck—and given Sam proper time to be emotionally scarred in private—he got back in and restarted the beast. He and Sam politely ignored each other until the darkness of backcountry roads gave way to a mecca of strip malls and traffic lights.

"Whoa," Sam said, sitting up straighter. "It's like a city."

"Not quite yet." Cade shifted gears, the vibrations of the truck rattling his teeth. "But they're doing their best to grow one in the middle of nowhere."

The little town of Gaiterville had become a hub of commerce, chain stores, and McMansions over time, with every spare corner of land being developed as fast as someone could snatch it up. Coming Soon! signs were everywhere, and after passing four strip malls and mega shopping complexes, they soon came upon the skeleton of yet another, right up against the beginnings of condominiums.

"When I was real little, all I remembered was two stoplights and a grocery store," Cade murmured. A new traffic pattern ahead, orange signs for men working, concrete barriers—coming soon, a new connection to the highway. "None of this was here, you know?"

"Mmmm." Sam looked out the window. "I never imagined living somewhere like this. It's got everything you need in one place!"

The stunned timbre of Sam's voice redirected his thoughts; for Cade's family, this was unwelcome progress. For Sam? This was a miracle of commerce and creature comforts.

"My mother is going to have fun spoiling the hell out of you," Cade murmured, taking a breath as he eased the truck to the turning lane.

Last leg of the trip toward home.

Interlude

CADE IS nine when he realizes he is gay. His cousin Vicki comes to spend the summer from the big city (Chicago) and regales him with stories about her best friend, whose name is Tyler. She shows Cade pictures on her phone—and Cade is overwhelmed. This boy is so… so handsome, and his smile makes Cade's face turn bright red. He thinks about Tyler before he falls asleep and when he wakes up. He imagines them being friends, hanging out together.

Kissing.

He probably had a feeling before that, but now he's sure. The final confirmation is when Vicki confides that Tyler is gay, making her a very cool person because they are best friends forever.

Feeling bold, Cade tells Vicki that now she knows two gay boys and therefore is extra cool. Vicki squeals with delight. It's the first time he's come out, and it's awesome. Vicki makes it sound like he's just discovered superpowers.

Confident, he tells his mother. She doesn't squeal or anything, but she does hug him and say she loves him. That's good enough. Then she says, "Let's wait to tell your father," and all of Cade's confidence quakes and shakes like the earth is moving.

So he waits.

And waits.

Loses his virginity to the sheriff's son and goes steady with his junior high principal's nephew. All of this is on the down-low because this is a moral, Bible-devout place, and all sin must take place in dark corners.

It's the law.

Cade regains his confidence—his cockiness. He has superpowers all right, and the boys—especially the ones who play straight and mighty—can't get enough.

He gets lax in that down-low part.

He gets brazen in the way he dresses and the way he gives the once-over to cute boys walking down the halls. The girls love him, protect him. The boys leave him alone, lest he reveal their secrets.

Everything is fine. Until his father finds out.

Whatever Cade had imagined, whatever he'd read in books or seen in horrible social-issue-of-the-week movies—it didn't prepare him for his father's reaction. No shotguns or threats, not even angry words. Just a look of disgust when he finds Cade and Louis Baker half-dressed in the barn loft.

And then it is never mentioned again.

His father's silence is loud—it reverberates through the house every time he found something to disapprove.

"Fuck you, old man" is Cade's only sentiment when he leaves for New York. His father doesn't bother to respond.

THE FIRE road hadn't changed much—Cade had fond memories of keggers and blowing half the football team back here, but he didn't bring that up to Sam as the truck rattled the last few miles through the trees and up into the old barn sitting on the edge of the Creel Farm. The double doors were open, so Cade just maneuvered inside.

"Great job," Sam said enthusiastically before smothering a cough in his hand.

Cade shut off the truck, and almost immediately cold began to seep in through the cracks in the window.

"All right, well. Here we are." Cade ran his hands through his hair and didn't bother to consult the mirror. Hot mess, with a side of home with your tail between your legs. He didn't have to look pretty for this.

He opened the door, then jumped out, hay and dust kicking up as he landed. "Stay in the truck," he called back to Sam. "Just hang on, okay?"

Sam gave him the thumbs-up.

After slamming the door behind him, Cade headed for the back of the truck. The doors were open, and Nox was already out, gun drawn. Mason followed, with Rachel and Damian bringing up the rear.

"Oh my God, where the hell are we?" Rachel muttered, brushing hay and dust and whatever the hell was in the back of that truck off her jeans.

"Welcome to Creel Farm, in lovely Gaiterville, South Carolina. You'll very shortly meet my awesome mom, my endlessly disapproving father, and whatever mood my brother is in this week," Cade said cheerfully. "Someone needs to carry Sam through this lung-murdering muck—I'm assuming Mason will volunteer."

"Can I go back to the place where people are trying to kill us?"

Nox turned around slowly. "You know, I can take care of that right now, Rachel."

"Hey, Damian, stand between these two until I get back. Please." Cade got about three steps outside the barn before footsteps alerted him to the fact that their arrival had indeed been noticed.

"Caden!" His mother flew through the dark, and Cade didn't even hide the fact that he ran toward her. In a few steps, she was hugging him tightly—and the welcome scent of her perfume drew tears to his eyes.

Home sure as hell didn't mean this farm, but her hug was everything he needed right now.

"Oh my God, I was so scared when those men showed up," Amelia Creel gasped. She pulled back enough to look up into his face, scanning him alertly for any signs of distress. He knew that look—it was the entire reason he'd known where they needed to go.

"I'm so sorry they came here, Momma, but it's okay now. We're going to straighten it out," he lied, even as she touched his face gently.

"You look like you haven't slept."

"Understatement, but we'll fix that too," he said, smiling. "I need to get everyone into the house, though. Is Dad around?"

Her smile faltered. "He went into town," she said, patting his cheek. "LJ's bringing the cart down so we can take that sick boy up. I have all the rooms ready, and dinner's in the oven."

It was like a slumber party; his mother could whip up hospitality in her sleep, no matter what the scenario. Fugitives from the law? He'd bet his boots there was going to be a cobbler.

"You're the greatest mother in the world," Cade laughed wetly, pulling her back for another hug.

A rumbling sound and headlights broke things up. Over the small rise between the house and the barn, the old golf cart rattled down to where they were standing. In the driver's seat was Cade's older brother, LJ.

The cart braked to a halt behind them, and then he jumped out, barely waiting for the rumbling to stop.

"Well this is a fucking mess," LJ drawled, opening his arms at the same time.

"Yes, you are. What's wrong with your hair?" Cade choked out before he pulled into LJ's embrace a second later.

"I puffed it up in your honor—used some of Momma's church spray," LJ said, pounding his palm against Cade's back. It was how Cade knew LJ was glad to see him. He stepped back, taking in Cade. "You okay?" he asked softly.

"Yeah."

"Caden, can we get everyone into the house, please?" Amelia said, rubbing her hands together. "It's cold, and I can hear that child coughing from out here."

The reunited Creels walked as a unit back to the barn. The semicircle of misfits—complete with Mason carrying Sam—greeted them.

"Very quickly—Amelia Creel, LJ Creel, please meet Rachel, Damian, Mason, Sam, and uh—that's Nox."

"Pleased to meet you all. You can remind me of who you are again when we're in the house," Amelia said briskly, rubbing her hands together. "Young man, put your sick friend in the back of the golf cart. We'll put the bags in there as well. Everyone else, follow me. LJ, shut the doors when they're out."

She turned, gesturing for Mason to follow her.

LJ rocked back on his heels; Cade looked at Nox, who was looking at LJ, who was—looking at Rachel.

"I'll remember your name just fine," LJ said as Rachel barely gave him a glance.

"Impressive, as I'm the only woman," she said dryly before picking up her bag. "Someone point me in the direction of running water, please."

She strode out of the barn, and LJ's gaze followed her intently.

"I like your friends, Caden."

Cade grabbed Nox by the arm and yanked him toward the house, calling a warning to LJ over one shoulder. "She'll eat your balls for breakfast, and that isn't a metaphor. Don't do it."

CADE WALKED everyone up the hill, following the taillights of the golf cart. No one talked, as the exhaustion and stress once again pulled at them. Nox huffed next to him, still limping from his brush with the nasty dock; Cade reminded himself to set Amelia and her first aid kit loose on the man once they got Sam settled.

The house hadn't changed much at all—everything warm browns and honey colors, family heirlooms mixed with the crafts his mother filled her time with when she wasn't hawking produce at the farmer's market. A wooden sign over the double windows in the living room said "Don't let yesterday take up too much of today." It was a favorite of his mother's—Cherokee wisdom, she'd say with a knowing nod. Between the Cherokees and Jesus, Amelia always had something to share, no matter the occasion.

"I sent the boys upstairs to get cleaned up. We'll bring supper up to them. Frankly they barely could keep their eyes open." Amelia's jacket was gone, an apron tied around her waist. Cade could see a few more strands of gray streaking her shoulder-length brown hair, a few more wrinkles around her eyes. Those he blamed on his father.

"LJ, you can show everyone else where they're stayin'. I put the young ones together in your room, and then you—Rachel, was it? You can stay with me. Caden, your room is made up, of course. And uh, the other two gentlemen, you'll be in the guest room."

Cade dropped his bag on the kitchen floor, seeking out Nox where he stood near the back door. "That's okay, Mom. Nox'll stay with me. Damian can have the guest room by himself," he said, waiting for Nox to flinch.

He didn't.

"Oh. Well. I'll have LJ put the rollaway bed in there," Amelia said primly. "Let's get everyone washed up and settled, shall we? I have a nice stew—warm you all up."

NOX FOLLOWED Cade quietly up the stairs, bags in hand. The silent thing was starting to wear on Cade's nerves. It made him nervous, what Nox thought of his family. He concentrated on the oval rugs on each step, remembering the creaks to avoid if you were, say, sneaking out at four in the morning to meet someone in the copse of trees near the creek.

The narrow hallway that led to Cade's old room featured an embarrassing array of photos—terrible bowl cuts and prebrace teeth, he and LJ in matching denim rompers as toddlers. His father's stern visage was in only a few photos; he'd grown weary of his wife's tireless documentation of their lives and began to skip the portraits. A person would think him dead before the boys hit puberty, going by the walls of the house.

Cade opened the door and stepped inside, then hit the light switch with his elbow, like he'd done a million times before.

Blue rug and wood panel walls twenty years out of date before he was even born. One window—near the big tree out back, a good backup plan when you couldn't sneak down the stairs—covered with the long navy drapes Amelia had made him when they turned this into a "teenager's" room. The matching spread on the queen-size bed, tall wood dressers still bearing his school awards and sport trophies.

Did anyone really care he was Most Improved Soccer Player anymore?

"There's a bathroom down the hall, opposite side. You probably want to get in there before Rachel," Cade said absently as he walked into the room and dumped his bags next to the bed. "I'm going to use the washroom downstairs."

"Are you okay?"

"Hmm?" Cade turned around and once again found Nox backed up in a doorway. With the fight-or-flight response etched on his face, Nox looked like he was floundering for something to say or do.

"Are you okay?" Nox repeated.

"Why are you asking me that? You look like you want to jump out of the window," Cade said, feeling irrationally annoyed. "Just get in here and shut the door."

Nox moved aside and did what Cade asked. He watched Cade like someone trying to figure out how to defuse a bomb.

Cade sat down on the bed, the shimmy and lumps in the mattress like a flashback. His entire body sagged.

"I am both really glad to be here and really fucking hating it," Cade said quietly, kicking the dirt-caked sneakers off his feet. He wanted a hot shower and food and to sleep for about a month. He wanted to wake up and realize this was all a really fucked-up dream.

"We don't have to stay long," Nox offered, sitting down next to him. Close but not touching. "Sam needs a few days at the most, and then...."

"And then what? Exactly." Cade's hands shook; he was discovering how fine he could be until he stopped moving, and then the walls fell away and reality kicked him in the teeth. "There are warrants out for us. We're six hundred miles away, but is that enough?"

"If they wanted to find us, they could have." Nox's expression flipped back to the one Cade had first seen in the city. The one that didn't see anything but a threat to assess.

"Is that supposed to make me feel better?" Cade laughed. He felt choked by the dirt on his skin. "I don't have a job anymore. I'm back home without a penny to my name. If I'm lucky, I won't get thrown into prison or, you know, murdered by fucking... gangsters." He spat the word, that edgy laughter shaking through him. "In a few days, what the fuck is going to change?"

Nox didn't move, not even a blink. Cade broke their mutual gaze and dropped his head into his hands.

"If I leave Sam here, do you promise to protect him?" Nox asked finally.

Cade turned to look at him. "What?"

"If I leave—I can't take Sam, not right now. Will you stay with him, make sure he's safe?"

The quiet pain in his voice pulled at Cade's emotions. "I didn't mean you had to leave."

"I'm the reason you're involved in all this."

"Yeah. And there's also a heap of me not staying away," Cade said with a tired sigh punctuating his words. "I said I would help you, and I will. Just—this is hard for me, okay? I left this shithole determined to make it on my own, to show my father I was just as fucking valuable as my brother. And now I'm back because I screwed up."

Nox touched him then, a big warm hand against the back of Cade's neck—and the bolt of heat that followed made his mouth go dry. "You're back because you didn't let a kid get killed. And you didn't let more people die in that casino," Nox murmured. "You're valuable to me and everyone else who's here and safe because you made it happen."

Cade wanted to laugh again, maybe cry for a while too. What was fucked-up was this man and the fact that nothing about their connection pointed to anything but heartbreak.

But Cade couldn't break this living, breathing thing between them.

"I already let you fuck me—you can stop with the sweet talk now," Cade whispered back.

Nox tightened his hand on Cade's neck and guided him closer. "Cade," he said, utterly serious, "if it gets too much, tell me to leave and I will."

The quiet words hurt, but Cade nodded, the pang in the center of his chest a feeling he was afraid he'd need to get used to.

CHAPTER EIGHT

A QUIET knock roused their tortured tableau.

"Cade, Daddy's home. You should probably come down," LJ said through the door.

"Comin'."

Hands still shaking, Cade kissed Nox on the lips—quick and simple, more for his own benefit than anything else. "Time to meet the man who made me what I am today."

NOX STRIPPED out of his filthy clothing and pulled on a pair of semiclean jeans and a gray sweater. He left his dirty boots in the corner as Cade rubbed nervous, damp palms against his shirt. Then Cade led Nox downstairs to the kitchen, where everyone save Mason and Sam was gathered. At the table, Rachel and Damian were deeply engrossed in bowls of stew while Amelia fussed around the kitchen. At the stove stood Lee Creel Sr., all rangy muscles and receding hairline, his face leathered and dispassionate.

"Dad," Cade said, extremely proud of the way his voice came out. Haughty, a little bratty—the voice he used with clients who wanted a reason to kick his ass.

Well, wasn't that a revelation for another day.

"Caden Lee, what the hell did you bring into my house?" It wasn't loud or even angry. Just weary and filled with disappointment, washing over Cade like an old lullaby. Oh yes, he knew that tone well.

Amelia didn't stop flitting around, but Cade saw Rachel's shoulders go up the tiniest bit.

This might be a race to see who punched out his father first.

"I brought my friends, Dad. And thanks for your concern—I'm fine."

"The FBI…," Lee started, and then stopped, both hands fisted and pressing against the dirty sides of his jeans. "In my house." He stepped into the center of the kitchen, rheumy blue gaze locked on Cade like they were the only two people in the room.

"Not the first time the feds were here—remember when Uncle Leon got caught skimming money off the books?" Cade met his father halfway; behind him, he felt Nox's presence, quiet and deadly backup. He wanted to tell himself to shut up, to approach this like a fucking adult, because, like it or not, he needed his father's help, but something mean and childish and hurt kept feeding him lines guaranteed to set off his father's temper.

"Don't be flip about this," his father snapped. Up close, Cade could smell a whiff of beer, really see the age spots and craters beat into his father's skin.

When the hell did Lee Creel get old?

"We didn't do anything wrong. It's… it's a misunderstanding, and we're going to straighten it out." Cade tried to sound reasonable, like there wasn't so much more to the story than those two sentences. "My friends need a place to stay."

"One of them is sick, Lee," Amelia said quietly. She stood at her husband's side, looking at him with a pleading expression. "If we could just let them stay a few days."

Lee turned to his wife, the change in his tone and expression one that didn't go unnoticed by Cade. "Amelia, I've been trying my best to keep those people off the farm, but if they realize they're here, they're gonna raid the place. You want to go to jail?"

"I won't turn them out." His mother's resolution was the only thing to soften his father, so Cade kept his mouth shut.

Clearly frustrated, Lee raised a finger in Cade's direction as he turned back. "You stay out of sight, and you make arrangements to move on as quickly as possible. I see a single fed heading down the road with a gun in his hand, and I'm telling them you're here. I won't put your mother in harm's way."

Cade didn't have much choice in the matter. Shame burned his face, licking a fire of regrets against his skin. Putting his mother and brother and yes, fuck, even his father in danger hadn't fully dawned on him. He wanted to be safe and to help Sam and Nox, and he'd brought this mess to his family's door.

Selfish, just like his father accused him of being.

"Fine," he snapped. "We'll be gone in a few days."

Lee threw a disgusted look at all of them, one by one. Silence followed him as he turned and stormed out the back door.

"Where is he going?" Nox's voice broke through the tension, a knife sharply cutting out words.

"The bars are closed," Cade said tiredly. "Probably a walk."

"Actually he's goin' home," Amelia murmured next to him. "He doesn't live here anymore."

RACHEL EXCUSED herself shortly after Amelia's bombshell. Damian followed, a quiet shadow in her wake.

Nox tasked himself to take dinner up to Mason and Sam; he left with an overloaded tray after a gentle brush of fingers against Cade's shoulder.

"So you kicked Daddy out," Cade said as he sat with his mother and brother at the kitchen table.

"His drinking has been... quite frequent lately. In the past few months." Amelia twisted her hands in her lap. "For the past two years, actually. As the farm has been failing, so has his will to resist."

"You should have called me. Told me what was going on."

"LJ was here to help, and we didn't want to bother you."

Cade threw LJ a nasty glare. "*You* should have called me."

"So, what? You could come back here? Let's face it—your paycheck is keeping this place afloat."

Cade felt sick to his stomach at the idea of his mother dealing with this—and even sicker to realize that without his money, they wouldn't have a choice about selling the place.

"I'm sorry—" Cade started to say, but Amelia cut him off.

"No, no, please. Caden, don't say that. I hate what you've had to do these past few years. It wasn't your fault."

"I'm not sorry for what I used to do at the Butterfly, Mom," he reminded her gently. "I'm sorry that I won't be able to contribute."

"We've just been prolonging the inevitable," LJ broke in. "Daddy knows it. That's why he started drinking so much."

Cade's head swam. He clutched at his mother's fingers and twined them with his. "Where does he live?"

"He rents an apartment over in the new development. They let him do handywork around the place so he can stay there cheap," LJ said.

At least they didn't have to worry about him being around.

But....

"Can we trust him to keep quiet about me being here?" Cade asked. Amelia tightened her hands around his. "Or is he running to the sheriff?"

She and LJ exchanged glances.

"He's the one who convinced the sheriff to distract those government assholes. Played up the paranoia, big-government thing so much the entire force is basically protecting this place." LJ sounded almost proud. "Daddy's had 'em in his pocket for years. Let's 'em keep their illegal arms on the farm—so everyone's paranoid they're gonna find out about all those guns in the second barn."

Cade stifled a half-crazed laugh. Well, Nox and Mason were going to have a fucking field day with that. Bless his father's manipulative bullshit. "Jesus Christ."

"But it is—it's good. I know it doesn't seem like it, but he's worried about you," Amelia said quickly. "We just want to make sure you're safe. And what he said—you don't pay him any mind. He won't give you up. So... you can stay here for a while, right?"

Her anxiety tripped a dozen switches in him. He just nodded and leaned over to press a kiss against the back of her hand. "Yeah, we can stay awhile."

NOX DIDN'T sleep as well as he had on the boat—ironically. In the soft bed, on the slightly musty sheets, he waited for Cade to join him.

He'd eaten with Sam and Mason in the bedroom, another ode to little boys who seemed to grow up in some sort of sitcom with Little League and country fairs. Sam conked out pretty quickly after a shower and change of clothes; Mason kept losing track of the conversation, so Nox took his leave and tried not to obsess over leaving Sam alone in the room.

With Mason.

But the siren call of a shower of his own pulled him back down the hall. He scraped off a few layers of dirt under the hot, weak stream, wincing as the water hit his banged-up knees. Blood and filth-stained water circled the drain of the old-fashioned tub, pipes rattling with the effort of cleaning so many exhausted people in one night.

He rebandaged his knees with a first aid kit he found under the sink and then dressed in a pair of thick sweats from Cade's bag. Back in the bedroom, he stowed the Sig under the right pillow, his knife between the mattress and box spring. The light left on, Nox climbed under the covers and resolved to wait.

He didn't last long.

Sleep pulled him under quickly; he floated in and out of wakefulness for a while, voices murmuring in the hallway outside the door. He thought he heard Cade but fell back to sleep.

When he woke again, Cade was curled against him, head on his chest, clutching him tightly around the middle. The tension in his lover's body made Nox think he was awake, but no—Cade breathed slow and deep.

Nox drifted away again.

IN THE morning Nox woke up to find himself alone again.

Or rather alone in the sheets. Amelia Creel was standing at the foot of his bed.

He sat up slowly, blinking as they made eye contact.

"Good morning," Amelia said politely. She was wearing another variation of her clothes from last night, a thin floral sweater over jeans. The resemblance between her and Cade was almost startling—the cheekbones and warm eyes, the smattering of freckles, the same steely gaze that seemed to be zeroing in on his thoughts.

"Morning."

They played the silent stare game another few moments. Nox shifted uncomfortably.

"There's breakfast downstairs."

"Thank you."

She gave him a shrewd glance. "There's no need for the rollaway bed up here, is there?"

Nox waited one beat. Then two. "No, ma'am."

"Hmmm." Amelia folded her arms over her chest.

"But if you wouldn't mind, could you put that extra bed in the room with my son and his friend? I'd prefer a little more distance between them."

"Your son? The sick one."

"Sam, yes."

"Mmmmm." Amelia gave him another appraising glance. "Where's your wife?"

"Don't have one. Sam was, uh—orphaned. During the storms. I took him in and raised him."

"I see."

Nox pushed the covers back, then moved his legs over the side.

"So you don't want your son and his boyfriend sleeping in the same bed?" Her dry tone made it very clear which of his parents Cade took after, right down to the inflection of bemusement.

"No, ma'am, I don't." He ran his hands through his bed head. "And I can go down and sleep on the sofa if it's a problem for me to be up here."

"I'm not sure Caden Lee would appreciate me moving you," she said finally. "So I'll pretend you're not doing anything up here that might make me blush."

"Yes, ma'am."

AFTER AMELIA stuffed him full of ham, steak, and eggs, Nox headed out to find Cade. Everyone else was still asleep, according to his hostess, but Cade couldn't seem to settle down past dawn, so he had gone with her to feed the chickens.

Nox tried to imagine Cade feeding chickens.

Outside, a chill sat in the air, not yet dissipated by the risen sun. Nox walked through the dewed grass, marveling at the stretch of land in every direction. Over the ridge and through the trees, he could see the encroachment of the developments; behind him was the small white farmhouse with a simple porch and flowering bushes. Ahead, cookie-cutter mansions played like game pieces on a board of green.

He staked out the various buildings on the property. A newer structure—a shingled one-story guesthouse—sat a few yards from the main house. Two huge barns, weary with age and neglect, and several sheds dotted the rest of the space, with small fields stretching out beyond them closer to the road, which seemed to cut unnaturally into the landscape. The aforementioned chicken coop was angled near the house, surrounded by raised beds currently devoid of flowers.

A tiny country oasis, squeezed on all sides by progress.

The Sig sat heavy at the back of his jeans, hidden by the windbreaker over his sweatshirt. Nothing looked familiar, nothing felt like home—except for the tendrils of paranoia that dogged his every step.

"Hey," a voice called out. From a copse of trees, half hidden by the smaller of the two barns, Cade sat, perched in the V between branches.

"You're up early."

"Farm living, resets my clock I guess," Cade said, swinging his legs gently. "My mother feed you an obscene amount of food?"

"Yes." Nox was still a little dazed by the fresh food, the alien lifestyle of normality. "I managed to escape before the coffee cake was out of the oven."

"Ohhh. Yeah, you don't want to escape that." Cade slid off the tree and hit the ground with a thump. "It's freaking amazing."

Nox joined him at the tree; they did their little maneuver where their bodies angled toward each other almost instinctively, and Nox felt the radiant warmth of Cade settling in his bones.

"Everything okay last night?"

Cade shrugged, leaning against Nox's side. "I can't fuck for a living anymore, so there's no money, my father is drinking because the farm is going under, and uh—yeah. Oh right, sorry—there are a shit ton of illegal guns in this barn."

"That might be the best news since the coffee cake," Nox said gravely.

Cade snickered against his shoulder. "I thought that would be your reaction."

"I'm sorry about the farm." He looked at the sloping hills and tall trees dwarfing everything with their sheer size. They'd been here so long, and now they were going to end up being cleared away so someone could build another ugly house.

"I'm actually not. I think this place is fucking cursed. Steal land from the Native population, grow tobacco, enslave human beings, then give people cancer. Seriously—becoming a prostitute was like a step up on the Creel family moral ladder."

The quiet of the farm sat between them, a layer of birdsong and the chickens, the wind through the trees.

"You really think there's a curse?" Nox asked, tipping his head back to look at the sky.

"Yeah, actually I do. I mean—when I left, my father was a taciturn dick, and now he's...." Cade's voice cracked. "I didn't even recognize him last night. It's like he aged ten years."

Cade took a big shuddering breath and pushed off the tree. "Come on, take a walk with me." When he extended his hand, Nox took it without a second's hesitation.

THEY WALKED to the edge of the property, until the buildings and the trees were far behind them. The ground got rockier, the slopes more dramatic. Clearly no place to plant crops or build homes as the tangled earth gave way to a wandering creek.

"I used to come down here all the time. I know you're never going to believe this, but I am a Grade A, top-of-the-line frog catcher."

Nox stepped over a large rock as Cade pulled him deeper into the woods.

"You're right, I don't believe you."

"Okay, LJ was better at frogs. I, however, could entice a jock behind the high school with one magic sway of my hips."

"That I believe."

Cade shook his ass as they walked along a pile of fallen logs.

CHAPTER NINE

AT THE end of their trek, Cade brought Nox to the shallow pool, where the creek water collected and went still. The quiet of the farm was a cacophony compared to this; the silence seemed to rise up from the ground and wrap its arms around Nox's body.

A jolt and Nox let out a breath.

They were in the middle of nowhere; what if someone went to the house and he wasn't there....

"Stop," Cade whispered.

They were standing at the water's edge, Cade's hand on his chest, and Nox sucked in a breath of cold, clear air.

"My brother is a crack shot, and my mom taught him everything he knows. Just... stand down for a minute, okay?"

Nox closed his eyes. The little paranoid voice in his head didn't stop just on Cade's word. The urge to run and check and hide didn't go away.

But oh God, it felt so good to breathe.

And focus on Cade's hand.

Just... stop.

He opened his eyes and found Cade's smile waiting for him.

"It helps me when you freak out, gives me something to do," Cade murmured, as if not willing to break the serenity of the moment. "Then I don't freak out."

"That's sort of insane."

"That's why we work together so well."

HAND IN hand, they walked back, following the path they'd made. Nox's neurosis hummed just under the surface, and he felt the gun at his back, the weight of Cade's palm against his.

Balanced.

"Maybe we work so well together because my family has a curse too," Nox said suddenly, as the buildings of the Creel Farm began to take shape. "All the money in the world and—look at where Sam and I are now."

"Two curses, balancing each other out." Cade stepped around a pile of decaying leaves. "That's romantic."

"Romantic?" It was a word so unfamiliar that Nox imagined it might be in a foreign language. "Like when I slammed you into a wall…."

"Saved me from a street gang."

"Handcuffed you to a bed."

"Saved me from asshole drug dealers."

"Got you accused of being an accessory to a crime."

Cade stopped and stood tall on the tiny rise beside Nox. Long gone was the slick boy in the tight clothes who had charmed him to distraction in alleyways and on the casino floor. They were in the midst of Cade's roots—the place that had created him and informed him and forced him out into the world. Nox was seeing Cade for the very first time.

"Granted, it's been a little top-heavy in the danger department," Cade said lightly, his expression composed of tired eyes and a simple smile. "But I don't do anything that I don't want to do. I made a choice to help you, and I'm not sorry."

"And what happens in the next few days? We can't stay here forever."

"No, we can't." Cade's grip tightened on his, their fingers twining together intimately. "We need to figure out how to disappear I guess. All of us." The pang of vulnerability triggered a tight pain in Nox's chest.

Are we disappearing together?

"Maybe we need to figure out how to clear our names instead," he said almost absently.

"What?" Cade laughed. "How the hell do we do that? Those feds are probably as bought and paid for as the cops in the District. You think a city like Manhattan gets privatized for sin without greasing every palm in the vicinity? We can't afford those kinds of bribes."

"Millions of people lost everything when the city fell to ruin. They didn't get a dime of what came later. Maybe some of them would be angry enough to create a problem for the people in charge...." The argument didn't even carry much weight in Nox's head; he just spun the words as an alternative that wasn't making him say *I want to kill them all by myself.*

"So what? We go to the press? We go to the government?" Cade's disbelief was written all over his face and woven through the incredulous tone of his voice. "Right after we convince them we didn't blow up a fucking casino and kill a bunch of people?"

Hysteria began to tinge the words, and Nox instinctively drew him closer. "Calm down."

Shaking, Cade pushed out of his arms. Something about the white pallor, the spots of red forming on his cheeks—Nox sensed a secret.

"What?"

Cade shook his head, digging his hands into his hair. "I don't want to talk about it."

"You can tell me."

And the second the last syllable fell from his lips, Nox knew Cade's response. He could see the frosty wall forming, feel the words he deserved coalescing.

"Like you tell me everything?"

Cade turned and hurried up the pathway toward the house, leaving Nox to follow in his wake.

BACK AT the house, life waited for no insane plans or crazy relationships. Amelia ran a tight ship, now and forever, and even fugitives were expected to pull their weight. Nox disappeared with Mason to check out the stash of guns; Amelia recruited Damian to carry up jars of food and extra supplies from the basement. Sam was propped up on the couch, heavily dosed with Amelia's best homemade remedies and covered with an array of colorful quilts.

At a loss for what to do, Cade went out to help LJ do the chores. Maybe normalcy would stop the itch of anxiety trying to burrow out of his chest.

"Where's that Rachel girl?" LJ asked as he swung an ax through another log. "What's her story?"

"Calling her *that Rachel girl* might get you killed, so I'd revise your way of thinking. Also, I can't prove anything, but I suspect she was hatched fully grown in a mad scientist's lab," Cade said, stacking the split pieces on the ever-growing pile. He set up another log and stepped back.

"Momma's got everyone working but her. That's pretty impressive. I think if the president came by for dinner, Momma'd have him shelling peas."

"Why do you care what Rachel is or is not doing?"

"She's gorgeous. And kind of a badass." The ax swung down as LJ whistled. "Like a secret agent or something."

"She's at least fifteen years older than you are, and once again, she is literally capable of killing you. Rachel's dangerous."

LJ gave him the suggestive eyebrows. "So's your boyfriend."

The ax cut through the air, and two perfectly even logs fell to the ground.

"He's not my boyfriend," Cade said archly. "He's just a—fugitive I happen to be keeping company with."

Another log. Another split. Another level to the pile.

Laughing, LJ rested the ax on his shoulder, doing his best Paul Bunyan. "Maybe you're the badass."

Something uncomfortable bubbled under Cade's skin. Was he dangerous? He knew he was capable of taking another life; he knew he could find a place of survival and brutality if pushed far enough....

He didn't answer, ducking his head to catch up with his stacking duties.

"Not as badass as your boyfriend, though."

Cade sighed dramatically.

"I don't know what we are, and right now I'm in no position to ask. Or offer," Cade said finally, when LJ's pointed silence was just too annoying. "I'm just... I feel like I'm supposed to be with him."

LJ whistled; he stopped chopping wood and leaned the ax against the stump they were using. "That's not like you."

"Yeah, well." Cade reached for another log, avoiding LJ's eyes. "I've never met anyone like him before."

"Don't doubt that. Which should give you some sympathy for my struggle—put in a good word for me with Rachel."

Cade threw some bark at LJ's head. "It's your funeral, asshole."

RACHEL, IT turned out, was setting the table when Cade and LJ got back to the house, sweaty and starving. The time with LJ had settled Cade down a bit; he knew he had to come clean about Billy to someone before it ate him alive—and Nox was the only person who could truly understand.

Amelia was at the stove, and his father was sitting in his easy chair, watching Sam sleep.

Hackles raised, Cade slipped into the living room and stood between Lee and Sam.

"What's wrong with him?" Lee asked quietly, looking up at Cade with clear eyes.

"He got kidnapped, beat up, and caught in a collapsing building," Cade said. "I think he has pneumonia."

His father nodded. "Your mother's Indian stuff'll clear that up."

"Why are you here?" He couldn't keep the irritation out of his voice.

"Your mother asked me to come for dinner." With an air of dignity missing from last night's confrontation, Lee stood up. He walked around Cade into the kitchen.

THE ENTIRE group came together an hour later; Lee sat at the head of the table, as if his drunken doppelganger hadn't appeared last night. Amelia led everyone in grace, even though the majority of the table were card-carrying heathens. They couldn't quite achieve the tableau of normalcy, even as they passed around bowls of mashed potatoes and platters of chicken.

A sleepy Sam poked at his food, every now and again resting his head on Mason's shoulder. Cade could see his father's eyes linger on Sam, then Mason, then over to Nox. Fingers tight around his fork, Cade tried to concentrate on the meal and not his father's irritation.

Amelia attempted to engage people in small talk, though only Mason and LJ seemed capable of answering.

"So are you all heading out together?" Lee asked suddenly, bringing a halt to the conversation.

"Dad, please," Cade muttered, matching his father's hard stare with one of his own. "This can wait until after dinner."

"It's a simple question. You leaving together or not?"

"I can't really speak for anyone else," Nox said, breaking the stare between father and son. "But Sam and I will be gone as soon as he's feeling up to traveling. Everyone else is free to make their own decisions."

Cade caught the emotional look between Sam and Mason from his seat across the table; his stomach sank with the pronouncement. That didn't leave much room for Cade in the equation—there wasn't even a space for him to jump in and say *sure, I'll go with you; what the hell else do I have to do?*

Lee seemed satisfied with Nox's answer; in the end, he was the only person who bothered to finish his meal.

CADE AVOIDED Nox after dinner. He helped his mother clean up, watched his father bid her—and only her—a good night, then head out the door to return to his apartment.

Surreal.

"Sam's all settled in," Nox said as he entered the kitchen. "Your mother's medicine cabinet is apparently full of magic."

Cade refused to turn around, up to his elbows in soapy water as he scrubbed a plate, furiously determined to wipe the stupid flower pattern right off it.

"How's the rollaway bed working out?" Amelia asked. He could hear the note of mischief in his mother's voice.

"Perfect."

The back door opened as LJ clattered back in after evening chores.

"Cade, you almost done? I want to show you somethin'." LJ wiped his boots on the mat. "You too, Mr. Mullens."

"Go on, I got this." Amelia waved them out the door—personally hip checking Cade away from the sink and forcibly removing the sponge from his hand. "Wipe your hands and go."

They grabbed their jackets from the hook and followed LJ outside. He led them toward the tidy guesthouse—where Rachel waited on the front stairs. Nox sighed heavily next to Cade.

"She's freaking everywhere."

"Well, it won't be much longer now. You can take Sam and disappear pretty soon, right?" Cade hurried past LJ, then up the stairs past Rachel as she stood up.

Irritated, Cade stepped inside the house—and did a double take.

Whatever he had been expecting behind that door, this was not it. The entire main room of the house, floor to ceiling, was filled with equipment—computers, scanners, monitors, printers, and cables of every possible color snaking around. The only furniture other than that supporting the computers was a futon covered in a quilt Cade recognized from the house and a rolling chair near one of the desks.

"What the hell is all this?"

LJ stepped in behind him and clapped Cade on the shoulder. "I'm a disinterested farmer, but fuck if I'm not a great hacker."

"Tell me you can make IDs," Nox said, stepping into the wonderland of computers.

"Oh sure, whatever you need. I figured you guys would be needing stuff."

"Yeah, Sam and I…."

Cade stifled a sound of irritation as he went into a far corner to poke at some laptops lined up on a wide shelf. He recognized his old one from college right up to the most recent model on the market. Each one ran a program, code scrolling by at a rapid pace.

"Why didn't I know you were a nerd, LJ?" Cade called, interrupting whatever LJ and Nox were talking about. "You didn't do this in high school."

He remembered field parties and some drag racing, football and baseball, and always girlfriends that changed with the seasons. The only time he saw LJ at the computer was when he figured out how much free porn there was.

"Nope. Community college." LJ came to stand next to him, hands tucked into his back pockets as he admired his setup of computers. "Business management and accounting were freakin' boring, so I started tinkering around with programming.... Then I uh... got a little obsessed."

Cade narrowed his gaze. "How much of this shit came from my money?"

"Enough that I'm beholden to you and your friends for whatever you need." LJ coughed, then elbowed Cade in the ribs. "You need a new ID?"

"We all do," Rachel said. The brothers turned in unison to regard her, lazily leaning on the chair like a '50s pinup. "Birth certificates, government identification cards, passports would be nice. I've always wanted to see Paris."

"Hmmm—me too."

Cade needed a drink, watching as LJ sashayed over to Rachel's side, voice honey-sweet. He stole a glance at Nox, who was regarding the entire scene with a measure of distaste.

"We need credit as well." Nox spoke loudly—clearly trying to wrestle LJ's attention from sampling Rachel's wares. "But that might be more complicated."

"They'll be watchin' your accounts."

Nox shook his head. "They don't know about the accounts I'm speaking of. They technically belong to someone else. Someone, uh... someone who is presumed dead."

Now he had Rachel's attention. The flirty air disappeared, a serious scowl turning her face older and harder. "That's crazy."

"It's been seventeen years. If it's still there, it'll buy us some safety." Nox took a breath, then finally met Cade's penetrating stare. "All of us."

Cade unhitched his anger by about 1 percent. He nodded. "Thank you. But exactly how dangerous is accessing this money?"

"If it's still there," interjected Rachel. "*If.*"

"Even if they follow the dots, I'm Patrick Mullens. That's who they're after," Nox argued. "Even if they run my prints, they're not going to get anything. I'm not in the system."

"I am, and so is Cade. You work in the District and they fingerprint you."

"How'd you get around that one?"

Rachel didn't even blink. "I have my ways, just like you do. We might have used the same guy," she said dryly. "Although I left him with a smile on his face. You probably shot him."

LJ watched them like a great tennis match was going on right in front of him.

Cade rubbed his eyes wearily. "Would you two please…?"

"So our prints can't be connected to those accounts," Nox went on, ignoring Cade's warning. "Which means they're fair game."

"They know who Cade is! They've already been here. That means if they're watching this farm, they're going to think it curious if bank activity begins in earnest and we start draining money from the accounts of dead people." Rachel all but threw her hands in the air. "It's too risky."

"Uh, excuse me. Hate to interrupt this little back and forth, but…." LJ looked at each of them, barely hiding a smirk. "What if I'm able to bypass their trace?"

"I'm sure you're very good, LJ, but this is the government we're talking about."

"Thanks for the vote of confidence, little brother." LJ poked at the keyboard behind Rachel. "But while you were off making friends with people havin' disreputable backgrounds, I was makin' friends with people who can get around a government trace." He sounded so proud that Cade's frown faded a bit.

"How do you know they won't turn you in?"

LJ gave Rachel a disarming smile. "'Cause they don't hate anything as much as they hate the federal government. I could tell 'em I was helping Satan run coke to an orphanage and so long as it was government run, they'd give me the passwords I needed. Probably throw in some beer too."

"Well, that's terrible," Cade sighed, even as Rachel and Nox looked interested.

"So am I getting a dead guy's money?"

Nox rocked back on his heels; Cade watched the muscles jump under his left eye, his hands twitching at his sides.

"Yeah. I'll give you the name and social security number," Nox said slowly.

Rachel's lips went into a straight line, and then she nodded. "And when you're done with the family fortune, I might have somewhere else you can look for money."

LJ gave an actual fist pump at the news. He gently scooted Rachel from his chair and pulled his keyboard to the edge of the desk. "Fire away."

Chapter Ten

Cade waited for some indication from Nox he should stay, that they had something to say to each other, but when his—whatever he was exactly—went deep into conversation with LJ and Rachel about overseas transactions, Cade left the guesthouse and slammed the door behind him.

Fuck this, all of it. Clearly his first mistake was believing Nox thought of him as something other than just a helper monkey he fucked on occasion. Cade had given up everything—willingly—to help Nox and his son, and this? This was the thanks he got. Dismissed as soon as he wasn't necessary.

Cade should have known better.

He breathed in the cold air, kicking rocks as he headed for the barn. Where did this leave him? Nox and Sam would disappear into the world with new identities, and what would Cade do? Stay here at the farm and wither away? Get his own fake identification and follow suit? Maybe somewhere warm, maybe a place no one knew he was a failed whore and everyone's second choice.

At some point—probably in an hour or two—Cade would hate himself for being so self-defeating and possibly irrational, but fuck it. Right now, he was going to wallow.

Then a flash of movement caught his attention up ahead. Every bit of anger drained out of him, turning to a knee-knocking fear as a figure walked through the shadows down the sloping hill. Cade was out in the open; his options were turning, running, throwing himself into the bushes, and raising an alarm—but panic locked him into place so his only choice was to wait.

The spill of light from the security floods meant he was seen, meant that this person could....

"Caden?"

Cade's heart thumped violently—he nearly tripped on the grass under his feet. It was his father.

"Yeah," he called weakly. "Yeah."

"You shouldn't be out walkin'." Lee Creel came into the light; he stood a few feet downslope from Cade, bundled in his heavy jacket and carrying a shotgun over his shoulder like the freaking Marlboro Man. "You don't know who's around here."

"You just called out my name, so even if they didn't see me, they heard you," Cade muttered. "You hunting in the dark?" he said, louder this time.

"Patrollin'. You brought dangerous things to this house, Caden Lee. I'm makin' sure your mother is safe."

"She'd probably be safer if you still lived here—or wait, is that why she kicked you out?" Cade laughed at himself. A few moments ago, he was afraid for his life; a few minutes before that, he was watching LJ start the process of fucking with the government. And now? Picking a fight with his father.

Maybe he had a death wish.

"That's none of your business," Lee said finally, his voice low and dangerous in a way that Cade had firsthand knowledge of. Usually the sound his father made right before Cade got a smack to the side of the head. "You're not in any position to be makin' judgments about other people's lives."

"I didn't do anything wrong," Cade snapped. "I didn't hurt anyone. I didn't set off that bomb. Shit, I helped people, okay? Got them out of a goddamned burning building. But you didn't even ask, did you? Just assumed."

"You went up there to whore yourself out and got mixed up with the wrong people—that wasn't an accident. If you stayed home—"

"If I stayed home, what? I could play disappointing second son to you for the rest of my life? No thanks." Cade turned to walk away but couldn't resist a parting shot. "The only good part of all of this is you finally lost your cash cow. No more pimping me out. Now you're going to lose this shitty farm, Momma's gonna leave you for good, and you'll be stuck with nothing."

Shaking, Cade aimed his angry steps in the direction of the barn. He could throw that shit at his father, but in the end, Cade wasn't going to end up with much himself.

"Caden!"

He disappeared into the inky shadows of the outbuildings, a child's sense memory of the corner of the barn's loft where he would escape when being *Caden Lee Creel* became too much.

"Stop walkin'—I want to talk to you," Lee snapped from somewhere behind him.

A few feet from the side door, Cade skidded to a halt, dirt and tiny rocks kicking up under his boots. His breathing shook and rumbled as his emotional state became seriously compromised. It was anger and fear and shame and a million other things that seemed to bang off each other with increasing fury until all he had was clenched fists and nowhere to go.

"You don't speak to me like that," his father said.

Cade didn't turn around, nails biting into his palms.

"I know we don't get along, but this isn't me punishing you for breaking curfew or cutting school." Lee came closer; Cade could hear his breathing.

"I didn't do anything wrong," Cade muttered. "I didn't. I could have walked away, but I thought I could help...."

His father's hand came down onto Cade's shoulder; he jumped, his stomach twisting with the memory of Billy's touch.

"You need to tell me the whole story."

THERE WAS a stone bench near his mother's flower and vegetable beds; they settled into the cold shadows, the space between them generous. Cade stared at his boots, just enough light from the house reaching them and giving some relief from the darkness.

He started with the letter, rambling on through the Byzantine roads of their journey over the past few weeks. Lee said nothing during Cade's monologue, didn't even make a disapproving grunt. The only thing that Cade tried to leave out was Billy—but the void of that incident seemed to overtake his narrative. He felt the hole, the weight of it under his skin.

"When you found that man dead, what did you do?" Lee asked, and Cade swallowed the sick lump in his throat.

"I… I got out. I uh… I got out."

His voice shook, a cough sputtering from the bile burning his throat.

"Caden"—and really, it was his father's shockingly gentle tone that pushed the words from his mouth.

"I killed him," he whispered. "I hit him until he let go of me."

His father sighed as Cade folded in on himself. The release of words dizzied him—like gravity shifted under his feet.

There was no comforting touch, no hug like a movie father might do. Lee tapped his foot against the ground, a quiet huff to his breathing.

"Anyone else know that?"

"No." Cade rubbed his face with both hands, shivering a little bit.

"Not even your…." He paused. "Boyfriend."

Cade laughed into his palms. "No, not even him."

Lee grunted. "I been reading about the explosion. The whole place came down, which means even if they find the body, they aren't gonna be able to tell what happened."

And then it dawned on Cade what his father was trying to get at.

"Oh God, Dad." Cade dropped his hands in his lap. "I'm not scared they're going to arrest me. Not for that anyway."

"Those feds said you were a witness."

"And the word back in the District is that I'm an accomplice." Cade sighed as he leaned forward, elbows on his knees. "Somebody's lying."

"So you leave—where you gonna go?"

"What the hell do you care? Didn't you practically kick me out two nights ago?" Cade's annoyance was rising again.

The butt of Lee's gun knocked against his boot. "Someone's gotta keep things together, Caden."

"Momma said you've been drinking, and she kicked you out—try again."

Lee stood up abruptly at that, the shotgun swinging dangerously before finding purchase on his shoulder again. "I left because I knew I had to get straight with myself. Doesn't mean I don't love your mother. And it sure as hell doesn't mean I stopped being head of this family."

"Yes, sir," Cade answered, giving his father a halfhearted salute.

The peaceable mood between them snapped and broke; Cade could feel his back going up, the distance widening, with each of them on the opposite side of the valley, not quite able to see the other.

"I'm gonna take another walk around the property," Lee said, his voice cool. "You get yourself inside."

Without another word, he turned and walked away.

CHAPTER ELEVEN

NOX FINISHED writing down all the information for LJ, avoiding the looks Rachel was shooting him over LJ's head. Accessing Boyet money was a risk, but it was a chance he'd take—money to send Sam somewhere safe, money to make sure Cade got something out of all this. Maybe enough to keep the farm afloat a bit longer.

Money to fund his way back to the District and find the people manipulating his life like unseen puppet masters.

Poetic justice.

"Anything else?" he asked, dropping the pencil on the desk.

"Nope." LJ picked up the pad, looking it over. "Gonna take me a while—might as well go find my brother and apologize for being a dick boyfriend."

Nox's spine stiffened; he set his face into something stern, only to see Rachel break into a grin.

"I don't know what you're talking about. Cade and I are just...." Nox started the sentence with a full intention of setting the record straight. Except he wasn't sure he knew what that meant. "Cade and I are fine."

LJ didn't look up from the screen that held his full concentration, but his smirk matched Cade's perfectly. "Uh-huh."

"Go. I'll help Mr. Creel with any information he needs," Rachel said sweetly. She pointed helpfully at the door.

Nox wanted to argue, but staying around Rachel for long periods of time made him crazy, and beyond that, if Cade was angry with him, well, he'd like to work out why. If they only had a few days left....

An awkward emotion tunneled up through Nox's chest; for all his logical decision-making, the part that related directly to Cade was the hardest to reconcile. He wanted to go back to New York. He wanted to keep Sam safe. He wanted—Cade.

"Fine," he mumbled. "Let me know when it's done."

He headed for the door, well aware of Rachel's amused stare following him.

OUTSIDE, THE cool night air smelled like nothing Nox had ever known—fresh and clean, completely devoid of the faint stench of decay he'd lived with for so long. The sky was vast overhead, tiny twinkling dots of light spread out as far as he could see. Maybe when this was all done—if he was still alive—he'd make a home for him and Sam somewhere like this.

The ground crunched under his feet as he paused on the tiny stone walkway.

Sam. The more he thought about taking him somewhere else, the more he realized how much Sam didn't want to go. He could pretend all he wanted that Sam was still a child, still beholden and devoted only to him, but that was a lie.

He'd be eighteen soon.

There was no mistaking the way he and Mason looked at each other.

What if he told Sam it was time to go and Sam chose Mason?

"You got your new identity yet?" a voice asked. Nox turned around slowly to find Cade a few feet away, slumped on a stone bench.

"Your brother's working on it." He kept his tone neutral, well aware of his hammering heart and the irritated look on Cade's face. "You're going to need one as well for when—"

"Right. For when you fuck off to parts unknown and leave me behind. Got it," Cade spat.

Nox's breath caught. "Are you sure you want to come with me?" he asked. He gazed at every shadow to avoid looking at Cade. "It's dangerous."

"Mmm, right. So dangerous you're dragging along a seventeen-year-old kid," Cade scoffed, walking slowly into the weak spill of light from the guesthouse. "Just admit you don't want me along."

"I'm going to take Sam somewhere safe. And it's not a matter of wanting." Nox's defenses began to ramp up, arming with ammunition. "It's what makes the most sense."

"Up until a few days ago, you ran around the city stabbing drug dealers—and now you're talking about making sense?"

"I did what I had to do."

"Well, I wouldn't know anything about that." Cade kicked a clump of dirt so hard it sprayed over Nox's boots. "Fuck you."

Anger boiled up; Nox could feel his face heating, a sour taste filling his mouth. "I appreciate your help. I couldn't have done this without you," Nox said, his voice measured and even. "But as far as the future goes, I have to look out for my son and myself. I don't want to mess up anyone else's life."

"And what are you going to do when he tells you he wants to be on his own?" Cade's anger seemed to fade. When he came into full view, Nox almost needed to look away. Because suddenly all those moments when he thought *I cannot resist this man*, returned with a rush like a tidal wave crashing into him.

"Sam and I—we are all that's left of my family," Nox murmured, unable to turn away from Cade's imploring gaze. "We have no one else in the world...."

"That's not true."

"Mason is just—it's a crush, okay? That's all." Nox tried to sound convincing, tried to convince himself. "Sam will see that."

"And what about you?" Cade closed the distance between them until Nox could feel the heat radiating from his body, tendrils of desire snaking their way under his clothes and into his blood stream.

"What about me?" he asked in a whisper. The pull of Cade's steady gaze locked him in place.

"You're not alone, in case you haven't noticed."

Nox wasn't sure if he moved first, or if it was just inevitable that he lean down, tilt his head, and find Cade's lush and searching mouth with his own.

Just like the first time, Nox convinced himself a taste would satisfy the urge—if he stole a tiny moment, he could wrestle himself away permanently, he could walk in the other direction with his thirst quenched. But Cade twisted against him, hot and dirty, teasing his tongue as he rubbed his hands down Nox's back. When he brushed over the gun tucked at his waist, Nox tried to push Cade away, but it only seemed to inflame them both, locking their bodies together even tighter.

The wet sound of their kisses obliterated everything else; Nox imagined eyes on them, danger around every corner, but it didn't stop him from sucking on Cade's bottom lip or letting his palms drag down to rub against his ass.

Cade pulled away first, a tiny moan escaping as he stumbled backward. Nox reached to drag him back, but Cade had other plans. He caught Nox's hand and yanked him into the shadows.

They tripped and stumbled around the corner, Nox trusting his night vision and Cade's familiarity; there was purpose to this, he could feel it, and it made perfect sense when the smaller of the two barns loomed over them a second later.

Cade fiddled with a side door for a moment; Nox crowded him from behind, unable to keep his hands from Cade's body. He molded himself against Cade's back, pressing and rubbing his hips against the curve of his ass.

"Stop, I have to get this open," Cade murmured, pushing back in his own hungry rhythm.

Nox couldn't suppress the nasty chuckle that welled up inside him. He ran his palms over the front of Cade's jacket, then dipped down until he could cup and tease at his erection straining against the zipper of his jeans.

"Fuck, stop." Cade's protestations were weak. He stopped trying to open the door, bracing himself on both hands against the wood, open to Nox's probing fingers.

It didn't matter someone might find them. It didn't matter that anyone could walk over here. The only thing that Nox's lust-addled mind could process was the loud sound of the zipper in the darkness, the raspy breath Cade took when Nox slipped his hand into the open V of Cade's jeans. The heated weight of Cade's cock against his palm as he tightened his fingers into a fist and began to stroke.

Nox buried his face against the back of Cade's jacket, held him around the chest, and rubbed his erection against Cade's ass with a breathless urgency. He could smell the desire, feel the tiny pearls of moisture as he cupped the head of Cade's dick. It spurred on the demanding rub of his hips, the way he panted in his lover's ear. He wanted to push Cade to the ground and tear away the clothing barriers. He wanted to open him up with his mouth and fingers and taste and....

Cade stiffened in his arms, a second's warning before he thrashed out his orgasm—wild in Nox's arms before Nox's hand was wet with come. Nox held on, absorbing every bump and grind, stroking through the mess in his hand until Cade was moaning, his body limp.

"Let me...," Cade murmured, but Nox didn't stop any of his movements; he jerked his fist and pushed the pounding of his hips to an uncomfortable burn of zipper against his painfully hard dick. Nox didn't come until Cade was almost crying with stimulation, and then he spilled in his pants so violently his legs felt weak.

CHAPTER TWELVE

AFTER SO much sleep, Sam found himself up early and unable to relax. A few feet away, Mason lay on the rollaway bed, curved in an S because the thing was about two feet too small for his lanky frame. Mrs. Creel had seemed amused—but insistent—when she showed up with it, and it wasn't hard to figure out his father was behind the change in sleeping arrangements.

Sam was just grateful Mason still got to stay in the same room as him.

Rolling over, Sam watched Mason sleep, excusing how creepy it might be. He was looking, and there was nothing wrong with that. In fact he was fully aware how many times Mason did the same thing, thinking Sam was completely out.

Maybe—just maybe—he faked sleep now and again, to bask in the warmth of knowing Mason wanted to stare.

Mason. Wanted. To. Stare. At. Him.

The tingling feeling of it, the way he felt when Mason looked at him—God, maybe he did want privacy because of the ache of it, the way his dick stirred at the very sight of Mason's strong features in slumber, wheat blond hair sticking up, his full lips....

If he wasn't so utterly horrified by the prospect, Sam would imagine reaching under the covers and into the oversized sweats he was currently wearing and—

No.

No, he couldn't do that. Staring was creepy, but jerking off with Mason a few feet away? That was just gross.

Being a virgin was slightly less terrifying, knowing that Mason hadn't been with a guy. Of course, that led to another set of concerns, about Mason liking girls and having experience with *them*. All of Sam's sexual knowledge was from books he'd snuck out of the library—Henry Miller was a perv, but he was the only reason Sam knew anything.

The guys from his messenger job talked crudely about women they'd slept with, so at the very best, Sam was operating from the same knowledge base as Mason.

This was the least of his worries—sex with Mason wasn't going to happen if his father dragged him away from everyone he knew and cared about.

Sighing, Sam pushed back the covers. He had to move very quietly and very slowly or Mason would wake up. And quite frankly, Sam needed some time to himself.

And not just in the bathroom.

It took him almost fifteen minutes to work his way out of bed and then down the hall. He moved slowly; his cough was rapidly improving thanks to Mrs. Creel and her medicine cabinet. They had so much food—piles of it heaped on his plate at every meal and then more pushed on him for snacks—that Sam felt better than he had in a week. He'd even gotten an old pair of Mr. Creel's glasses from the family's junk drawer, and while they weren't exactly like his old ones, it was enough for him to feel a bit more in control of his surroundings.

After peeing and washing up, Sam took a breath as he headed for the stairs. For all the good side of things, his body was still bruised and battered. He considered it a blessing he didn't really remember much from the kidnapping or the casino—mostly flashes of pain and fear, the smell of smoke. He didn't poke the memories, though. The residual injuries were plenty.

He could smell something yeasty and delicious as he reached the bottom of the stairs. This whole house was like something out of a movie—warm and cozy and filled with good scents and candles and pictures and a nice lady in an apron who petted his head a lot and praised him when he finished a plate of food. For so long Sam'd carried around the fantasy of "normal" life, and now it was both a curse and a blessing to know that it really was as lovely as he'd imagined.

Sam didn't want to leave this behind either.

"Good morning, Sam." Mrs. Creel poked her head around the corner. Her smile reached her eyes; she was wearing yet another brightly colored patchwork apron, her hair tied back and sleeves rolled up. "I hope you're hungry."

At the table, Mrs. Creel settled him into a chair, then filled his cup with hot water and a homemade tea bag. "For your cough," she said, patting his head. Next came a small plate with two hunks of homemade bread, fragrant with pools of yellow butter and a heaping of fresh strawberry preserves.

Sam's stomach practically screamed with delight.

He stuffed his face with the bread—and oh, that was what smelled so delicious. Sam's body almost convulsed with pleasure at the yeasty taste. Everything he'd been calling bread up to this point in his life was a lie.

Sam was still swallowing the last bite when Mrs. Creel appeared again, holding a plateful of scrambled eggs, tiny chunks of potatoes, pepper, onions, and a pile of bacon. "There's more if you're still hungry," she said happily, laying the platter on his placemat.

"Oh man, Mrs. Creel, I might never be hungry again," he laughed.

"You're a growing boy, and you've been sick. Your body needs extra fuel." She ran her hand over his hair. "And a haircut." Amelia Creel clucked her tongue at him. "I'm gonna go into the attic, find you some decent clothes to wear. I have a ton of the boys' stuff up there."

She puttered away back to the stove, and Sam attacked his meal with his fork and a mission. The more food he had, the more fuel for his body to heal. The more healed his body, the stronger he would be...

To stand up to his father and tell him what he wanted.

Toward the last third of the plate, Sam started to feel a little woozy. He obediently drank his tea, then a second cup. His stomach full and his body warm was so lovely a feeling he wanted to curl up under the table and nap until the next round of feeding began.

"You sure you don't want more bread?" Mrs. Creel asked, but Sam shook his head.

"It's all so good, thank you. But I'm full." Sam gave her his best smile, which she returned, her hand stroking his hair. The desire to purr and bat his head against her palm like a cat had never been stronger.

"I'll save you some for a snack," she said; her smile faltered slightly as she stared at him, but a second later she pulled back, lighting up again. "It's nice having a boy around the house again. LJ comes in for meals and then disappears in that computer house of his. Caden's been so far away for so long and, well...." Mrs. Creel sighed. "It gets a little lonely here."

"I understand that." Sam ducked his head. "I mean, I have my dad, but no friends or anything. At least not till Mason and Cade." He gave her his most sincere smile when he looked back up. "Cade is a great guy. He's helped me and my dad so much."

This seemed to please her. "Thank you for telling me that," she murmured. "I know it to be true, but it's nice to hear from other people."

"I hope—like I don't know what's going to happen, but I hope that me and Cade can continue to be friends." *And that he can stay with my dad because he makes my dad happy.*

"I'm sure Caden would like that." Her lips curved into an amused grin. "Seems like he's quite fond of your dad."

"Uh, yeah." Sam wasn't sure how much to mention to Mrs. Creel. Like, should he mention they were totally sleeping together? Although she probably knew that—there wasn't any rollaway bed in Cade's room, that much he was sure of.

"Is that coffee?" LJ sauntered into the kitchen, rubbing his hands together. "And bacon?" He sniffed dramatically. "Momma, did you make bread?"

Sam excused himself when Damian and Cade joined the breakfast table. He felt good but a tiny bit antisocial. As much as he was loving the feeling of not being lonely, that didn't change the fact that he simply wasn't used to this many people.

Moving slowly, Sam made it to the porch without incident. He settled onto the porch swing, perfectly angled to catch some sun.

The warmth and the sway of the swing put him out, because he woke with a start, aware of being watched. When he looked over, he saw Rachel leaning against one of the pillars, her gaze directly on him.

She blinked when she realized he was awake and flushed a little at being caught.

"Morning," Sam said politely, struggling to sit up straight and collect all his scattered thoughts.

"Good morning." Rachel had sort of disappeared since they'd been at the farm, mostly staying in her room. The only person he'd seen less of was Damian, who seemed to emerge for meals and chores—only to slink back upstairs as soon as he was done.

"You uh… you want to sit down?" Sam pointed to the open seat next to him.

Rachel took a while to decide; she stared at him, her coffee cup, the lightly stained floor of the porch, and then she walked over to settle down next to him.

They rocked in silence for a few minutes before Rachel cleared her throat. "So, you like it here down on the farm?"

"Yeah actually. It's so different than home. I feel like I'm in another world," he said, answering honestly. "Trees and grass and plenty of space," he murmured, lost in the rhythm of the swing. "So much food and…." Sam stopped. "It's just different."

"I know you haven't had it so easy," Rachel said softly. She rubbed her fingers on the half-drunk cup of coffee in her lap. "Must've been hard, growing up with just your father."

"He's the best dad." Sam felt a little defensive. "I mean—he works really hard to take care of me, to keep me safe."

"Mmmm." Rachel didn't answer, she just brought the cup to her lips and took a sip.

"You and him don't get along so well." Sam's hands were getting cold; he twisted them together in his lap. "I don't know why exactly."

"That's something to ask your father," Rachel said. She turned to look at him and scanned his face. "Are you still eager to find out who your birth parents are, Sam?"

The question took him aback. He wanted to say yes, but guilt over their current situation and his part in it triggered a wave of shame. He should have thrown that letter away, burned it and forgotten everything but how his father had taken care of him all these years.

"No. I don't care about that," he said finally, his voice cracking. "The only person I need is my dad."

Rachel regarded him, curiosity all over her face. "Growing up, that's all you had. I imagine it's the most comfortable of all the other options."

"Well, yeah. Dad and I kept to ourselves, because you can't really trust people. They might seem like they want to help you, but in the end, they're just using you to get what they want for themselves."

Something flickered in Rachel's eyes. "So you don't trust Cade."

"I didn't say that." Sam's cheeks grew hot. "And anyway, my dad trusts him. So that makes it okay for me to."

"I don't know if he trusts him—they're fucking; that doesn't necessarily mean trust."

Sam's entire face caught fire.

"Oh, I'm sorry. I see by your blush you don't care for my frankness." Rachel was teasing him, he knew that, but he couldn't help looking away. "But you do have things to learn about life, Sam. Like the fact that your father doesn't trust a soul, not even you."

"That's not true at all. My dad and I are a team." Sam felt perilously close to arguing, his annoyance rising. "And the only person he really doesn't trust here is you."

Flustered, Sam stood up, the abrupt movement making him dizzy. He shook off Rachel's steadying hand with a huff, then made his way into the house, and the door clanged shut behind him.

CHAPTER THIRTEEN

BEFORE DAWN, Nox had gotten out of bed, dressed, and armed himself, then crept downstairs and out the back door.

The normal cycle of sleep he'd been on the past few days had only increased his anxiety; to know there was danger out there, potentially lurking behind trees and buildings he didn't know like the back of his hand, made him jumpy and unsettled.

And the fact that Cade soothed some of the insistent burn? Well, that just drove him out the door even faster.

Nox walked the property line, slower than he'd like, but he was still learning the slope and drop under his feet. He checked both barns, the guesthouse, the sheds, and the trucks in the driveway. He walked all the way to the edge of the land, slinking behind a copse of trees near the road to observe.

As the sun rose over his shoulder, Nox's gaze was locked on the comings and goings on the public side of the Creel Farm.

A few cars, two joggers bundled up and lost in the rhythm, completely unaware a man watched them from afar. The property across the way was under construction; only stumps and a half-dug foundation could be seen. If surveillance was ongoing, the feds weren't having an easy time of keeping a low profile; there wasn't much space for someone to hide and still have a line of sight on the house.

When the light was finally bright enough to expose his hiding place, Nox stood up, brushed the dirt and leaves from his pants, then headed back to the house.

LJ met him at the back stairs, startled momentarily by Nox's appearance. He gave him a head-to-toe look-over before shrugging and gesturing toward the guesthouse. "You wanna come sit while I try to steal you some money?"

IN THE guesthouse, LJ immediately sank into his office chair, running his hands through his wild shock of hair. He muttered to himself as he checked three of the screens surrounding him.

Nox settled onto the futon, his own gears turning. When the money and IDs were ready, he needed to know his next move. Finding a safe place for Sam and then leveraging himself back to the District to begin his search.

Maybe LJ could help with that as well.

The door rattled and then opened, admitting Mason carrying a large carafe and a handful of cups.

"Your mother sent me out here with coffee," he said to LJ, who just waved him in before clicking away at the keyboard.

Mason nodded at Nox, the faint look of panic making Nox feel a bit better—so long as Mason was at least a little afraid of him, the less likely he would do anything to hurt Sam.

Or anything else *with* Sam.

"I'll take some of that." Nox gestured toward the silver-and-black carafe. "Then I wanted to ask you a few questions."

Mason poured them each a cup, after choosing from the mugs he'd deposited on top of a filing cabinet, each boasting a computer company or superhero logo.

"The police are on the take," Nox said as he and Mason sat angled toward each other on the sloped futon. "Everyone knows that. They protect the casinos that throw them the most bribes. But you—you can't be the only cop who isn't just a glorified security guard."

Mason contemplated his coffee cup. "Some departments—well, some are worse than others. Narcotics is a joke. Homicide, it depends on the shift. Most of the senior detectives are cashing two paychecks, one from the department and one from the casinos." He sounded weary, and Nox knew that feeling well.

"Who decides which cops get in on the action?"

"The chief, I guess." Mason shrugged. "I don't know. Some people never get asked and, well, I assume no one's ever said no."

Nox shifted his weight, tapped his boot against the floor. Finding honest cops like Mason might not be as hard as he'd thought.

"Francis, the one who tried to frame Sam for the construction site bombings…."

"Oh man, he's the worst. He doesn't even pretend, you know? He brags about how much he makes off the casinos, how he can do whatever he wants."

I'd like a few hours with him, Nox thought. *I'd make him tell me what I want to know and enjoy every second of it.*

"But he was forced to let Sam go," mused Nox. "Someone higher than he was got Sam out of jail."

"The mayor?" Mason asked. "He and the police chief are always together, thick as thieves."

Nox stood up, unable to keep still another second. "So the police chief gets his orders from the mayor. The mayor gets orders from the casinos…."

A small object plunked against his side. He looked down at his feet to see a fat black marker.

"Write it down. Draw a diagram," LJ called, already back at his computer. "Use the wall. Stop talking so loud." He gestured wildly, leading Nox to walk around to the far wall, where he discovered a large empty room with just four white walls—no windows—and an overhead light fixture in the center of a ceiling fan.

Mason joined Nox, sharing his bemused confusion. "Use the wall, the man said."

Nox shrugged. "What the hell."

He put his coffee down, uncapped the marker, and went to work.

Nox started with some simple organizational charts based on Mason's observations. The mayor to the police chief, to each of the crooked departments and the names of the people involved. Judges were next, in a set of squares to one side. By the time he'd filled half the wall, sweat crept under his arms and over the back of his neck, and Mason had had to go back to the house for more coffee. Twice.

Standing back, Nox stared at the compiled lists and various arrows. He felt almost… unburdened by the act, as if seeing it laid out made it somehow less threatening than the incredible force of the unknown he'd been fighting.

It made him think of his father. And Jenny. Mr. White.

LJ had left a small pile of markers in different colors in the corner; Nox grabbed a dark blue and moved to a second wall. At the top, as far as he could reach, Nox wrote his parents' names: Natalie and Carson Boyet. He added the years they were born and the year they died. He wrote his name and then stilled his hand from adding Sam's.

A moment of sorrow blurred the wall in front of him, and then Nox began to write once more. The chronology of his mother at Morningside Sanitarium. His father's ever-increasing hours away from the house. The years after the storms, his encounters with the Dead Bolt dealers in his neighborhood.

The escalation made his hand shake.

Interlude

NOX IS thirteen. His mother is having a good month, and that is rapidly turning into a good two months, a thing almost unheard of these days. It means his father has started coming home for dinner twice a week, and Nox thinks his heart might explode from happiness.

His friends bitch and moan about family dinners and vacations, complaining about all the time they're forced to spend with their parents. Nox never says anything—he's not going to reveal the delight he feels when his father is at the breakfast table or his mother sits down with him to watch television at night.

He doesn't know what it's like to get too much parenting, only too little.

It's summertime and gorgeous out. His father is wearing casual clothing so alien that Nox wants to take a picture—this is how Carson Boyet looks without a tie. His mother puts on a green dress, and when his father says, "Nat, you look gorgeous," she blushes and giggles. They hold hands walking down the street, with Nox in tow.

Tonight they'll eat and laugh, and Nox will see his parents kiss for the first time in so long he can't remember the last time. They'll sit on the stoop when they get home, eating frozen yogurt and talking about maybe taking a trip over the Christmas holidays. Skiing or maybe Europe or someplace tropical. Nox doesn't care—he'll gladly stay home if he can have this forever.

And if his father takes a phone call after they return to the house, a call that leaves him locked in his office until after midnight—that's fine. It doesn't mean that things can't stay as wonderful as they've been.

The weekend is coming. They'll spend time together then.

Two days later the UPS driver drops off thirty boxes as Nox is coming home from school. The man's expression of sympathy is all too familiar. Hair dank and eyes dull, Natalie flits around the house in a nervous panic, wringing her hands and checking the stove for a gas leak five, ten, twenty times an hour.

Carson doesn't come home for two days. Two weeks later, Nox wakes up to find his mother gone and his father packing a bag in the master bedroom.

And Nox is left alone again.

CHAPTER FOURTEEN

WHEN MASON returned for coffee a third time, Cade followed him back to the guesthouse. Since their little sexual encounter the other night, he and Nox had been doing an odd dance of silent intimacy. They took every opportunity in private to touch and be close, but the second they stepped outside the bedroom door, Nox threw up every wall he could until Cade felt like he was circling a fortress, futilely looking for an opening.

He couldn't find one.

Inside his abode, LJ furiously worked on his computer, muttering into a wireless headset. Mason led Cade into the adjoining room with a quirk of his finger—and Cade's jaw dropped.

Neat and efficient handwriting covered two of the four walls. Squares and arrows linking dates and names and locations in carefully ordered rows. And in the middle of it, Nox, stripped down to his tight T-shirt and jeans, the ever-present Sig at his back, writing what looked to be a chronology.

A timeline of his life.

Cade swallowed. He saw Sam's name. Jenny. Mr. White. And then his, neatly tucked toward the bottom third of the wall.

The Iron Butterfly. Alec.

"Rachel said Alec left on his own," he said suddenly, "because he was asking too many questions."

Nox's hand faltered for a second, and then he turned around slowly. "What else did she say?"

"People came to Zed. They wanted to deal Dead Bolt through the casino...."

Cade talked and Nox wrote everything down, eventually sinking to the floor to use the space. Cade paced, his hands shaking slightly when he mentioned Billy and finding Zed's body.

He stood facing the untouched wall, back to Nox as he breathed deeply.

"He brought me to Zed's rooms, I guess to turn me in," Cade murmured, hands flexing into fists. "Billy was shocked when he saw Zed had been killed, and I managed to get away. But he uh... he kept coming after me. I made it to the closet, and then he was there. I grabbed the first thing I could find, an umbrella I think, and I just...." He choked as saliva filled his mouth; he didn't want to be sick on the wall, so he breathed and breathed, big gulping heaps of air until he could speak again.

"I killed him."

"You protected yourself," Nox murmured, closer than Cade thought, and rested his hand gently on Cade's shoulder. "He would have killed you—all you did was fight back."

Cade nodded. Because logically, yes, he had defended himself. He took no pleasure from Billy's death. But for all his nausea and sickening memories, he wasn't sorry, and that was actually the scariest part. Because he was becoming more aware every day that he'd do it again—and not just because he was in danger himself.

Nox's arms circled his chest, pulling their bodies close together.

"I'd do it again, if I had to," Cade whispered, quiet in his confession. He leaned his head back, letting Nox take his weight for a moment.

"Good." Nox's breath was warm against his ear. "Because I don't want anything to happen to you."

Cade couldn't resist turning in his arms; he liked the look of bashful surprise on Nox's face when they were facing each other.

"I don't want anything to happen to you either," Cade said, close enough for a kiss.

The quick flash of guilt in Nox's eyes was unmistakable.

"Whatever you're planning—" Cade started, but Nox silenced him with his lips.

Cade almost fell for it, almost fell into the slick heat of Nox's mouth and Nox's hands tightly clutching his back, but the distraction wasn't enough to silence the nervous voice in the back of his mind. He pulled away, far enough from the temptation.

"What are you going to do?"

Nox took a shaky inhale, closing his eyes to Cade's expectant gaze. "I'm going back to the city."

The bottom dropped out of Cade's stomach. "You're wanted on a federal warrant," he started, but Nox was already shaking his head.

"We have to clear our names. And I refuse to let them get away with what they did to my family."

"Your family is here, right now. Sam is your family." Cade's voice faltered; he felt the anger and panic turning his face red-hot. "I...." He couldn't make himself say it, fear cutting his words off at the source. "If you go back there, they'll throw you in jail. Or worse. Is that what you want? For them to put a bullet in your head?"

"If they were going to kill me, they would have already."

"You can't think—"

"Rachel was right. She asked me the night we sailed away—why didn't they just kill me? All those years, all the money I cost them by destroying shipments of Dead Bolt." Nox's bewilderment was palpable, but Cade could see him building a head of steam over this train of thought. "I got in their way, and they let me live. I have to know why."

"You have to know why you aren't dead? How about this— you're goddamn lucky. You are lucky to be alive. You have your son, and you have friends." His voice cracked on the word. "You have a fucking chance to start over, and you would give that all up, for what? An explanation? Words? You want an apology because you're alive?" Cade pushed out of Nox's arms, bouncing off the wall behind him. "This is crazy. You cannot go back."

Nox let him go. But the tone of his voice stopped Cade from storming out of the room. "I can't go forward until I know," Nox said quietly. "I can't tell you what you want to hear until I know."

Cade faltered at the doorway, unable to stop from looking back. Nox looked smaller, almost cowed by his admission. The pleading expression in his eyes made Cade's stomach twist.

"You can't tell me what I want to hear if you're dead."

CHAPTER FIFTEEN

DINNER WAS a quiet affair, as half the party remained holed up in the guesthouse. Damian and Rachel, Sam and Mason, and Amelia had a pleasant meal, with sporadic polite conversation and a great deal of "pass the potatoes" filling in the quiet. Afterward Amelia sent the "boys" out for a walk before dark, with orders to get fresh air.

They made it just down off the porch before Mason reached out and took Sam's hand in his.

Sam tried not to spontaneously explode on the spot.

They meandered over the property, trying and failing to make small talk, because Sam was too distracted by the way their fingers and palms curved together, the way his lips buzzed and his heart beat quicker, as if this were an intimate act and not just a simple touch of their hands.

"Let's sit down?" Mason asked, startling Sam out of his daydream. He indicated a small copse of trees ahead, a canopy of branches over a thick felled trunk.

"Sure."

Sam followed Mason's lead until they were situated side by side on the log, the shadows chilling their hideaway.

"Why did you pick—" Sam began. Lifting his chin to look at Mason, he was quickly swept into a tender kiss. They'd kissed before, but not with this urgency, this sense of need. Sam leaned into Mason's body, thrilled when Mason's arms circled his chest. The bite of bark against his legs was the only thing that kept him tethered; he wanted to fly up and sing with delight at the soft press of his lips against Mason's.

The tongue tracing the seam of his lips—that was a jolt.

Sam didn't think, he just instinctively opened his mouth, gasping when Mason tilted his head and pushed in, sucking on the tip of Sam's tongue.

Mason made a delicious noise, and a warm palm pressed against the inside of Sam's thigh. The hot-cold flares of desire in the pit of Sam's stomach became almost painful as Mason traced his fingers inside Sam's pants, closer and closer....

Sam pulled away, trying to get air into his lungs.

"Um...."

"Sorry—I'm sorry." Mason pulled his hands away, scooted his body until they were no longer touching.

That was not what Sam wanted at all.

He followed Mason, ignoring the roughness tearing at his borrowed jeans, the light-headed blur before his eyes as he moved too fast; Sam pressed against Mason's body, trying to pull his mouth against his once again.

"You're not making it easy to be responsible," Mason whispered, his breath warm against the side of Sam's face.

"You started it." Sam made a decision, a second's thought, and then he was straddling Mason's lap, tucking his knees against Mason's hips.

He hadn't calculated Mason's surprise, or the delicious rub of their bodies against each other. They tilted toward the ground, and Mason slid his big hands around Sam's waist to try to steady them.

"Sam." It was a glorious whisper; Sam's chest heaved with effort and lust—he was pretty sure that's what it was. Lust and pneumonia and being pressed up against Mason, chest to chest....

"I wish we knew what we were doing," Sam whispered, slipping his hands into Mason's hair and holding on for dear life. He wanted to be embarrassed for how turned-on he was, but Mason rocking his hips told him he wasn't alone.

"We're doing fine," Mason said softly before slotting their mouths together once again.

As THE sun set, Cade walked back to the house to return the basket of dirty dishes to his mother. There was a strange intimacy to watching Nox fill the walls with the narrative of this journey so far—odd to see so many terrible things reduced to squares and arrows and names.

Caught up in his thoughts, Cade almost missed the emergence of Mason and Sam from the trees, clothes rumpled and faces bright red. He didn't need full sunlight to catch those details—they were bright and shining as the neon signs in the District. They didn't see him, hand in hand as they walked in the opposite direction, off toward the barn.

Oh crap was all he could think. Nox wasn't going to like this one bit.

In the kitchen, Cade found his mother serving coffee and cake to Rachel, Damian, and his father, whom he ignored entirely from the second he walked in until he was done filling the empty carafe.

"What are you crazy kids up to?" Rachel asked, breaking the silence sitting heavy over the room.

"Just putting together some notes." Cade screwed the top on the carafe and then glanced at Rachel. "Maybe you can help, actually."

There was a hint of strain around Rachel's eyes and mouth— maybe it had always been there, hidden by makeup, or maybe everything was catching up with her. Whatever the reason, she had knowledge, and if he could keep her and Nox from killing each other, they might just solve another piece of the puzzle.

CADE KNEW Nox would make a face when he entered with Rachel, but it was far more muted than he had expected. Another half of the wall had been filled, this time with a map of the island. Nox glanced over his shoulder briefly, acknowledged Rachel, then turned back to where he and Mason had labeled casinos and neighborhoods.

"What the hell?" Rachel asked, even as she drifted closer to the walls, her eyes going wide. "This is...."

"I was thinking you could add some stuff," Cade said, sinking down onto the floor, out of everyone's way. "You've been there for most of this."

That got another head turn from Nox; he locked gazes with Rachel, their expressions similarly matched—a little pissed, jaws locked. Then Nox reached into his pocket and pulled out a red marker.

"I'd love to see what you know," he muttered.

RACHEL STARTED in the middle.

She added three names next to Nox's family tree—Marat Aglaya, Vera Aglaya, Galina Aglaya.

"Galina," Nox said as Rachel wrote out *Jenny* below it.

She drew a line between Carson and Jenny, then began to draw boxes in a new pyramid format.

"So here's a little story about how some Russians freelanced their services out to a Dominican drug cartel."

Interlude

JENNY IS fifteen when her parents die. She comes home from school to find the door of the Brighton Beach cottage kicked in, the smell of blood choking her as she wanders into the bedroom. Marat and Vera are dead on the bedroom floor—head shots, then two to the heart. She is dazed and devastated until a calm falls over her.

They had prepared her for this possibility since she was six years old.

Jenny takes her bag from the closet, the money tucked in the freezer, and the Beretta from the hollowed-out Bible on the bookshelf.

Her father was a Krysha—an enforcer. His job was to protect the cartel from other groups who wanted a piece of the business. Vera's father had been a Pakhan, and while it afforded her protection in Moscow, that didn't extend to America.

They were living on borrowed time and trained Jenny accordingly.

She takes the subway to Manhattan, then down to Wall Street. Once a month Marat took her on the trains, and they mapped out every route she could take—straightforward and to lose a tail—to get to the offices. Once there, she'd invoke a promise made to Marat and Vera by the American contact for the cartel.

Chin up, shoulders back, Jenny tells the guard she is there to see Carson Boyet.

Carson is handsome and neatly dressed, regarding her with curious blue eyes over his glass-topped desk. He doesn't ask many questions except "Can you use a computer?" and "Do you speak Spanish?"

Yes and yes.

Two years later, she doesn't remember her life before being Carson Boyet's assistant. She spends every waking hour in the office, answering his phone in her cheerful fake voice, or running "errands" around the city, a gun in her pocket and a cool smile on her face.

She sits in a car and snaps pictures of a member of the city council trolling for crack in the Village. She bugs hotel rooms and cyberstalks politicians and the city elite. She knows everyone the mayor fucks, including his stepdaughter. She has files on everyone.

When she isn't creating a blackmail database, Jenny is dealing with things Carson doesn't care about. Like paying the household bills and making sure Natalie's stay at the mental hospital is always the deluxe package.

Carson doesn't share what he's doing, but Jenny slowly comes to realize that all his hustle and bustle isn't for their Dominican bosses.

He's got a plan.

So Jenny creates a database of her own. Insurance, in case something goes wrong. And when, a few years later, a man calls one day, when Carson is at Gracie Mansion with the mayor once again, Jenny answers his questions truthfully. She knows what happens to snitches—but then, she knows even better what happens to people who skim off the top.

One head shot, two to the heart.

CADE HELD his breath as Rachel finished her story.

"My father…," Nox began, then stopped.

"He laundered money for a Colombian cartel," Rachel said, still staring at the wall.

"They had him killed."

"Skimming profits is frowned upon."

Cade held his breath, watching Nox and Rachel in a frozen tableau.

"I didn't do it, if that's your next question." Rachel recapped the marker and dropped it on the floor. "The cops came and told me to identify the body. Then when I got back to the office, there was a gun on my chair and a message on my phone."

"Go and take care of my mother." Nox's voice dropped to something low and dangerous, but Rachel, clearly weary, didn't even take a step back.

"No, that was something I decided to do on my own."

"Kill her."

"Hey," Rachel snapped. "I wasn't going to kill her. I just wanted to get her out of there, okay? But you were there, and the baby…." Rachel's voice cracked, her face pale and damp. "I didn't know she was pregnant, or I would have gotten her out sooner."

The air crackled; Cade could feel his chest heaving with tension. Out of the corner of his eye, he saw movement—Mason, who must've come in unnoticed while Nox and Rachel squared off. He didn't know how long, but Mason's fingers fidgeted at his side, like those of a gunslinger unsure of what would happen five seconds from now.

And then realization fell over Mason's expression.

"Oh shit," he murmured, scrambling to his feet. "Nox…."

Mason kept blinking, then took a hesitant step back, as if his brain were clicking everything into its uncomfortable place. Cade tried to decide if he should grab Mason or throw Nox in the opposite direction, so unsure of what his reaction might be.

"You can't tell him," Nox started, but Mason's face cracked from surprise to a firm-lipped refusal.

"I won't lie to him." Mason's shoulders went back, the recurrent tremble to his voice gone. "I won't do that."

"He would be devastated to find out...." Nox was moving across the room, past the stone-still Rachel, past Cade, who couldn't block his desperate stalk to stop Mason from walking out that door.

"Find out what? You're his brother? No—he'll be devastated to find out you lied to him."

The whiplike strike of the remarks hit Nox; he stumbled a little, but even that didn't stop him from grabbing Mason's arm.

They were evenly matched—size, strength—and both, Cade realized, were fighting about the person they loved most in the world.

Sam.

"Hey, hey, let's just—let's just relax, okay," Cade said, getting between them as quickly as he could. "This isn't going to help the situation, and it's sure as hell not going to help Sam."

Gazes locked, neither man reacted to Cade's words. Frustrated, he shoved at Nox's chest, breaking his hold on Mason. Cade kept his hands on Nox's trembling body, as if he could contain the anger and fear boiling below the surface.

From around the wall, a wide-eyed LJ stared, and Cade tipped his head toward the front door.

LJ disappeared quietly—Cade assumed his psychic plea to lock them in had been received.

"You tell him or I will," Mason said finally, when the suffocation of silence and heavy breathing reached its breaking point. He was quiet and sure, his face the picture of disappointment. "My loyalty is with him, and I won't let him keep on believing you're a freaking saint when... when...."

"Hey, you don't know the full story, so shut up."

The three men turned; Rachel stood, framed by the words on the wall, arms folded over her chest.

"You think everyone has the right to know everything? That's bullshit. Maybe Sam doesn't need to know because the story is so fucking horrible it'll ruin his life. Maybe not every kid has to know where he came from, okay?" she snapped. "Hey, your mother was crazy and your father was a fucking rapist—wow, what an amazing gift."

Nox sagged against Cade's hands, then straightened up again, eyes glittering as he glanced over at Mason.

"He's my son, and I would do anything to protect him," he said finally, the threat spelled out in every ice-cold syllable. "Don't underestimate me."

Mason shook his head. "Aren't you just protecting yourself? He blames himself for all this, you know that! He thinks because he wanted to know who his parents are, that's what got you into trouble! You can't let him drag that around."

A sudden commotion from the other side of the wall broke the moment. LJ popped around the corner, a frantic expression on his face.

"The feds just pulled into the driveway."

CHAPTER SIXTEEN

THE BLACK SUV didn't have a front license plate; it was a behemoth of tinted windows and vibes so dire Nox already had his gun drawn. He watched from his perch inside LJ's house, tucked down between two desks piled with old computers and parts. Rachel and Cade were in the corner of the empty loft bedroom, while Mason—the only other armed person in the house—was at the back door.

LJ, scratching his stomach under his T-shirt and ambling like he didn't have a care in the world, walked down the pathway to where five men in gray suits were getting out of the SUV.

Nox controlled his breathing as he monitored LJ's deceptively casual movements. The bombardment of Rachel's revelations and Mason's knowledge set his teeth on edge—he almost welcomed the chance to rush through the door and engage in some sort of violent defense, if only to release the gathering force of his anger.

From the house, Amelia Creel hurried to meet the group, hands frantically fluttering. Before she even arrived, Lee Sr. came around the side of the house, the ever-present shotgun in his hands.

A conversation ensued; the tallest of the gray-suited men came forward, facing the menace of Lee Sr. without even bothering to acknowledge LJ or Amelia. The gun stayed pointed at the grass—just barely; it would have taken a twitch for Lee Sr. to blow the guy's legs off—but there was no mistaking the firm set of Lee Sr.'s shoulders.

Three minutes passed. Five. Sweat pooled under Nox's arms and down his back, his gun heavy, itching his palm. Amelia buried her face in her hands at one point as Nox kept his eyes trained on the four men who stood like silent witnesses to the conversation.

Seven minutes. Suddenly Lee Sr. stuck his hand out, and the fed shook it heartily. After a few nods, and just as quickly as they had come, the SUV of agents backed down the driveway and out onto the road.

Nox shook his head. A trick maybe? An ultimatum?

The Creels, however, didn't seem to be panicking anymore. Nox watched Amelia and Lee Sr. embrace, and LJ turned toward the house with a huge smile on his face.

What the hell?

"What's going on?" Mason whispered from behind him, but Nox was already up, already headed for the door. It flew open and LJ greeted him with a punch in the arm.

"Congratulations, asshole—they think you're dead."

ONE BY one, they converged in the space in front of the guesthouse. Damian and Sam emerged from the house, as shell-shocked as the rest. When Mason made a beeline for his son, Nox not-so-subtly beat him to it, laying a comforting arm around Sam's slender shoulders.

"You okay?" he murmured as Sam nodded nervously.

"Yeah. That was just a little scary."

Nox rubbed Sam's shoulder, glancing toward Mason at the other side of the group. The kid looked pissed, but he wasn't moving from his spot.

"What happened?" Cade asked, directing the question to LJ, who couldn't seem to wipe the grin off his face.

"He said there was a raid up in the District," Lee Sr. answered instead, his voice gruff. "Police got a tip, went into this house, and found the Vigilante fellow. Got killed in a shoot-out."

The bottom dropped out from under Nox's feet. His gaze went immediately to Cade, who was dead white.

"What? That's not possible."

"Said the guy was dead. They found enough evidence to prove he set the bombs," LJ interjected. "Said it looked like he worked alone, which means...." He ruffled Cade's hair like his little brother had just gotten an A on a test.

"Which means there are no warrants, which means y'all are fine. Praise God," Amelia said delightedly, throwing her arms around Cade's neck.

Sam whooshed a sound of relief next to him, folding into Nox's embrace. "Oh my gosh," he mumbled into Nox's shoulder. "We're safe."

Nox didn't celebrate, but he hugged his son tightly, his focus on Rachel, who stood on the other side of the little celebratory huddle of Creels between them. Her expression was like the visual of how his insides were twisting and calculating at this very moment.

For the second time in his life, someone was making sure Nox was safe by claiming he was dead.

"WE HAVE to talk," Rachel murmured to him as they went into the house with Amelia. "This isn't good."

"Give me a few minutes."

Nox kept walking past her, locked in on Sam, who'd already circled back around to get to Mason.

"Mason? That's your name, right?" Lee Sr. suddenly called out. "Come here."

Detoured, Mason walked over to the back door, casting a glance over his shoulder at Sam.

"Why don't you ask Amelia if you can help her with feeding everyone," Nox said quietly, and Sam—being Sam, kindhearted and unquestioning and eager to contribute instead of lying around—perked up at the idea. "If you're feeling up to it."

Sam gave him a dazzling smile. "I feel so good right now."

He shuffled over to the stove, where Amelia already had Damian on fetch patrol to the pantry.

Cade ducked around LJ and the suddenly crowded kitchen to reach Nox's side. "My father's going into town to speak to the sheriff, make sure the feds aren't setting a trap." A tiny smirk—a smirk Nox had dearly missed—twitched against his lips. "And he's taking Mason as company."

"What a great idea." Nox reached out to touch Cade's face but at the last second realized the crowd and the moment.

Cade's expression fell slightly. "Rachel's in the sunroom waiting for you."

The fact that it was Rachel he needed at this moment....

Nox swallowed the irony that burned his throat. His stomach bubbled unpleasantly, even as the reassuring sound of Lee Sr.'s pickup leaving the farm echoed. A little more time, another set of stories to weave, another layer to protect Sam.

In the sunroom, among the plants and tidy wicker furniture, Rachel waited, perched on the edge of a sofa that had seen better days. She still carried herself like nothing fazed her, nothing could touch her.

He knew better.

"I'll just skip accusing you of this," he said lightly, clearly catching her by surprise.

"Did you just make a joke? Fuck, it is end times." Rachel sank back into the blue calico cushions, weary. "What do you think that was about?"

Nox shrugged. "Smells like a trap. Why would they make a show of coming here and telling the Creels?"

"They want us to think we're off the hook. I'm pretty certain they're going to come back from Sheriff Cornhole's office and tell us yes, the District police are saying the Vigilante is dead. And that means someone is manipulating us."

"Maybe they're trying to smoke us out."

"This is like the guy on the boat—why send the least logical and efficient way to get us? I'm not convinced these people are bumbling idiots." Rachel picked at the fabric of her sweater, arms crossed over her chest. "That leaves yet another version of my question, Nox. Why haven't they just killed you? Who the fuck is protecting you?"

The note of hysteria in her tone—Nox felt it up his spine.

"You know."

She shook her head wildly. "No."

"You suspect."

Her eyes grew wide, and when she looked away, the hair on Nox's arms stood up.

"We need to go back to the guesthouse. I... I need to figure something out," she finally answered.

They didn't give much explanation as they breezed through the kitchen. Cade and LJ hovered behind them, but Nox didn't invite them to follow. He couldn't afford to pause for Cade's angry expression or the stares they received as the door slammed behind them.

Rachel practically ran to the house, and Nox stayed at her heels, resisting the urge to grab his gun from the small of his back. The danger that had followed them from the city, the things he'd been hiding from for so long, seemed more present in that tiny guesthouse than they had at home.

The gun would do him no good anyway.

They hurried into the house and then around to the wall with their notes. Rachel fumbled on the floor for a marker, the orange one in her trembling hands as she picked a clean section.

Down the middle she drew a line, shaky and uneven.

"Why did the Colombians kill your father?" she asked, startling Nox from his rambling mind, his fantasies of grabbing Sam and getting the hell out of there before Mason came back.

"What?"

"Why did they kill him?"

"You said… you said because he was stealing," Nox spat. He hadn't processed that accusation; that his father would work for these people was horrible, but the fact that he stole from them….

"Right."

Rachel wrote *Colombians* at the top of one column.

Then: *Carson*.

"Why did they kill my parents?"

"How the hell would I know?"

She wrote their names under *Carson*.

"Why did they want to kill you?"

"Jesus Christ, Rachel." Nox wished there were something in the room to throw or kick. His lack of answers already tasted like poison. More questions plucked at his sanity.

Nox. His name in orange with the rest.

"You're alive because I lied. You're alive because of a fluke, them thinking you were on the ferry with Jenny. But they wanted you dead," she murmured. He could see her shaking, the hunch of her shoulders.

Nox bit the inside of his mouth. "They wouldn't be protecting me now."

"If they wanted you dead at sixteen and stupid, why the fuck would they want you alive full-grown and meddling in their business?" Rachel turned around slowly.

"The Colombians aren't running Dead Bolt."

"No, I don't think so."

"The man who grabbed me, who warned me off—he knew about Sam, and he knew about my mother." Nox walked backward until he could point at the timeline. "Someone from my father's office, someone he trusted."

"There was me and there were freelancers when we needed something. After my parents were gone, Carson moved everything a little tighter together. He wanted as few people involved as possible."

"What about someone from the cartel who—I don't know, changed their mind about me?"

"Do you think they were hanging in our office, drinking wine?" Rachel scoffed. "You don't socialize with the guy laundering your drug money."

"So you never met them?"

Rachel's frown deepened. "Just phone calls."

She turned back around, marker poised.

In the second column, she wrote *Carson*.

"What...?"

Rachel ignored him.

She started writing a list, her handwriting sloppy as she hurried from one line to the next.

Mayor's office.

Gabron Holdings.

Mutual Holdings Ltd.

American Patriot Insurance

"Rachel."

"I wish I had my fucking files," she muttered. "I should have made a copy. I thought there would be time...."

Roland White

Nox stepped forward.

"You knew him, from before?"

"He was a board member of your father's company. Crazy but with enough connections to make him valuable. They gave him side projects to keep him busy."

"He said...." Nox swallowed, wishing he could kill the man a second time. "He said he flooded the sanitarium to kill all those people. My mother would have died either way."

Rachel sighed. In the first column, she added *Natalie*, then the word *Morningside*.

Then she wrote *ferry*, her hand shaking wildly.

"The ferry?"

"Right before... there was all this commotion. The National Guard was freaking out, shoving people on board. Then someone started shooting," Rachel whispered. "We sank so quickly afterward—it must've been the crew they killed."

A chill rolled through Nox. *What better time to commit a crime?* he thought, his mind racing. In the middle of a natural disaster, when your guilt would be washed away or crushed under a fallen building.

"A couple thousand people dead—no one's going to notice a few more."

Rachel dropped the marker on the floor. "If they flooded Morningside, if they capsized the ferry—the question is why."

"The question is who. Who would gain from inflating the number of people who were killed?"

A cough caught Nox's attention; he and Rachel turned to find a pale Cade at the edge of the wall, with LJ hovering behind him.

"Come and look at this."

CHAPTER SEVENTEEN

CADE COULDN'T wait in the kitchen another second; Amelia and Sam were bonding at the stovetop as Damian excused himself to lie on the sofa. He and LJ exchanged looks and seemed to be twitching as if synchronized—finally he grabbed the doorknob and burst into the backyard.

"What the hell is going on, Caden?" LJ's long legs caught him up to Cade's side in a few steps. "I thought you'd be glad to know your name is cleared. You and your friends can—"

"Can what? Go on with our normal lives? The fucking feds were an afterthought, LJ. Of all the people who have wanted to get their hands on me, law enforcement outside the District was pretty much bottom of the list."

"Who the hell is after you, then?" LJ's tone stopped Cade dead in his tracks. Because it was a good question—a great question even. He wanted to say drug dealers and organized crime, but those were just words. They were plots from a television show or vague warnings about bad things.

He didn't know who these people were. And worse, neither did Nox.

Cade couldn't look at LJ, even in the face of expectation. He kept walking, heading for the guesthouse.

"THERE'S A message from one of my contacts," LJ whispered as they heard the rise and fall of Rachel's and Nox's voices on the other side of the wall. He sat down at his desk, clicking on his mail as Cade walked over to press against the wall between him and the conversation.

He didn't understand about the ferry—though suddenly Rachel's behavior on the boat made sense. The idea that people were purposefully killed during the storms and evacuation floored him. Mass murder, undetected....

"Cade, Cade!" LJ frantically waved from his seat, urging Cade over.

Words were unnecessary a second later as Cade leaned down to read over LJ's shoulder.

The numbers.

The zeroes—Cade had literally never seen sums so high on a bank statement in his life.

Nox and Rachel followed them back to the desk; LJ didn't even bother to sit down—he just pointed to where Nox should look, with Rachel peering around his side.

"What the hell is this?" Nox asked, bewildered, as he glanced back at Cade and LJ. "This can't be my trust fund."

"Move." Rachel shoved him aside and dropped into LJ's chair. She grabbed the mouse and scrolled down to the page where recent transactions were shown.

Cade couldn't bear to stay away a second longer; he pushed into the tight circle, up against Nox's side.

No one breathed as Rachel revealed line after line of steady transactions.

Money deposited at astonishing rates, with almost no withdrawals. Month after month, year after year, far beyond the time when Nox and Carson and Natalie Boyet were all presumed dead.

"Who does it say is making all those deposits?" Nox asked. His voice was steady, but he grabbed Cade's hand and twisted their fingers together.

Rachel clicked a few times, then let out a string of expletives in what Cade deduced was Russian.

"I am."

Cade kept a tight hold on Nox's hand as a tremor ran through them both. He waited for Nox to explode, to threaten Rachel's life, but nothing, just shocked silence.

"Who knew your log-in?"

Rachel swiveled in the chair to look back at him, eyes narrowed. "Are you fucking kidding me?"

"It's not that hard to figure out if you know what you're doing," LJ piped up.

"Fine," Nox snapped. "Can you tell where the money is from?"

"Yes, Nox, in the little line that says memo on the checks, we can see it's drug money. Hey, wait, let me see if there are names and addresses there too!" she yelled. "How the hell am I supposed to know?"

LJ made a gesture with his hands—like Moses trying to part the Red Sea. "If y'all could move...."

Rachel got out of the chair, shoving it into Nox's knees. LJ dropped down in her place, then began to open other documents onto the large screen. The monitor above, mounted to the wall, displayed lines of code, which he began to search.

Cade bit his tongue until he just couldn't take another moment of incessant clicking. "What the hell did you two figure out?"

"We have a lot more questions than answers," Nox muttered, then began to walk away—with Cade's hand still linked to his.

On the other side of the wall, Cade got up close with the new notes.

His palms itched until he grabbed a black marker resting against the baseboard and began to add a few notes of his own.

Nox started to pull away, but Cade held tight.

"LJ asked me who was after us," he murmured. "And I thought—organized crime and drug dealers, which tells us nothing."

The point of the marker rested on the wall, the smell pungent. "So let's get simple. Dead Bolt is only on the island—why? Why the distribution through the casinos?"

Nox pressed up against him until Cade could feel his breath across his ear.

"Control."

Cade wrote it down.

"If I'm already in the drug business, I have avenues. I have a way to move my drugs, get them distributed anywhere I want," Nox whispered—but Cade could feel the excitement building.

"Not the Colombians," Cade answered.

"Not the Colombians."

"Or the Russians or the Dominicans or the Chinese," Rachel's voice called out from behind them. "There wasn't money to be made on the island for a long time after the storms."

Cade leaned back against Nox's body, their breathing in tandem. The puzzle on these walls wasn't just about breaking the danger following them—it was his future. The prize for solving it meant he got to move on.

"So there's no money to be made until Freck shows up," Nox said, resting his forehead against Cade's temple before moving away, their fingers unwinding at the last possible second. The mayor who resurrected New York City from ruins to Las Vegas's slutty cousin was lauded a hero, but Nox knew he was only a savior for investors, not citizens. "What were you doing then?"

Rachel made a face. "After I got out of the Red Cross tent, I grabbed someone else's ID, because they wouldn't be needing it." She tossed her hair. "Then I made friends with a nice young man who was doing search and rescue in the city. He got me a job."

"Why the hell didn't you run?" Cade asked.

"With what? I didn't even have anything but the clothes on my back. No insurance policy, no money. I thought maybe I could get into the building, maybe salvage something."

"You could have come to the house," Nox started to say, but Rachel just laughed, bitter and loud.

"Uh-huh. Because of that death wish of mine. No, thank you. I realized there wasn't anything for me to find, no one left who I knew, so... I stayed. I managed until the casinos started building."

Cade opened his mouth to question, though it was clear "I managed" was all Rachel was willing to share.

"And no one ever came after you."

"Just you, honey."

RACHEL REJOINED LJ at the computer after that, leaving Nox and Cade alone. Cade slid to the floor, his back against the little space not covered with notes and words and diagrams of a mystery that seemed to grow more out of control with each new question. Nox stroked his beard, walking in a circle for a few moments.

"What?"

Nox tangled both hands in his hair and did a step and pivot, then turned to face Cade. "I have to know what to say before Mason gets back," he said. "He wants to tell Sam."

"So you tell Sam first," Cade said gently.

"No."

"Why? Because it's terrible? Yeah, okay, it is. Rachel's right about that. But if you don't tell him first, if you let Mason...." Cade stopped and took a deep breath. "Sam's in love with him. And Mason is the big strong knight in shining armor. Your kid trusts you, adores you, but...."

"I can't compete with Mason." Defeat seeped into Nox's words.

"You can't compete with the guy treating him like a man," Cade corrected. "You continue to treat him like a child and you'll lose him."

"I have spent seventeen years keeping this from him." Nox sank to the floor, as if pressed down by the weight of it. "I killed...." He caught himself as Cade tilted his head to one side.

"You're going to have to narrow that down," Cade said lightly, but the expression on Nox's face didn't break even for misplaced humor.

"Mr. White. For what he did to my mother."

Cade swallowed hard. "What he...." He remembered Rachel's outburst about not telling Sam the truth, and his gut rumbled, bile in his throat. Mr. White, gentle and crazy, pushing money into Cade's pockets, the reason he ended up at the door of Nox and Sam....

"Oh God." The room spun as Cade dropped his forehead against his knees, swallowing frantically. He'd let that man touch him. For all the douche bags he'd fucked over the years, nothing made his flesh crawl like the one who had never wanted him like that. "I'm sorry...."

Cade felt a gentle hand on his ankle, his thigh. Nox touched his shoulder until he tilted his head up, blinking back tears.

"I brought him to your door, to Sam," Cade choked out.

"No—he sent you there. He already knew where I was, where Sam was living. Someone told him. The fact that he sent you—" Nox shrugged as he ran his fingers across Cade's jaw. "That's the only part of this I'm glad about."

Squeezing his eyes shut, Cade counted to fifty before he could speak, his breath coming in ragged spurts.

"You can't say stuff like that and expect me to let you walk away," he said finally, averting his eyes to avoid Nox's reaction.

"I won't drag you back into that mess."

"Where do I go? Do I stay here? Me and Sam and Mason and Rachel, bunking down with my family, waiting in vain to hear if you're dead or not!" Cade kicked his feet, trying to get out of Nox's hands, but Nox wasn't having it.

"Yeah. Why not?" Nox argued, pulling Cade closer. Cade struggled until Nox forced him down on his back, then he fought only halfheartedly as Nox pinned him to the ground.

It wasn't sexual.

It robbed Cade's breath.

He kicked his feet again, but Nox couldn't be budged.

Cade turned his head, gaze trained on the wall.

"I have to go. I have to—"

"To what?" Cade surged with anger, fighting to throw Nox off him. "Who are you going to kill? You don't have a name. You have nothing. You're running back into that mess, daring them to fucking kill you! You're running so you don't have to tell Sam the truth!"

The struggle turned into near violence as Cade's body reacted like he was back in the closet, back at the Butterfly, trapped under Billy. Frantically he went for Nox's head, trying to get him to move. In the distance someone called his name, then hands pulled at his arms. His chest seized, and for a second, unable to draw a breath, he thought he must be having a heart attack. He kicked harder as a rushing sound overwhelmed him.

Drowning, he was drowning.

CHAPTER EIGHTEEN

CADE WOKE up in his bed, stripped down to his underwear and draped with blankets. The flashback to waking up in Nox's house didn't escape his groggy mind as he fought to sit up.

"Caden," his mother murmured as she appeared at his side, her face drawn and worried. "Lie back down."

"What happened?" he asked, settling among the pillows. He noticed the room was dark—drawn curtains, low lights. And then he spotted Nox leaning against the wall near the door.

"Panic attack, I think," Amelia said quietly, stroking his cheek with her fingertips. "You blacked out."

Embarrassed, Cade turned his head in the opposite direction. "Sorry."

"Stop it. You've been through so much, Caden Lee. Close your eyes and get some more sleep, all right?"

Part of him wanted to lie here and hide under the covers, let his mother baby him for a while. He wanted to ignore the room of questions, the millions and millions of dollars filling the spreadsheets on LJ's computer, the threat circling over them like buzzards over a carcass.

But Nox's silent vigilance pulled him back to reality.

Not enough blankets in the world to hide him from all of this.

"Give me a few minutes," he said, stretching under the covers, working out the angry stress squeezing his limbs. "I'm going to take a shower, and I'll meet you downstairs."

His mother murmured her displeasure with this plan, but under her breath and as she dropped a kiss on his cheek. "All right, then," Amelia said aloud. "I'm gonna make you some of my special tea, for your nerves."

That meant whiskey, and he wanted her to skip the tea part of it— fill up a few tumblers and drop them in a row.

Cade waited until his mother left, well aware of the glance she and Nox shared before she disappeared down the hall.

"I'm sorry I kicked you. And punched you in the face," Cade muttered as Nox pushed off the wall to saunter to his side.

"I deserved it." Nox sat down on the edge of the bed. "Sam will probably do much worse when I tell him," he added, resignation in every syllable.

"He'll...." Cade stopped himself from lying. He pulled his hand out from under the covers to take Nox's, tangling their fingers together. "He'll probably hate you for a while. But then he'll forgive you—because you raised him right."

Nox's shoulders slumped, but he nodded.

"Come here, come lie with me for ten minutes," Cade whispered, pulling Nox down next to him. "Just a few minutes."

Nox went willingly, curling around Cade's blanketed body, his head on Cade's shoulder. Cade smelled the farm and sweat, the sour tang of fear that permeated his lover's body. It was only going to get worse, and nothing they did could stop that.

NOX SHOWERED first, leaving Cade to watch him idly through the frosted glass of the door. Cade leaned against his mother's girly pink vanity, arms crossed, cataloging a familiar body and keenly aware that his first time falling in love was an unmitigated mess. No dates, no getting-to-know-you stage. He couldn't even blame sex at this point—Nox made him crazy and emotional and angry...

And caught.

A smarter man might be chewing his leg off to escape, but Cade just couldn't seem to make himself go.

They passed at the edge of the tub, an intimate moment of Cade's warmth brushing against Nox's dripping wet skin. When Nox angled them into a kiss, Cade's heart pounded out a steady beat of acquiescence. There was no walking away from this.

He stood under the lukewarm water, washing everything twice. Clanging and water running alerted him to Nox still being in the room, but Cade concentrated on the water, on the calm before the storm.

When he slid back the door, the stall chilled from the last rush of water, he spied Nox at the hair-filled sink.

"You clog the drain, my mom's gonna be pissed," Cade said.

Then Nox turned to give the big reveal—and Cade's knees went a little weak.

If Patrick Mullens from that night in the Butterfly looked like a movie star, a clean-shaven Nox—in just a low-slung towel—looked like a god.

"Jesus, that's what you've been hiding under there?" Cade asked lightly, stepping onto the shag rug.

"I almost forgot what I looked like." Nox turned back to the mirror, rubbing his palm across his jaw.

"You're fucking gorgeous." Cade joined him at the vanity, slipping his arms around Nox's muscled torso. They were quite the picture in the half-fogged mirror, like the start of a porno as Cade dropped a line of kisses at the back of Nox's neck. The effects of the cold shower couldn't stop the ache of his dick pressing against the roughness of the towel and the perfection of Nox's body.

Nox moaned a little, but Cade didn't push. They rocked together for a few minutes, Cade finding comfort in the warmth and connection at every point they touched.

"'M gonna get dressed," Cade whispered, another kiss to Nox's shoulder. "When this is over, we'll come back up here and just...."

Nox stiffened a little, nodding as he unwrapped Cade's hands and arms from his waist.

"When this is over."

DOWNSTAIRS IT felt like a funeral was in progress.

His father and mother sat at the table with coffee. Mason—his face set in a stern rictus of disapproval—haunted the corner of the kitchen, pacing nervously. Rachel and LJ were nowhere to be found, and Sam—Sam was in the living room, looking half-terrified and faintly ill.

"Dad?" he asked, standing as soon as they entered the room. "Mason said you needed to talk to me."

Cade touched the small of Nox's back, willing strength through his touch. Nox didn't move or speak for a moment, then took a huge breath.

"Yeah—can you come with me?" Nox's voice rattled as he made his request.

Sam's eyes went wide behind his glasses as he nodded.

Cade watched them go, Nox's arm strong around his son's shoulders and Sam tucked into him, and he wondered if he'd ever see that closeness again.

"I SHOULD…," Mason started, as the door closed behind them, but Cade just shook his head.

"Sit down and have some coffee. Sam's gonna need you in a little bit, but right now—this is between him and his father." Cade dropped into the chair between his parents, well aware of their interest.

"I talked to the sheriff," Lee Sr. said. "Feds told 'em the same thing they told us, then packed up and left."

"That is good to know." Amelia poured Cade a mug of coffee, then did the same for Mason, who'd come a bit closer but still not taken a seat.

"You stayin', then?"

Cade wrapped his hands around his coffee mug, watching the plumes of steam and tiny bubbles. "No."

"Oh, Caden."

"Momma, I'm sorry. There's just some stuff that has to be taken care of, and I need to…." *Go with Nox? Do something crazy?* "I need to figure out what to do next. I don't have a job anymore, and maybe it's time for a change."

Lee Sr. huffed from beside him. "You have a perfectly good degree," he grumbled, tapping his fingers on the table.

"Sure, Daddy—I'll just see who's hiring ex-whores with a BA in English."

They lapsed into silence for a few moments until Cade realized they were one person short.

"Where's Damian?"

"Oh, in his room. He was saying all this drama had him feeling unwell," Amelia said. She glanced at the clock. "Let me take some tea up to him."

TEN MINUTES later, his mother came down, a concerned look on her face. Interrupted brooding aside, Cade picked up on her distress the second she walked into the room.

"What?"

"He's not in the guest room," she said slowly, the tea tray awkwardly full in her hands.

Cade stood up the same time as his father.

"So maybe he's—"

"There's—there's something in there, Cade, something I've never seen."

Cade jogged up the stairs, anxiety pricking at him. He pushed open the bedroom door slowly, wishing for a gun but well aware his father and Mason—both armed—were hot on his heels.

Inside the blue-toned guest room, nothing was out of place. Pin neat, except for the small black box sitting in the center of the bed.

A green light blinked, and for a split second, Cade thought it was a bomb.

"Transmitter," Mason said from over his shoulder.

Unease filled Cade as he stepped farther into the room. Damian's bags were gone, all trace of him removed. He imagined if there were a black light sweep, he'd never even find fingerprints.

"What the hell is that?" Lee Sr. asked loudly, bringing up the rear.

Mason, kneeling near the bed, poked it as the green light continued to blink steadily.

"Definitely a transmitter. Old, though," Mason said. "Was this something—"

"Not ours."

"I never saw him with it," Cade said, echoing his father. "We need to tell Nox, right now."

Chapter Nineteen

SAM LET himself be led to the tiny guesthouse, where everyone had been hanging out for hours and hours lately, coming back with grave expressions. Mason refused to tell him what they were doing there—and worse, today Mason had been keeping his distance. He could barely look at Sam, which turned his stomach. And now his father, silent and sad, was bringing him to the house.

He couldn't imagine what was inside.

Rachel and LJ sat at the desk. Seeing Nox and Sam in the doorway, they exchanged glances—then LJ pushed back his chair.

"We'll just leave you two to things," LJ said quietly.

Sheer panic overwhelmed Sam as LJ and Rachel made to leave; Rachel's expression was... angry. Then she brushed her hand against his father's arm as she left.

The door slammed behind them, and Sam started to babble.

"What's wrong? I don't understand," Sam croaked. "Mason is so upset, he won't tell me why."

"Sam, please, just—let me show you something."

Sam followed Nox around the corner and into a large empty room. At first Sam thought it was wallpaper, but then he realized there was writing on the walls—floor to ceiling, lists and diagrams and a map....

"What is this?" he asked, drawn closer to the far wall. He could see his name at the top, grouped with his dad and his dad's parents.

"This is something I should have told you a long time ago.

"I didn't find you abandoned. I watched you be born.

"Our mother died.

"I protected you."

There were other words, but Sam could only hear the worst part—his father, no—no. His *brother* knew.

When those letters arrived from Mr. White, he had known they were a trick. A trap. And instead of telling Sam, Nox let him have hope.

Rage—an emotion so rare, so absent in Sam's soul—began to roil up inside him. He'd been moving since Nox started talking; his back hit the wall, and he pressed all his weight there, leveraged to keep himself standing.

"I blamed myself," he whispered, interrupting his father's....

No.

No.

His *brother's* narrative.

"Sam," Nox implored, as open and emotional as Sam had ever seen him. "You need to understand."

"You could have just said—it's a lie, Sam. It's a lie, and I know it is because I've been the one lying," Sam rambled, his palms flat against the wall. "Why would you do that?"

"I was trying to protect you."

Sam knew that was true. He knew in his bones his father—no, his brother—loved him so much and would do anything to protect him.

Except tell him the truth.

"How dare you?" Sam screamed, because if he didn't let out the anger, he was going to burst. Tears choked his throat, his nose, a tight fist of heartbreak in the center of his chest.

Nox took a step forward to touch him; it triggered something deep and ugly in Sam, and he threw himself at his father.

No.

At a stranger.

He shoved him hard, with both hands, pushing him out of the way. Pushing him out of his life, because no—no. He wasn't going to take this a second longer. He couldn't bear the betrayal....

Stumbling, Sam fled the room and blindly headed for the door. He wanted air and freedom and Mason—because now he knew why the man he loved couldn't look at him. He knew.

The grass was rough under his knees, and it took a second for Sam to register that he was on the ground. He dug his hands into the dirt, gagging on spit and tears as he tried to get himself under control.

"Sam, it's okay, it's okay." Hands soothed him, stroking his back, and oh thank God.

Mason.

"Come on, here you go," Mason murmured, helping him sit up. Sam fell into his arms, crying against his shoulder.

He cried until it hurt to breathe.

"We're going to get up, and we're going to go to our room, okay?" Mason was talking, helping Sam to his feet. "We're going to get you cleaned up, and then we'll… we're going to ask Mr. and Mrs. Creel to help us get to Boston."

"Boston," Sam croaked, clinging to Mason as they walked to the house.

"My parents will take us in, okay? We'll stay with them."

"You're not leaving me here?"

Mason stopped their slow progress, looking down at Sam with a gaze of such devoted tenderness that Sam's eyes burned with another wave of tears.

"You're stuck with me," he said gently. "I love you."

The kiss wasn't pretty, but Sam slipped his arms around Mason's neck and held on tight, sure Mason was the only person in the world he could trust.

Chapter Twenty

"WHAT THE hell?" Rachel asked as she and LJ examined the transmitter, now in residence on the dining room table. Lee Sr. had returned from a walk around the property with LJ, having determined that Damian was nowhere to be found.

"Do you recognize it?" Cade stood at the head of the table, arms crossed tightly over his chest.

"No."

An anxious quiet descended on the house.

Amelia broke the silence with a worried sigh.

"Your mother and I are leaving for a while," Lee Sr. said finally. "We'll go to her Aunt Belinda's cabin. You all are welcome to come along."

Cade looked at only one person in the room—Rachel, who seemed lost in contemplative thought.

"Maybe it's better if we split up." Cade stuck his hands in his pockets. "You and Momma go to the cabin, maybe take the boys."

"What about you, Caden?"

Rachel finally met his gaze, a fiery flash that he knew echoed what was going on in his head.

They weren't headed south to his aunt's cabin in Alabama. They were going north.

THE DOOR banged open, revealing Mason and a devastated Sam; Cade's stomach plunged at the look of betrayal on Sam's face.

"Sam," he said gently, but Sam shook his head before Cade could move.

"He's still in that room," Sam choked out. "I... I don't want to talk to him."

"Okay, I understand." Cade's hands fluttered helplessly at his sides. "Can I do anything for you?"

"No." Then Sam looked up at Mason; they shared a loaded and silent conversation before Sam spoke again.

"We need a ride or a car, because we're… we're leaving."

CADE FELT like he was running on fumes of insanity and sheer will.

Amelia took charge of Mason and Sam, leading them upstairs with food and quiet talk of plans. Going to Boston right now might not be wise—maybe they should come to the cabin, wait a little while. Her gentle tone and soft hands kept Sam calm as they disappeared onto the second level of the house.

His father made noises about gathering his things; he left his gun on the table in front of Cade before heading out the door.

Cade said a few nice words to Jesus—help, guidance, safety— then took a huge breath of air. Time to find Nox.

He didn't have to go far. At the bottom of the stairs sat Nox, shell-shocked as he stared out over the farm. Wearily Cade dropped down next to him, pressing against Nox, shoulder to hip.

"He hates me," Nox murmured. "He and Mason are leaving."

Cade nodded, resting his head against Nox's shoulder. "Give him time—and he doesn't hate you."

"I'm going back."

Biting his lip, Cade nodded again. "I know."

Dusk fell over the Creel Farm; Cade watched the sun set with the quiet realization that it would probably be the last time he saw it. When Nox left, he would be following, whether Nox liked it or not.

CHAPTER TWENTY-ONE

NOX KNEW there was one thing left to do before morning—talk to Sam.

"He's in the kitchen," Amelia told him as he came down the stairs, his mind full of facing Sam for possibly the last time ever. "I made tea, and there's a plate of sandwiches in the fridge," she said briskly, wiping her hands on a towel. "Everyone's out at the guesthouse, packing up the computers."

"Thank you for everything you've done for him, Amelia."

She shrugged, her smile indulgent. "Sam's a special young man. And awfully mature and levelheaded for a teenager, but…."

"I know." Nox jammed his hands into his pockets. "This isn't going to be easy for him."

"Not for you either." Her expression was so exactly like Cade's at that moment—indulgent and exasperated. "Explain it to him, man-to-man. He needs to know you're telling him the truth this time."

"You're right."

Amelia's shoulders went back, her chin high. "Always."

Impulsively Nox kissed her cheek, something he'd done to his mother on occasions when she was grounded in reality and he wasn't hiding.

Embarrassment burned his face as he pulled away, but Amelia was beaming.

"You're a very nice man, even if you hide it under that scowl all the time," Amelia whispered, as if sharing a secret. She leaned in to return the kiss, rubbing his arm affectionately as she did. "My son made a good choice," she added before turning to walk up the stairs.

Nox tried to clear his head as he moved toward the kitchen.

Sam was indeed waiting for him, seated at the large wooden table with a steaming mug of tea in front of him, hands folded. He looked so serious and… mature. Nox felt the rush of years whisk by, and he had small comfort in the knowledge that maybe—just maybe—he hadn't screwed up that badly.

Maybe Sam would forgive him one day.

"Amelia said you wanted to talk to me, so…." Sam nodded toward the empty chair across from him. Cool, collected. Still simmering with anger.

"I was hoping you wanted to talk to me as well." Nox settled down, crossing his arms over his chest. "About tomorrow."

"Mason and I will be fine. We're going with Mr. and Mrs. Creel and then, then we're going to Boston when things are safe." Sam lifted his chin, defiant.

"I know. I'm glad you have him—he's a very good person."

"He always tells me the truth."

Nox played with the edges of the tablecloth, tracing the huge floral as he let Sam's shot reach its mark. "Yes, he does. And maybe he'll never have a reason to lie. But if he does—if he makes a mistake? Try to find it in your heart to forgive him."

Sam swallowed hard as his eyes got damp, and he twisted his fingers together. "I know why you're saying that. You want me to forgive you."

"Yeah—I'd love that. But I know it's not that easy. I know you have the right to be mad. It doesn't change how much I love you, Sam."

Sam made a little choking sound.

Nox leaned forward, sliding his hands across the table toward his son, feeling a pang of sadness when Sam didn't reach for him.

"What you did, it's too big for I'm sorry, D—" The slip knocked Sam's anger out of him; he seemed to collapse in on himself as the word tried to break free. "I can't do this right now."

"Sam, please."

"I don't want to do this. I don't want to hear it." Sam struggled to stand up, knocking the table and rattling the dishes as he did.

"Sam, I might not come back," Nox finally shouted, anything to keep him from leaving.

Sam froze.

"I'm going to the city because I need to be free of it. I want to be done so I can move on and maybe—maybe, find you in Boston. To say I'm sorry until you believe me."

Sam wiped his eyes angrily. "Don't guilt me, don't, okay?"

"If I don't come back—"

"Shut up!"

"Sam! If I don't come back, I need you to understand one thing. Even if you never forgive me." Nox stood up slowly, until he and Sam were face-to-face. He absorbed every detail of his son's profile, flashing through every Sam he'd known and adored for the past seventeen years. "The most important moment of my life was when you were born. I didn't realize it then, but in that exact second, I truly became a man."

"Dad." Sam started to cry in earnest. "I can't...."

"Sometimes you're still that little baby, Sam. I'm sorry—but you are. I've spent eighteen years making sure you stayed alive, and I feel like—the only way I can be free of all of this is to know these people are not a threat to us anymore."

Sam shook his head, choking down his tears. Wet-eyed and devastated, he reached out to touch Nox's hand.

"You have to swear to me that you will come back. That you will get these men put in jail, and then you'll come back. We—we can make a date and a place, and you'll come back, and Mason and me will meet you there," he said in a rush. "And maybe then we can talk and...."

His fingers clenched and released over and over; Nox reached out and laid his hands on top of Sam's.

"I promise, okay? I'll come back."

"Swear."

"I swear...."

"Swear on something that matters. Don't just say words," Sam demanded. "Make a promise you won't break."

All that Nox loved in the world was Sam. Cade's face flashed in his mind a second later, and he blinked back the emotion that threatened to spill out of his eyes.

"I swear on you—okay? I swear on how much I love you that I'll be back."

Tears tracked down Sam's face as he squeezed their hands together.

"Okay, I believe you."

Nox pulled at Sam's hands; his son got up without breaking contact and came to Nox's side of the table. He threw his arms around Nox's neck and held on for dear life.

"Remember your promise," Sam cried as Nox held him tightly.

"To you? Always."

SAM FOUND his way out to the guesthouse after his talk with his father. His chest hurt like the pneumonia had come back; behind his glasses, his eyes were dry and stinging.

For all his talk of anger and being unable to forgive him, the thought of his father leaving—it made him sick inside. He knew what was back on that island, and now it was worse—because Nox wasn't a hidden nuisance. He was a man with a price on his head, and worse, he was a man who wanted answers.

What if something went wrong?

What if they caught him?

"Hey, you okay?" Mason, of course, coming to him as though a homing beacon shot out of the top of Sam's head.

"Me and my dad talked," Sam said, coming to sit down on the front steps of the house. "He's leaving in the morning."

Mason dropped down next to him, his arm automatically coming around Sam's shoulders and pulling him close. They clicked together like perfectly calibrated magnets.

"I'm sorry," he murmured and pressed a kiss to Sam's temple.

"I'm still so mad for what he did," Sam whispered. "But I don't want anything to happen to him."

Mason stroked his back tenderly. "I know."

NOX WATCHED from the window of the Creel home. Sam and Mason, twisted up in each other's arms, entwined in a lover's embrace.

The urge to pull them apart fluttered and died.

A hand touched his back—Cade, wrapping an arm around his waist and peeking out the window around him.

"How'd it go?"

Nox shrugged. "He's still furious, but I'm pretty sure he doesn't want me to die."

"Good, that makes two of us. Three—my mom likes you."

They stood together, watching the boys get up, then walk toward the guesthouse.

"LJ has a gizmo phone for you. He's very proud of it, so try to look impressed."

Twisting his body, Nox turned so they were nose to nose—or nearly so. He looked Cade right in the eye, bullshit detector in place. "Who are you going with?"

He got an eye roll for an answer.

"Come on—LJ has to explain the gizmo to you, and then we're eating dinner." Cade stepped out of his arms, but Nox was quicker and pulled their bodies flush together.

"You're awfully calm about this."

Defiance and amusement lit Cade's eyes, a smile so sweet and dirty Nox thought he'd burst from it.

"Would you prefer I weep and wail, throw myself at your feet?" Cade drawled, letting his tongue play across his lips as if savoring a feast. "Maybe rip my clothes in grief? I told you before—I make up my own mind when I want something."

Nox couldn't hold him this time; Cade broke out of the embrace and turned to walk out of the room without another word.

CHAPTER TWENTY-TWO

NOX LEFT the farm at dawn.

Tendrils of orange-yellow sunlight stretched over the quiet house as he paused on the front porch, taking a final sip of good coffee from the mug Amelia had left him. Good-byes had been said and now it was done. Nox was going back to New York.

He knew his loved ones weren't pleased with his decision. Their support was conditional and begrudging. He'd sworn to his son he would be back. They would meet at the rendezvous point—Boston—in six months' time, and Nox would be in touch before then, updating everyone on his investigation.

Nox walked the pathway toward the road, measured steps taking him away from a place that, despite its faults and dangers, actually felt like home. The memories, he tucked in his mind for the journey ahead—quiet moments with Cade and seeing Sam blossom into an adult. These times were all they would have in the future; in a few hours, the house would turn into an empty shell as the inhabitants left for safer climes.

In the privacy of the barn, three packed vehicles waited: Amelia and Lee Sr.'s truck filled with memories and treasures—and a few shotguns; LJ's beast of a Denali, holding all his computer equipment; and finally the farm's small pickup, which Sam and Mason would drive.

Cade never told him which vehicle he'd be riding in, but Nox hoped it would be with his son.

The spring air felt damp and heavy already; he'd conceded to the weather and wore his boots, blue jeans, and a gray T-shirt. Everything else—his hood, his weapons, money, and food—he'd stuffed into the hiking backpack strapped to his body. He felt prepared for the trip; the walking, the hitching, the covert borrowing of a car or motorcycle. What lay beyond that, on the island, was a mystery waiting to be unraveled.

The dark place inside him said he wouldn't ever see Cade and the others again. Nox buried that and kept walking.

LJ'd given him a sophisticated new phone with bells, whistles, and tricks so complicated it had taken almost an hour to explain. "The latest in high-tech communications," made LJ's eyes light up, but Nox just needed directions to his destination.

The rest he knew made his little band of loved ones—save Rachel—feel more secure about him leaving alone.

An earpiece connected him to the phone buried in his pocket. A soft voice gave him updates on his course—"keep walking straight for the next twenty-eight miles" was particularly amusing—and Nox breathed in the still South Carolina air with each long stride.

On the island, he'd find his answers.

BY NOON Nox was walking along the highway, rattled as the semis flew by him, bringing wares to all points of the Eastern Seaboard. In the distance he could see the tall buildings of Charleston, his destination for today. The phone vibrated against his thigh; he almost missed it with all the traffic, but that soft voice came back into his ear to say:

"*On our way.*"

A pang of regret surprised him—Nox knew they were leaving in a little caravan, seeking out Amelia's family cabin in the Alabama woods. Off the grid was their only choice, and the farther they could get from Nox and his plans, the better. It was what he wanted, what he'd fought for, but the pulse of sadness in his heart didn't listen to his brain.

He was walking in the opposite direction of everything he cared about.

Was revenge really worth it?

Caught up in his brooding, it took Nox a second to register the rumble of a vehicle pulling up next to him. He stepped through a clump of garbage and weeds, pausing as he slipped his hand into his pocket to secure his knife.

When he turned, a flash of annoyance stayed any smile that might be fighting to come out.

Cade leaned out of the window of the Denali, grinning like an idiot.

"Hey, sexy. You need a ride? I'll let you sit on my lap," he growled, drawl and lascivious eyes completing the picture.

"I thought I fucked you good-bye already?" Nox asked, walking slowly toward the truck.

Cade threw his head back and laughed.

Then LJ waved from the driver's seat, and Rachel flipped him the finger from where she was sharing a seat with Cade.

Idiots.

"I thought we agreed...," he started, but Cade rolled his eyes.

"We agreed you needed to do your whole macho-loner-asshole thing and pretend it was even remotely intelligent to walk into a clusterfuck without backup." Cade sighed, opening the door and nearly knocking Nox on his ass. "And then we had a meeting and overruled you."

"I voted to let you die a martyr's death," Rachel called, "but apparently you're worth the effort or something." She slid through the gap between the front seats and into a small space Nox could see had been carved out among the boxes and bags.

Nox leaned into the truck, half in Cade's lap and half still out.

This was ridiculous. He had suspected Cade would follow, but this was fucking ridiculous.

"You're all insane," he murmured.

LJ flicked his Ray-Bans onto the top of his head, gesturing to the three occupants of the truck. "You need us."

"I can—"

"You can kick things and kill things and shoot things. I can give you the interworking of the casinos and identify the people who are actually in charge," Rachel recited as she examined her nails. "Cade's got a nice mouth, and he knows half the whores in town, so that might be helpful. LJ...." She paused for a moment, casting an almost sickeningly sweet smile in his direction. "LJ is a fucking genius and can get us into the city computers. Can you do any of that?"

"His mouth ain't bad," Cade snarked, and bussed a kiss on his cheek. "But for the record, I'm not blowing anyone for information."

LJ put his sunglasses back over his eyes, a grimace across his mouth. "Thanks for that."

"I might blow you, however," Cade said to Nox, who honestly couldn't decide if he wanted to laugh or curse them all out, "for relaxation purposes."

Nox sighed. Rachel was right, and goddamn, he hated that.

"I hate all of you." Nox pulled off his pack with a sigh.

He crowded into the passenger seat with Cade as his pack got stored in a slender rectangle of space next to Rachel. They were a tight fit, and it was a long ride—which was going to seem longer, as Cade couldn't stop giving Nox an impromptu lap dance.

"Cut that out," he whispered into Cade's ear as he wrapped an arm around his lover's waist.

"Just trying to get comfortable," Cade said dryly.

IT WAS as they stopped to fill up the Denali in Charleston—at a seedy little diesel station near the new docks—that Nox relaxed a little. Logically LJ and Rachel would be of great help as he navigated the city's dense underbelly. They'd need to find a secure location, a place to pull electricity off the grid without being noticed by the city or anyone else. As Nox thought of potential hideouts, Cade came back from the "restrooms"—a tree behind the tiny station—and leaned against the truck.

"How long have you had this planned?" Nox asked, watching the numbers on the pump flip.

"Since you made your little pronouncement." Cade produced a chocolate bar from his pocket, then concentrated on the wrapper, tense across his shoulders even as his face belied casualness.

"And last night was...."

A gorgeous and amused smile crossed his mouth. "Last night was some great fucking," Cade said, fluttering his lashes as he looked up at Nox. "I figured it would be a while before we did it on a mattress again, and I wanted to make the most of it."

Nox fought off a smile. "You're crazy, you know that, right?"

"And you keep saying that. When are you going to learn that I don't back down when something is important to me?" A slight flush bloomed over those high cheekbones, illuminating his freckles. "And when are you going to figure out you're not alone anymore?"

Instinct overruled everything; Nox leaned over and pressed their mouths together, kissing Cade deeply. It wasn't a kiss that led to sex or even having to readjust your jeans—no, Nox just didn't have the words to say *I know* and *thank you.*

And maybe—*I love you.*

As THEY passed over each state line, the chatter in the truck grew quieter and quieter. Nox, LJ, and Cade switched off driving—Rachel laughed when they asked if she wanted a turn—and didn't stop for anything but gas and food. Every mile northward revealed a bit more damage, more abandoned towns, growing colder, seemingly by the hour.

Winter wasn't quite through with this part of the world yet.

"You think we should set up outside the city?" LJ asked the following evening as they cruised through the tiny corridor that was Rhode Island. "Like Jersey or something?"

"I was thinking the same thing," Rachel said. "Storming the island doesn't make much sense."

Cade squeezed Nox's hand, a warning to head off any expressions of disgust at Rachel's contribution. They were working in a state of truce here—three states without a war breaking out between them was their standing record.

"It's actually a good idea. Keep him off the NYPD's radar." Cade turned in the seat enough to make eye contact with Nox.

Keep him safe, Cade thought. The same reason Sam, Mason, and his parents had gone to Alabama.

The same reason Nox had tried to ditch them back in South Carolina.

"Yeah, that makes sense. You and Rachel can stay with LJ while I go into the city."

"I already hate this plan," Cade interjected, frowning.

"Give me a few days to set up a place for us, then you can join me," Nox continued, as if Cade hadn't spoken.

"Thanks, but no." Rachel shifted among their gear and bags. "I'll find my own way onto the island, and I'll find my own place to hide."

"Rachel," Nox started, twisting around Cade's body to look at her.

"*Asshole*. Stop acting like this isn't my area of expertise. What's going to happen is, you're going to wait with LJ, and I'm going into the city to establish a safe space. Then you can show up and stomp all the drug dealers you want," Rachel snapped.

Cade put his hand up to forestall any war between them. "Everyone's going to get what they want," he said, switching his glare between the two of them. "But we need to be smart about this. First, we'll set up the location outside the city. Then we will make our move."

"Fine. Then I know a place where we can go." Rachel's voice went cold and deadly, the temperature inside the truck dropping with each syllable.

Nox grunted.

It was the closest to agreement Cade was going to get, so he wisely took it.

They stayed silent right up until they drove into Jersey.

They reached West New York after midnight. The former refuge of Cuban immigrants sat atop a hill, its once busy urban streets and packed apartment buildings reduced to a ghost town. With work in the city nonexistent, the blue-collar residents had packed up and moved closer to cities like Montclair, which boomed years ago as businesses flocked to higher and safer ground. Towns like WNY now housed mostly addicts and those who didn't do much legal business to make money.

A shivering Rachel crawled into the front seat—banishing Cade to the back, as he let his feelings be known through a constant stream of muttering—as they left the highway and began traveling

152 | Tere Michaels

on empty, unlit streets. She directed LJ to an abandoned block full of boarded-up houses and an empty school high up on a hill; across the way, they could see the bright lights of the District.

"What is this?" Nox asked as Rachel pointed out a gap in the fencing, a place to drive the Denali into. She shook her head, processing the memories before she could speak.

"This is where they brought the bodies from the ferry accident," Rachel said finally. LJ took one hand off the wheel to touch her knee, and she exhaled through the cold fog that appeared to squeeze her.

"What is it now?" Cade murmured from the backseat.

"Someplace for us to wait before we make our next move."

THEY MADE camp on the second floor, in a pair of classrooms that sat back-to-back, end-to-end. Nox put LJ and Rachel on the water side, while he and Cade took the view of the street.

"I'll take first watch," he said as Cade unpacked sleeping bags by dim lantern light.

"I'm not even going to try and argue." Fully dressed, Cade settled down in the downy warmth, pulling his hood over his head.

Nox pocketed a flashlight, then sat to watch out the window. Nothing stirred and no vehicles drove by. Now and again light flickered in a nearby building as drug dealers and their clients made deals in near darkness. No one came close to the abandoned school.

His eyes grew heavy with exhaustion—the drive, the emotional weight of the day. As much as he was used to doing things alone, it was a comfort and a curse to have Cade and the others here.

At least Sam was safe.

The low rumble of a truck caught his attention; it drove past the school to the end of the block, headlights off. It paused, idled at the intersection, then slowly began to drive backward.

Adrenaline pumped through Nox's veins; now wide-awake, he was already reaching for the Sig at the small of his back.

Quiet footsteps alerted him—LJ had entered the room.

"Nox," LJ whispered anxiously.

"I know. Might be nothing."

Even as he spoke the words, the truck stopped, then pivoted, driving the same route they had with the Denali—effectively cutting off their escape route.

"We need to go," Nox said as the doors of the truck opened and men in dark clothing emerged from the vehicle.

NOX RAN down the hallway toward the center stairwell; he dropped to peer over the side and watched as the men poured into the first floor. This wasn't a quiet recon—this was a full-out assault.

One of the shadowy figures paused—Nox couldn't make out what he was doing. A second too late, he realized the man had reached his arm back and flung something up the stairwell.

The smoke bomb hit a few feet away from where Nox was hiding.

He ran in the opposite direction of where Cade, LJ, and Rachel were presumably hiding. Every footstep was exaggerated as the plumes of smoke followed him. He kicked over a broken chair, hopefully alerting the people downstairs to his presence. If he could just keep them occupied so the others could escape....

Hearing the thumps of people coming up the stairwell, Nox pulled his hoodie up over his mouth and slid into an open doorway. Through the smoke he caught the outlines of at least three men running in his direction. He aimed carefully, then took down the one in the middle.

Shouts followed him as he dropped and rolled across the hallway, then slid into another open doorway—the emergency stairs.

COUGHING, EYES stinging, Nox ran down the stairs, dodging debris, and plunged into the darkness. Above him the thudding sounds told him he was being followed. At the bottom, he ducked and felt his way to the door handle. The rusted handle didn't move.

Pushing deeper into the shadows, Nox hastily wiped his eyes. The men had slowed their rush and were easing down the stairs with methodical steps. He aimed his gun, ears trained; whoever got closest died first.

It would reveal his position.

And the second person who would die would be him.

He wanted to know that Cade and the others were safe. He wanted to be sure before he sacrificed himself, that there wasn't more he could do....

A radio crackled in the darkness and gunshots echoed through the static.

Someone else was shooting, and from the sound of it, it was a massive amount of gunfire.

Nox held his breath as the men murmured among themselves. A few sets of footsteps clattered back up the stairs, and he had a glimmer of hope he could escape this death trap....

Until the sound of gunfire surprised him again, this time as the bullets hit his body. The flash of violent pain, the shock, and then Nox hit the floor, unconscious before he formed a single curse.

NOX FLASHED between consciousness and blissful darkness, registering movement as he was dragged roughly across the rocky ground. When he opened his eyes again, he lay on the cold metal floor of a moving van. His body ached; he could feel the sticky flow of blood seeping into his clothing, the moments when his body went numb, and he guessed the bullets had damaged something vital.

A weird peace came over Nox.

He couldn't see anything, his vision clouded by blood loss; his ears buzzed with overload, everything a fuzzy murmur. Above him the chatter of conversation, below him the shakes and rumbles of a moving vehicle.

Nox was fucked.

Whoever these men worked for, they weren't here to help. He might die before they arrived at their destination, right here on the dirty floor of this van.

He didn't know if Cade was all right.

I'm sorry, he thought.

He didn't know if Rachel and LJ had made it to safety.

He would never find the people who hurt his family. He would never stop the destruction of his city.

The cold crept up his limbs and along his spine. All sight and sound began to sputter, like a candle in a draft unable to hold its heat. He felt himself flicker and fade, every breath a painful chore.

This was it. This was how he died.

CHAPTER TWENTY-THREE

THEY LEFT everything behind except the guns; Cade and LJ flanked Rachel, each of them armed. Cade watched as the crush of men ran down the opposite hall, saw when one of them dropped to the floor in the spreading smoke.

Nox. Nox was leading them away.

"Goddammit," Cade spat. When they got through this latest round of shit, he was going to handcuff their wrists together.

They were almost down the hallway when gunfire erupted, a spray of bullets sending plaster exploding over their heads. Cade dropped to the floor, pulling LJ and Rachel with him. In the smoke and darkness, he couldn't see where the new rounds were coming from—but he could tell where they were going.

In their direction.

"Back in the room," Cade rasped. They crawled—LJ, then Rachel, then Cade, gun nervously aimed at an enemy he couldn't see.

"Can we get out the window?" Rachel whispered, coughing between words. LJ angled his body in front of hers, and Cade had no doubt his brother would take any bullet intended for her.

"Too far a drop." Cade slid through the dirt, around them, then crawled to the window. The gunfire and shouting weren't getting any closer, but that was clearly only temporary. They had to get out of there.

"Our choices seem to be taking a chance with the concrete or facing the guys with machine guns." LJ pushed Rachel to follow Cade toward the window. "I think I know what I want to at least try."

"You could break your leg or your neck, and then you'll be praying for someone to shoot you," Rachel hissed.

"That leaves surrendering."

Cade put up his hand. "I'd like to know who I'm surrendering to before that's an option."

He put his handgun in LJ's lap, then got a little closer to the window. In the distance, the bright lights of the District. Boats patrolled the water. Everything below their window was dark concrete, the remnants of a basketball court.

"Maybe we can jump toward one of the trees," Cade mused.

Then he stopped.

Because the gunfire stopped.

LJ was the first to move; he jumped up, a gun in each hand, positioning himself in front of Rachel and Cade.

"Throw your weapons out of the door. Come out with your hands up," a disembodied voice crackled and pinged over a loudspeaker. "We are federal agents. If you cooperate, you won't be harmed."

Cade's heart pounded; Rachel grabbed his jacket, and LJ trembled above him. No one moved or said anything, and he knew they were waiting for him.

"Do it," Cade murmured. He prayed Nox was long gone.

LJ walked slowly to the doorway, then into the other room.

"I'm doin' it," he yelled. "Two guns, coming out."

Rachel slid her handgun into her pants as Cade took her free hand.

LJ leaned down, then slid the guns across the floor and through the doorway. They clattered into the hallway.

"Thank you. Now if you would instruct Rachel to do the same with hers, we can get started."

An itch of remembrance shaded the voice from mechanical and crackled to a memory....

"Oh my God," Cade murmured, but Rachel seemed to be one step ahead.

"Son of a bitch," she spat. Cade was already on his feet, pulling her with him as he all but ran to the doorway.

A bright beam filled the room; Cade, Rachel and LJ covered their eyes, straining under the intrusive light. Cade blinked, lifting his hand to block out the worst of it. His eyes watered as a figure walked through the brightness and into their midst.

"Hello, my friends."

Alec.

FEDS IN flak jackets led them down the stairs to the front of the school, where a trio of SUVs waited, lights flashing, and more men with guns circled.

"Did you find him?" Alec called out, leading the way.

"No," someone called back.

Alec paused and turned to Cade, who tried to keep his face neutral—all the joy at seeing his friend alive turned to distrust as soon as he realized the truth.

"Where is he?"

"Who?" Cade asked, batting his eyelashes.

"Cade, please. I'm not joking around here." Fun Alec, sarcastic Alec—none of them were here now. The serious expression and shoulder holster over his Kevlar took all illusion away.

"I don't know what you're talking about."

Alec stepped closer, nearly nose to nose with Cade, brows knit together. "You better hope I find him before they do," he whispered.

"What?"

Alec didn't answer. He pivoted on his heel and disappeared into the morass of cars and lights and chaos. Behind Alec, agents pushed LJ and Rachel toward the open doors of one of the SUVs.

Another agent put his hand on Cade's back, guiding him toward a second vehicle. A moment before Cade ducked in, he heard another shout.

"We found blood!"

Struggling against the man behind him, Cade tried to break away. "Alec! Alec—what's going on?"

No one answered, and the agents overpowered Cade, shoved him in, and slammed the door behind him.

THE HOUSE seemed entirely out of place in the rough landscape—a charming Victorian perched alone on the corner of a street high on the cliff overlooking the city.

Cade, who'd spent the entire ride shouting obscenities at the agents, nearly fell out in his anxiousness to find Alec.

"What blood?" he yelled, as soon as he saw Alec across the yard. "What did you find?"

"Enough," Alec snapped, striding over to grab his arm. "Stop shouting and get inside."

In all there were eleven agents for the three of them, all heavily armed and serious as death. LJ kept Rachel at his side, glaring at anyone who came near her. They weren't handcuffed, and Cade took that as a good sign.

The furnishings were sparse. Alec called out some orders—set up a patrol, get communications up, put LJ and Rachel upstairs—and then turned his attention to Cade.

"We need to talk."

"You need to tell me what blood. Did you find him? Is he all right?" Cade resisted the urge to run out the door, take his chances that Alec wouldn't shoot him in the back.

"We didn't find him, or a body. But there was blood in the stairwell. And no trail, so we're thinking they drove off."

Cade's throat closed in fear. "They?"

"Sit down, okay?"

On a dusty Queen Anne sofa they sat, strangers wearing familiar faces. Cade shook with fear as Alec—not dead but very much a lie—faced him.

"Before I get all official on you, Cade, I wanted to tell you how glad I am to see you." The charming smile Cade knew so well made a reappearance. "When I got pulled out, there wasn't time to get you a message, and I've done what I could to help you."

Cade shook his head. "I don't understand. I really don't. You were a… a fed? This whole time? They let you do…." His voice trailed off.

"Yeah, well, not many people volunteered for that sort of deep cover. Except me." Alec winked at him. "I was there to collect information, to observe, to try and find the connection to the source of Dead Bolt."

"So they pulled you right before you could find out? They killed Zed! They blew up the Butterfly and killed God knows how many people!" Cade's anger flared again.

"My cover was compromised."

"They killed our friends, Alec. Our customers. Innocent people just trying to make a living vacuuming up the fucking place and they're dead!"

"Cade, please. It wasn't my choice. I went to my apartment and had a bag thrown over my head." He laughed mirthlessly. "I'm lucky I was able to get that kid out of the police station."

"You got my messages?"

Alec reached over and laid a gentle hand on Cade's knee. "All of them. I hated how worried you were, and I really wanted to get you a message."

The intimacy of the moment soothed Cade—before he realized it was a lie.

He jerked back. "How did you know we were at the school?"

The serious façade fell back over Alec's expression. "We've been tracking you since you left the island. The captain put a transmitter in your bag."

Cade barked out a laugh. "You were our fucking guardian angels. Except for the guy who tried to kill us on the boat."

"Mr. Wick wasn't one of ours. We're not sure who he was working for exactly." Alec flicked some invisible lint off his pants. "But we've kept an eye on you."

"Damian?" The transmitter at the house suddenly made sense. "I never made him for a fed."

Alec gave him a strange look. "Damian definitely never worked for us."

The mention of him seemed to halt the conversation; Alec stood up, then gestured toward the staircase.

"Why don't you join your brother and Rachel upstairs?"

"That's it?" Cade didn't move. "That's all you're telling me?"

"I've given you all the information I'm authorized to share." Alec put his hands in his pockets. "In the morning we'll be escorting you to the airport and getting you to Chicago."

"Chicago? What the hell are you talking about?" Cade grabbed at Alec's elbow as he tried to walk away. "Where's Nox?"

Alec's expression flickered from cool to nervous for a split second. He ignored Cade's expression entirely. "You're federal witnesses now. In the morning you'll be in Chicago."

CADE, RACHEL, and LJ sat in a tiny clump on one of the double beds, heads together as they whispered.

Cade shared the little Alec had told him, with Rachel swearing furiously the entire time.

"A fucking fed," she muttered, as LJ petted her hand.

"I'm not going to Chicago," Cade whispered. "I have to find Nox."

LJ and Rachel shared a look; Rachel bit her lip, then nodded.

"We're sticking together," LJ said. "You're not going anywhere without us."

In the end, it wasn't difficult to come up with a plan.

A wild thunderstorm rolled through, shaking the ramshackle house with torrents of rain and wind. Alec sent them sandwiches and drinks, two of his agents standing watch at the door.

"Can I see Alec, please?" Cade asked, all docile and polite as he stood in the open doorway.

An agent—who he was fairly certain never said a single word—gestured toward the stairs.

"Alec?" Cade said, looking down over the railing to where Alec, still neat in his suit jacket, watched him warily from the foyer.

"Are you going to be honest with me?" Alec asked.

"Are you going to afford me the same courtesy?"

Alec's grin was familiar. "I'm sorry. My job prevented me from telling you certain things."

"I spent a long time being really worried about your sorry ass," Cade said lightly. "And here you are, some sort of special asshole with a badge. Commanding pretty boys in nice suits to make sure I don't leave."

"You're a material witness," Alec apologized. "You all are."

"He's out there alone, and you're not looking for him."

"Cade...."

"Why aren't you looking for him, Alec? He didn't do anything wrong. He's on your side, okay?"

"He's not my problem right now. You are." With a regretful look, Alec turned and walked out of sight.

Just outside the bedroom, Cade paused. The rain pattered down on the roof, wind whistling through the cracks; the twin sentries gave him a once-over nod before the one on the left opened the door.

As he stepped through the doorway, the screaming began.

Rachel had the lungs of an opera singer; she shrieked, furious at LJ, throwing everything not nailed down at Cade's brother. He ducked and dodged, calling her "baby" with the convincing air of a man who'd said exactly the wrong thing.

"Hey, hey," Cade called out, walking between them to break up the mock fight.

"Shut her up," one of the agents snapped.

Rachel flung a lamp in his direction.

The man pushed past Cade, heading for Rachel with a determined air and zero fear; his partner smirked in the doorway, observing the scene with amusement.

The man who put his hands on Rachel clearly never anticipated the tiny woman's move—she kicked him so hard in the balls he went down like a sack of rocks. When his partner shouted out in his defense, she was already halfway across the room, doing the same. They knew the sounds of chaos would draw attention—which was why LJ already had the window open.

Cade shoved Rachel over the sill as LJ hit the ground; he heard the sound of feet hitting the stairs and shouts as the other agents drew closer. Cade held his breath, threw his leg over the sill, then jumped into the pouring rain.

He had the overwhelming urge to search his pockets for magic beans, because that was the level of bullshit he was currently experiencing. A fractured fairy tale but no fairy godmother in sight.

They ran through the rain in the opposite direction of civilization and into the destruction that was once a hub of homes and condos and a direct artery to New York City. With the tunnel destroyed, no one had bothered to reconstruct the roads or businesses, leaving it for dumping of debris and construction mess.

They hiked down the hill—part construction refuse, part landfill—to the lowest point near the water. Construction trailers dotted the landscape, giving the illusion the area was being redeveloped. An easily jimmied lock on the trailer gave them some shelter—and gave Cade an idea.

"Strip off everything," he panted, throwing assorted clothing from a locker toward his shivering compatriots. "We don't want them tracking us."

In between lightning flashes, they tore off everything and quickly changed into overalls and boots, heavy slickers, and gloves.

Every sound outside made them jump; Cade pressed up against the window, watching for signs they were followed, but nothing. Antsy, he located another trailer farther down near the water—they made their way to that one through mud and mess.

For hours they sat on the floor, keeping watch for Alec and his men. LJ found a laptop and some food; Rachel filled a plastic bag with box cutters.

"Until we find something that does more damage," she said grimly, as Cade played sentry near the door.

The rain stopped before sunrise; they left the trailer and started walking.

"Where would he go?" LJ asked, perched on the concrete barricade at the end of what was formerly an entrance to the Lincoln Tunnel.

"The house. He'll go to the house first," Rachel said, her voice coming from deep inside the oversized rain slicker currently wearing her. She curled next to LJ, her feet not even touching the ground.

Cade wasn't listening—he kept his eyes on the island, the lights of the District like an ugly beacon calling him home. He tried to convince himself that Nox was okay, that they would find him at the house, making plans and gathering supplies. But the blood and Alec's indifference ate at his confidence.

He didn't voice his fears.

He kept his eyes trained toward the lights.

CHAPTER TWENTY-FOUR

NOX OPENED his eyes.

The lights above him swam in hazy circles until he thought he might be spinning. No—no, that was a ceiling fan.

Too weak to move his head, Nox blinked and breathed, the only two things his body could manage. He felt his pulse, unnaturally loud and ugly inside his head. One leg throbbed, and the other he could barely register, let alone move. He moved his fingers, wrists; he tried to shrug a shoulder and nearly passed out from the nauseating pain that seared through him.

Shot.

He remembered being shot.

The van moving—now somewhere bright. Still.

Quiet.

Warm.

"Nox?" a voice asked from somewhere beyond his vision. "Nox? Can you hear me? Blink once for yes, twice for no."

Someone laughed in the distance.

Nox swallowed as he tried to turn his head, but he barely moved a few inches before his neck locked up. With a moan of pain, he closed his eyes against the light.

When he opened his eyes again, very little had changed—except for the fact that he was in a bed.

Under a blanket.

A sudden surge of hope ran through his battered body.

They'd found him—Cade and LJ and Rachel. He was safe, and as soon as he'd gotten a little rest, they would be on their mission.

Someone called his name.

"C-Cade," he managed, a croaked whisper as he tried to open his eyes again.

"No." The voice came closer, and a hand touched his shoulder. "Not Cade."

Fighting against the darkness, Nox forced his eyelids to obey. Every flicker got him another piece of light, another sliver of his surroundings. A face swam in and out of focus.

A familiar face.

The jolt of fear and confusion brought everything into a moment of clarity.

"Dad?"

THE SHOCK of the hallucination—dream?—pushed Nox back into the darkness. His brain threw nightmares at him; history and fiction mixed together until it was Rachel bleeding and dying as she gave birth to Sam, and Cade on the deck of the ferry as it went down.

When he swam back up into the light, Nox braced himself for reality. Maybe he was still on the floor of the abandoned school. Maybe he'd never made it out of the Iron Butterfly, and the past few weeks were a fevered second before his life extinguished entirely.

Because his father was dead, and this could not be real.

Eyelids like concrete, Nox blinked into painful existence. The bright overheads were gone, replaced by a muted glow from a wall lamp across the room.

A hospital room.

The hint of artificial roses tickled his senses further; he managed to turn his head to one side, to where a shadowy figure sat, back to the door.

Lips glued together, throat tight and scratchy, Nox watched his guard stir and then slowly rise from the chair.

"You awake?" the man asked, a booming whisper from very high up.

No words formed from Nox's tired vocal chords, just a noise. The man stepped into the weak puddle of light, and Nox saw a mountain of humanity, ripples of muscles trapped beneath an expensive sports coat.

And the unmistakable bulge of a firearm under his arm.

"I'll tell the boss," the man intoned, looking down at Nox with a curious expression. After a weighted pause, he turned and left Nox's sight.

The door opened and closed.

He wondered where the hell he was.

The wait was long enough to allow him to drift back to sleep. When Nox woke up again, a young man in white scrubs and gloves was peering under the dressing on Nox's side.

"Oh, good morning, Mr. Boyet. Nice to see you awake," he said cheerfully, his whole Midwestern demeanor and rosy cheeks at odds with the cold terror that enveloped Nox at the sound of his name.

"Wh…." He coughed, crumpling in pain as he jarred every muted injury awake with the force.

"Easy, easy. Let's try a little water, okay?" The nurse put a straw to Nox's lips, and Nox slurped enough to ease the sandpaper of his throat, the burning sensation down to his stomach.

"There you go, lie back now." With pleasant efficiency, he got Nox back in a comfortable position, with pillows rearranged to raise his head a bit more, and the thin blanket pulled up to his shoulders as the exertion made him shiver. "You've been through quite a trauma, Mr. Boyet. You need to take it easy."

"Ssstop…." Nox shook his head, aggravating the ache. "Not… my… nnname," he said, a mouthful of gravel and the desperate need to protect himself.

The man gave him a strange look. "Let me get the doctor, all right?" A quick pat to the arm and he was gone, just like the armed man from before.

Nox didn't even try to move, but that didn't stop his mind from imagining a scenario where he threw himself off the bed—the IV and catheter lines miraculously disappearing—and dashed out the door….

To where?

He didn't know where he was or who owned this hospital. He heard nothing beyond the door—no sounds of rattling carts or announcements over the PA. What if this was a private house?

Did he make it out of Jersey?

A small flicker of fear began to bubble up, thoughts speeding up and crashing together.

Cade.

Did he make it out of the school?

Even premature, unsubstantiated, the flurry of grief threatened to drown him. Thoughts of rolling out the door, grabbing a gun, shooting his way out—they were overwhelmed by the idea that Cade was dead.

And Sam.

Headed to the mountains with Cade's family and Mason, away for a new and safe life with a new and safe family.

Nox was alone.

The scrape of the door startled him; the cast of unknown characters returned. The mountain with a gun. The cheerful nurse. Behind them, a gangly figure in a white coat, sporting a thick gray beard and a Sikh Dastaar.

"Mr. Boyet!" His accented voice boomed through the room. "Good morning to you. We were afraid you might sleep another week."

The name made him wince; the length of time filled him with dread.

"I...."

The doctor put up his hand. "No, no. Don't strain yourself. I'm going to examine you, ask a few questions. I am Dr. Khanna. You are a patient at my clinic."

Nox nodded, his gaze drifting to the large man who rested against the closed door.

A clinic with an armed guard.

"Mr. Sutherland says you were a bit confused about your name," Dr. Khanna said, conversational and chatty as he felt Nox's pulse. "Nox Boyet is not your name?"

The tone was light, but Nox tensed under the man's fingers; he saw the flicker in Dr. Khanna's dark eyes, even as he smiled.

"P-Patrick Mullens," Nox answered, defiant even in his weakness and fear.

The resulting smirk from Dr. Khanna didn't help to soothe him.

"Now, now, there's no need to lie here. You're safe, Mr. Boyet." The doctor took the chart offered to him by Mr. Sutherland. It was large and silver, like a set relic from an old television show. Dr. Khanna flipped through, nodding occasionally.

"Do you remember what happened to you?"

A calculated risk, but Nox shook his head.

"You were shot by undercover federal agents who were seeking you and your party for the bombing of the Iron Butterfly," Dr. Khanna said matter-of-factly. "You were rescued by...." He trailed off for a moment but found his footing quickly. "You were rescued and brought here, to be made well under my care."

He snapped the chart shut.

"Five bullets removed, the torn ligaments in your knee stabilized, and a severe concussion we have been keeping an eye on." Dr. Khanna's eyes twinkled. "That would account for your confusion, I'm sure. Do you have any questions for me?"

The swirl of questions was almost too enormous—Nox was in the center of a tornado and had no way to remove himself physically. There was only one question on his mind.

"When... can... I... go?" he ground out.

The sharp bark of laughter from the door made him jump.

Above him, Dr. Khanna sighed. "That is not a question I can answer."

He patted Nox's shoulder. "Rest. You'll have some important visitors shortly."

Nox closed his eyes; he listened to the three men take their leave, a murmur of voices and the door opening and closing. Alone, he breathed as deeply as his injuries would allow.

A momentary setback.

He would get better.

He would get the hell out of here.

He would find out what happened to Cade and the others.

He would finish what he set out to do.

CHAPTER TWENTY-FIVE

CADE LAY on his back, staring up at the construction trailer's ceiling. The torrential rain had driven them back into a trailer, this one a bit farther down, where Hoboken used to be, and clearly abandoned for a long time. The refuse of squatters was unmistakable both in smell and debris; Rachel claimed she would sleep outside in the mud, but another thunderstorm pushed her inside.

She and LJ were curled up under the window, illuminated by the newly revealed moon. His older brother formed a protective barrier around Rachel, putting her between him and the wall, as they slept in a nest of tarps and canvas drop cloths. It would be both sexist and tender—except Cade knew Rachel had at least three box cutters hidden on her tiny body, and anyone stupid enough to look twice at LJ would end up dead before they hit the floor.

If he weren't so terrified about Nox, he would think it sweet.

Getting back to the District was proving to be difficult. After the bombing of the Iron Butterfly, security had been ratcheted up to a near state of emergency. From the vantage point of an abandoned construction skeleton, LJ had observed water patrols around the island, armed men on boats seemingly on alert for an attack. Checkpoints were going up on the ferry side of the city.

Even increased patrols here in the middle of a coastal wasteland seemed to point to a heightened sense of urgency.

Cade couldn't figure out how to get them across the water.

In quiet dark moments, he considered going back to Alec, pleading and begging and playing on their past connection for help in finding Nox. He thought about stripping down to nothing and dropping to his knees, coaxing cooperation with his mouth and pretty eyes.

He'd do it if he thought it would work.

They'd snuck back to the school where Alec had captured them, and found a carnage of broken glass and busted doors and, yes, blood in the far stairwell where Cade knew Nox had been.

But if the feds didn't have him, who did?

Sleep eluded him until he could barely put together three lines of intelligent thought before his mind drifted to worry and panic and confusion.

He needed to rest. He couldn't rest.

The damp, dirty smell of the trailer, the rot of the pile of molding refuse they sat on—Cade closed his eyes against LJ and Rachel, against the teasing moonlight, praying for just a few moments' respite.

None came.

Rachel stirred first, appearing from the cocoon of LJ's body like a grumpy-faced butterfly.

"The accommodations just keep getting shittier," she murmured, rubbing the sleep out of her eyes. Her red hair a tangled mess over her shoulders, Rachel pressed the heels of her hands against her temples. "I need coffee in the worse way."

They were subsisting on tepid bottles of water, granola bars, and bags of crushed chips liberated from one of the trailers. The eeriness of the lack of people was outweighed by the supplies they were able to find—clothes, backpacks, sharp objects that Rachel seemed to take extra delight in, another laptop, tools, bottled water, and food. Now they traveled with full backpacks and claw hammers in their back pockets.

Just in case.

"No one's around here," Rachel said, crawling over a still-sleeping LJ. "That's weird, right?"

"It was all over the news—a month? Two months ago?" Cade sat up, twisting around until he could lean against the trailer wall. "New developments on the waterfront."

"Another ferry." Rachel walked on unsteady legs toward him, her small body buried in layers of men's work clothes in an attempt to stay warm—and pass for a man. "No one's here."

"The weather, maybe." Cade shrugged. "I don't know. It looks like people just didn't come to work one day."

"Mmmm."

Cade looked at Rachel's expression; he knew what calculation and suspicion meant.

"Something scared them off."

Rachel dropped down, mirroring his position so they were shoulder to shoulder. "Looks like it. Everyone left stuff behind. Valuable stuff. They know how shitty this area is—just junkies and squatters. They shut the door and assumed they'd be unlocking it the next day."

"Security maybe—the explosion at the Butterfly, everyone thinks it's dangerous to build right now."

"Mmmm," Rachel said again. "The patrols look like they're here more to keep folks from working—not destroying the buildings. I mean, do you think we've just been lucky no one has found us?"

"It doesn't make any sense." He laughed mirthlessly, looking at his dirt-black hands, the too-long cuffs of his olive jumpsuit, the boots so big he needed to stuff them with extra socks. "Nothing makes any damn sense."

Rachel sighed next to him, echoing his sentiments without speaking. He felt it in her slumped posture, matching his own.

ANOTHER TORRENTIAL rainstorm kept them indoors for the day. LJ had both laptops gutted, each piece carefully laid out on a bright blue tarp, a pile of the most delicate of the found tools nearby. Rachel had fallen asleep after their lunch of bottled water and beef jerky, curled into a tiny ball under the window like a cat.

Cade pressed the end of his pen against the watermarked pad of legal paper in his lap. He wanted to get his thoughts down, out of his racing, aching head. Formulate a plan, come up with other ideas—because sitting and waiting was starting to sliver off bits of his sanity with each passing day.

They needed money, first off. That was LJ's current assignment—get a laptop running and into a hacked network so no one could find them. His antigovernment friends just needed the impetus to start drilling holes in secure sites and finding them leads.

A way into the city. Cade scratched "workers" on the top of the page, underlining it twice. With some fake IDs, maybe they could get at least one of them through security. Bribes would be difficult since they had credit not cash—the latter definitely preferred by those getting their palms greased in the District.

LJ again. The only one of them without a recognizable face.

Once inside, LJ could arrange transportation—except he didn't know anyone in the District, and everyone Cade trusted was either in this shitty trailer or....

He choked down another sigh and began to draw a passable version of the Iron Butterfly going down in flames.

Cade dozed off, his "work" for the day just a pile of words and sketches, each crossed out with an increasing amount of pressure, ink blotting the pad like droplets of blood.

"Got it," LJ said, delightedly, startling Cade out of his hazy state. "We'll be up and running in a few minutes."

Cade looked over to find Rachel at LJ's side, the closest thing to a look of affection he'd ever seen on her face. It hurt so much he looked away.

"My contact is waiting for me. We'll get what we need," LJ muttered, already clicking away on the keyboard. "I just need this security to hold until I get into their...." He drifted off in midsentence, biting his lip as he concentrated.

"IDs," Cade said as Rachel stared intently at the screen.

"Yeah, but they have to be better than these yokels can manage. They're used to getting past government checkpoints. This is the best money can buy."

"They're city cops," Cade started, but one deadpan look from Rachel shut him up.

"You really think the District security is from the government? They can't afford what guards the city. It's private, paid for, and the only people who can break in are the people they have working for them."

"They hire hackers," LJ added, finally ungluing his eyes from the screen. "If you have a rep you can break them, they put you on their payroll."

Cade shook his head, a hand going to his exhausted, gritty eyes. "And if you say no?" But he already knew the answer.

"If you say no, you're still in no position to hack them, because you're dead," Rachel said slyly.

"What about Nox's guy? He managed to have passes and credit that got him into the Butterfly. They had to be the best...."

Rachel perked up at that. "True. Unless Damian...." She said the name with a steely, venomous hiss. "Maybe he knew it was fake and let him in anyway."

That didn't make sense to Cade. But then again, neither did Damian's betrayal. He had been sending information to someone—who's to say it wasn't someone inside the city?

"Alec said Damian wasn't a fed."

"And he clearly wasn't just working for Zed." Rachel tapped her heavy boots against the floor. "The drug people?"

"I'd ask for a raise—he was still in the casino when the bombs went off. And with the doors locked, he would have been killed if we hadn't gotten him out."

The *tap, tap, tap* of Rachel's boots got louder. "Maybe he works for the cops?"

"I thought the cops worked for the drug people," interjected LJ.

Cade groaned. "It's like a fucking chess game. Why isn't this like the movies where someone just declares they're the bad guy?" he bitched tiredly. The paper and pen went flying across the room and hit the wall with a satisfactory thump.

"I wish we'd been able to bring the wall with us," he said eventually. "All that information—"

"Is photographed and uploaded to LJ's server," Rachel added. When Cade looked up, she shrugged. "What? That was a lot of work and valuable information. After I was finished, LJ covered it all with paint."

LJ gave Cade a thumbs-up from over the screen of the laptop.

"You guys are good at this stuff." Cade threw Rachel a shrewd look. "Well, *you* I knew about." He didn't know the full extent of her past, but given her actions since everything went to shit, he knew he wanted her to always be on his side.

"You have no idea," Rachel drawled before dropping her head against LJ's shoulder. Her gaze didn't leave Cade's face, though, and he thought maybe he could read her mind a little bit better.

If Cade didn't know, then LJ most likely didn't either.

Finally Cade broke the staring contest. He felt restless, sluggish—tired of waiting for something to happen. For a man who'd spent so much of his life with his head down, Caden Lee Creel had forgotten what it was like to not step into the fray.

He struggled to his feet, his lower half pins and needles from sitting so long. The ten-foot-wide trailer didn't provide much room to pace; a huge desk and piles of boxes (files, plans, tools they had no interest in) created a cramped path—certainly not conducive to pacing.

Cade considered outside, but the rain cut that option out of the picture. Instead he leaned against the small north-side window, his vision locking onto the misty outline of the city.

Somewhere in that mess of corruption and chaos was Nox. He'd come this far—no way he was going to stop until he found Nox.

The rain lulled him into a state of drifting, brushing against memories, until the first blow came against the door. Pounding soon followed, as if someone on the other side wanted to bring the cheap door down with the power of his fist.

Interlude

HER NEW name is Rachel Moon, and all the identification Mitzie Haze pushes across the pockmarked desk says so. Buying fake credentials in the basement drug den of a former strip club feels like the most normal thing Jenny—Rachel—has done in forever.

The National Guardsman—Scott, kind and idealistic, utterly foolish, and enraptured with her body—is being deployed elsewhere. New York City has been declared a lost cause for the moment, and there are too many other cities still limping toward recovery, with many more citizens living in crisis and itching to riot. He asked her to come back with him—to Connecticut—and for a moment, she almost said yes.

But Jenny—Rachel—can't be sure what lies beyond the borders right now. She has nothing but a price on her head, and far too much information to be left alive. Making herself known would be suicide, and no fucking way is she going out like that.

No way.

Mitzie's parents had been friends of Vera and Marat; they'd come over for arguments about Russian politics and strong black coffee every few Sundays. Ever the rebel, Mitzie chopped off all her black hair, dyed it white, and ran a strip club in Hell's Kitchen with her girlfriend Ursula. Her parents declared her dead and went into mourning.

Now they were actually dead, swept away in floodwaters that had surged through their neighborhood in Brighton Beach. Mitzie and Ursula survived, staying in the city and refusing evacuation.

They had their reasons—they weren't asking questions about hers.

"I don't have money," she says as Mitzie lights a cigarette. Her eyes are dark, sweeping over Rachel's ragged hoodie and jeans, lips pursed as she leans back in her chair.

"You can work for me, Galina," Mitzie murmurs in Russian, in a way that pricks at the back of her neck.

"My name is Rachel," she answers, running her fingers over the documents.

"Raaachel." Mitzie sounds out the word, and then Rachel knows exactly how she's supposed to be paying for the documents.

She doesn't hesitate, standing and reaching for the hem of her hoodie in the same motion. When her nude torso is revealed, Mitzie makes a soft sound of interest.

Rachel—Jenny, Galina, all of them—can work with this. She earns the fake documents on her knees with Mitzie's fist in her hair.

By crawling and purring and being the perfect girl, she earns a cot in an abandoned top-floor apartment of the building Mitzie and Ursula have claimed as their own.

She takes over running the strippers—those that are left— and keeping the linens clean in the back when the National Guardsmen come in for some recreational fun.

A lonely general takes a shine to her, so she picks up some extra food and a whispered reveal across the pillows of several locations where supplies can be purloined and when patrols will not be around.

In less than two years, Ursula is gone and Mitzie is crawling around for her.

Rachel Moon rises from the ashes like a fucking phoenix.

CHAPTER TWENTY-SIX

"MR. SUTHERLAND is my dad—I'm Kyle!"

Nox had no interest in anything that perky, particularly not when a man he didn't know was checking his catheter and smiling like an idiot. Nox turned his head to one side, trying to ignore the invasive tug. He gripped the metal railings on each side, attention on a small watercolor painting where a window should be.

His room had no windows.

No glimpses outside the door gleaned more information. He'd seen no one but Dr. Khanna, Kyle, and the mountain with the gun since he'd woken up. Weak tea and soup—provided by the ever chattering, no substance nurse Kyle—went ignored, and Nox kept his eyes closed as much as humanly possible.

Somewhere after his fifth nap of the morning, Nox realized the steady drip of his IV was more than just nourishment for his body. Through lidded eyes he'd watched Kyle inject something into the tubing, and almost instantaneously, Nox had drifted off again.

They were keeping him drugged.

Unable to fight it, he slept, long and blessedly dreamless, not fraught with violence or hallucinations of his dead father—at least until Kyle arrived for another round of uncomfortable touches.

"I'm going to give you a sponge bath, Mr. Boyet. You have a visitor coming later." Kyle winked at him. "We want you looking your best, don't we?"

Nox scowled. "Don't... fucking... touch me," he muttered, struggling to pull himself up into a seated position. The bed—and his body—didn't cooperate, and he fell back down in a panting heap.

"That's really no way to behave," Kyle said sadly, shaking his head as he fussed with the blankets. "But no problem really. I'll just get the restraints, and then I can take care of your... needs." He licked his lips slowly.

A surge of anger drove Nox to move again. This time the adrenaline defied his injuries, and sweat-drenched and gasping, he pushed himself up.

"I… will… kill… you," he spat.

Kyle's face went white, and he stepped back, momentarily forgetting he had all the power. He said nothing, his pale face and red-spotted wide eyes betraying his confusion.

Did he take the chance and fight back, or believe exactly what Nox was telling him?

The latter won.

"I'm going to get clean linens," Kyle whispered, then fled the room and slammed the door behind him.

Nox fell back, hazy with pain. The weakness overwhelmed him, the throbbing of his leg, his side, his head—he had to get out of this bed before someone a lot stronger than Kyle challenged him.

A subdued Kyle returned with linens and the large man with the big gun—who seemed amused to be standing guard for a sponge bath. Kyle didn't even make eye contact with Nox; he carefully divested Nox of his sweaty hospital gown one corner at a time, going over his skin with a large damp sponge. As quickly as he could, he finished and then got Nox into another pristine white gown.

"Underwear," Nox muttered, but Kyle shook his head.

"Your leg…."

Nox let out a growl, and their guard began to chuckle.

"Get the man some fucking drawers, *Kyle*." His emphasis on the nurse's name—the derision—sent Kyle scurrying once again, darting around the man and out into the hall.

"Fucking pervert," the man said, shaking his head.

Nox observed him carefully; he was middle-aged but massive and clearly in control of his movements and power. Everything about him screamed professional, and Nox had no doubts he'd killed many times and with great enjoyment.

"Not my type," he said, cool as he could croak in the man's direction, testing the waters.

The muscle regarded Nox with an impenetrable expression, then walked toward the bed with slow deliberation.

"Mine neither. Pain is business, not pleasure," he said finally, flashing a shark's smile.

Nox felt a sliver of relief—and an overwhelming need for a gun in his hand.

"Better with you here, then," Nox offered.

"Don't get your flirt on—you're not my flavor either." The man cocked his head to one side. "You got a sister?" he asked before tipping his head back and laughing loudly. He slapped his hand on the metal guardrail, sending the bed shaking.

Nox waited for him to stop, his face still locked in an unemotional mask. "You got a name?"

"Yeah."

Nox rolled his eyes, eliciting another chuckle from the man.

"Name's Antonio. You call me Tony and I let the pervert have at you with a sponge behind a locked door."

"Duly noted." Nox shifted uncomfortably, then sent a glance toward the door. "Are my visitors coming soon, Antonio?"

"Not my call." Antonio regarded him with keenly interested eyes, tapping his meaty fingers on the metal railing. "You have no idea, do you?"

Unease pooled in Nox's stomach. "You mean where I am or who my visitors are—I have some ideas," he said, lying confidence with each syllable. "I'd like to thank my host of course—maybe see if I can get upgraded to a room with a view."

Antonio's predatory grin appeared again, crinkling his eyes and earning Nox an approving nod. "You got balls, I'll give you that."

The door opened to reveal Kyle, now pouting and silent as he returned with a pair of nondescript white boxers. Nox kept his eyes locked on the nurse's face and projected a look of sheer disdain as the man's shaky hands got the undergarments up his legs—including the one with the stabilized knee—and up over his hips. Antonio watched from a few steps away, clearly amused.

Kyle didn't make eye contact—or stay. He rearranged the blankets once again and then fled, nearly getting brained by the door as he attempted to escape.

"I'm impressed you scare the shit out of him when all he has to do is press a pillow over your face to shut you up," Antonio observed dryly, situating himself back in the "guard" chair near the door. "Glad I have a gun," he added, extending his tree trunk legs out and crossing his arms over his chest.

"Maybe after I get a view, I can get one of those," Nox muttered. He turned his head away from his guard and waited.

EVEN ANGRY men sleep; Nox woke up yet again, fuzzy-headed and dry-mouthed, to an empty room. Antonio was gone, his IV was full, and a spray of white roses sat on a rolling table at the foot of his bed.

The bizarreness of his current confines seemed to be pushed over the edge by those goddamn flowers; they reminded him of the ones his mother had gotten when he was little, when his father would have to stay late "one more night" and she'd cry over the phone. It was among his earliest of memories—his father's absence, his mother's tears....

The memory of his father made that days ago—or was it hours, weeks?—hallucination of Carson Boyet all the more uncomfortable. He'd like to think in his hour of sadness he'd only think of Cade. Or Sam. Or his mother. A weird prickling sensation began to crawl over Nox's skin like tiny electrically charged ants. Nausea began to build, a pressure behind his eyes.

No—it was a hallucination.

No—Rachel said the bosses Carson had double-crossed had murdered his father.

An unexpected memory forced Nox to close his eyes; the phantom pain of the man who'd grabbed him, the one who'd told him to back off his vigilantism or Sam would be prosecuted. He scoured every second he could remember—the man's voice, what he knew. He knew about Natalie, he knew about Sam, but no. The voices—they didn't match.

They didn't match, did they?

Could they?

His turmoil reached the point of physical illness, the room swimming and pulsing around him. The urge to get out of the bed overpowered him as his breath caught.

No air, there wasn't air....

"Shhh," a male voice murmured, and a second later, a flood of warmth from his arm to his chest made the presence of medication known. Nox found his breath again, spots dancing before his eyes when he finally pried them open.

Dr. Khanna stood above him, his dark eyes holding warmth and sympathy.

"A bit of panic—unsurprising for what you went through." Dr. Khanna patted at his wrist. "I gave you something to ease your mind. There you go—keep breathing."

It got easier, the knots loosening. Nox felt the edges of sleep reach their arms out for him, but once again the doctor touched his wrist.

"No, no. Don't fall asleep. It might not be the best time, but you have a visitor." Dr. Khanna's voice held a note of disapproval, but Nox had no time to try to make sense of it. He heard the door open, a quiet creak, and then the doctor moved away.

The man who took his place was tall and of slender build, with neatly tamed graying brown hair and serious blue eyes. He looked down at Nox with a guarded expression, his mouth pulled in a tight line.

"Hello, Nox," he said finally, a voice familiar and foreign, so much a distant memory that Nox couldn't remember the last words his father had spoken to him. But he knew that sound right down to his DNA.

Nox couldn't speak. The medication thrumming through his veins stopped the well of panic, the shock, but Nox's throat tightened because his brain threw up a wall so high he couldn't see over it.

He shook his head, just a tiny motion that seemed to break Carson Boyet's stoicism into something else. Something… fond.

"I've wondered what it would be like, seeing you again. So strange," he murmured.

Blinking, Nox felt the muteness spread over his body. He couldn't move as his father leaned closer.

"I'll explain everything, I will. Right now—right now, let's just have this moment of being a family again."

It was like a key, unlocking the deep freeze and letting Nox back into the sunshine.

Family?

A muscle began to twitch in Nox's jaw; he swallowed, willing himself a voice.

"Not my family," he muttered, spittle gathering in the corners of his mouth. "Not—Mom died. You let her die."

Carson was already shaking his head, putting up one well-manicured hand in protest.

"I had nothing to do with that. Circumstances beyond my control, Nox, you must believe me. I didn't even know she was pregnant."

Nox wanted to kill him. He wanted just enough energy to rise out of this bed and kill his father, the way he'd killed that piece-of-shit rapist, Mr. White. Because White had violated her, but Carson was the abandoner. He was the one who had delivered a defenseless Natalie to her abuser.

"You left her there! You left... her. And me. And...."

Sam's face—baby to the young man he'd left behind in South Carolina—pierced Nox's brain.

Carson narrowed his gaze, but he didn't utter the name. "Yes. I did. And I am truly sorry for that. If I'd had a choice...."

Nox rolled his eyes. "Your choice to work for murderers and drug dealers. Your choice to disappear."

"I let them think I was dead to protect you," Carson said, soothing and lying in the same breath. Now Nox remembered that sound—the sound of his father placating him, placating Natalie, pretending his absence was anything other than calculated. "I thought it would keep you safe."

"Safe until the storms killed us?"

A flicker behind his father's eyes was like a lie detector test spiking.

CHAPTER TWENTY-SEVEN

"OPEN THE door, Cade!" The sound of the voice coming through the flimsy door stopped Cade in his tracks, midscramble, as he was reaching for the claw hammer in his back pocket.

LJ—in the midst of gathering up the laptop and supplies—froze as Rachel began cursing.

"Goddammit—I'm just going to crush his skull," she hissed, and Cade went for the doorknob.

He exchanged a look with Rachel, who took position behind him, box cutter in hand.

LJ's eyes went wide.

"He's a fed!" he whispered frantically as Cade unlocked the door and Rachel slipped into position.

On the other side, Alec stood in the pouring rain, his hands raised as water streamed down his overcoat. Mud coated his dress pants and nice shoes, his dark hair plastered down over his face. He looked like shit—but Cade didn't lower the hammer.

"I thought you'd be long gone by now," Alec said, still surrendering.

Cade said nothing, carefully checking in either direction to see if this was a trap.

"They think I'm on my way back to Chicago." Alec began to lower his arms. "I left my car at a rest stop and walked."

"Why are you here?"

"I came to warn you, Cade. You and Rachel and your brother—you're playing in a dangerous game and—"

Cade stepped back and slammed the door. He turned to face Rachel, who seemed peeved she wasn't going to get to kill Alec, and LJ, who was still stunned into silence.

"Let's move. I'm going to assume they're following him."

"No one is following me. They think I'm on my way to Chicago," Alec yelled through the door. "I told them you were headed back to South Carolina."

Rachel shrugged, as if she wasn't able to weigh in on the chances of him telling the truth. But she didn't put the box cutter away.

Cade took a calculated risk. "So now you're helping us?"

"No, I'm protecting you."

"Bullshit," Rachel shouted. "You arrested us."

"I took you into protective custody. For the love of God, open the fucking door. I'm drowning out here."

"Probably better he's inside than yelling out there," LJ pointed out.

Cade nodded, then waited until Rachel looked ready to gut their "friend" if need be.

"You armed?"

"Of course."

"I want the gun before I let you in."

Cursing followed, then a thump as Alec gave the door a hard pound.

A crack of an opening and Cade saw a holstered gun just outside on the front step, currently getting drenched in the deluge. He leaned down to pick it up, gaze locked on Alec.

"Come in."

ALEC STOOD on the tarp in the corner, with Cade holding the gun on him and Rachel stripping him down to his shoes, shirt, and pants while simultaneously searching him.

She was thorough, and Alec didn't flinch.

"He's clean," she said finally, retreating to the corner with a fierce look on her face.

"That's my standard-issue weapon. I don't carry anything else," Alec said.

"Oh right, we should believe you because you aren't a liar or anything." Cade kept the gun trained on Alec's face.

"I was undercover, Cade. There was no way to tell you what was going on." Alec started to raise his hands, but Cade waved the gun until he got the message. "And when we picked you up at the school, I had to make sure no one on my team thought I was compromised."

"They must be pissed you let us escape," Rachel piped up. "Is that why you've been summoned back?"

Alec didn't answer, but the slight downturn at the corners of his mouth was an easy tell—he was charming and proven to be a skilled liar, but everyone had their tells.

"So you're in trouble now. Figure you'll get us to surrender and take us back?" LJ entered the conversation from where he watched, leaning against the far wall, arms crossed over his chest.

"It wouldn't be the worst thing," Alec said, a faint smile on his face.

"Fuck no."

"I guessed as much, but thanks for articulating it, Rachel." The quip was lighthearted, but Alec's eyes looked sad. "My secondary plan would be to advise you not to try to get onto the island."

Cade shook his head, about three seconds from handing the gun to Rachel and letting her blow off some steam. "This has nothing to do with you or your investigation. Nox is innocent and he's out there— we're going to find him. So put your coat back on, get your car, and go back to Chicago."

"Unless you have some information you can give us," LJ added. "What are all those patrols for?"

Alec cocked his head to one side. "You're kidding, right? I'm not sharing anything. I just wanted to warn you because…." He looked directly at Cade, almost imploring in his tone. "You need to leave as soon as possible."

Rachel stepped out from her perch behind Cade. She walked between the two men, until she was right up in Alec's personal space. "When's the raid scheduled for?"

Alec looked uncomfortable.

"Soon, I'm guessing. You evacuated the waterfront, which must've alerted the District police, because they're going crazy shoring everything up. Which means…." She tilted her head, and Cade saw Alec's dusky skin go a little pink.

Another tell.

"It's happening from the inside. More undercovers? Hmmmm." Rachel turned back to Cade, her expression one of calculated delight.

"Maybe that sort of chaos is just what we need to slip in without anyone knowing."

It happened in a quicksilver minute; Alec moved and grabbed Rachel around the neck in a choke hold, her throat trapped under the pivot of his elbow. She fought against him, kicking backward with fist and foot, trying to break free.

Paralyzed for a second—because stupid, stupid, he'd forgotten this wasn't Alec, his Alec, because that person was a lie—Cade threw himself at the melee, even as the sonic boom of LJ rushing into the fray nearly knocked him down.

"Don't!" Alec yelled, inexplicably loosening his grip as he stepped back and hit the wall in a few steps. No way out. "I just—you need to listen! Get out of here, forget your friend. If he's not dead, he will be in the next forty-eight hours! I'm trying to help you!"

Rachel struggled harder as Cade continued with a wavering arm to train the gun on Alec's rapidly paling face.

"Let her go, right the fuck now," LJ warned, his voice low as he inched closer. "You don't have anywhere to go."

Alec's gaze darted from the menace of LJ to the gun in Cade's hand. Everything seemed to slow down, an overpowering stench of tension and fear filling the trailer.

Alec seemed to make a decision; he squeezed Rachel a fraction tighter, then threw her to the ground.

Down on her hands and knees, Rachel choked and gasped, fighting to regain the lost air. LJ seemed momentarily torn between grabbing her and murdering Alec, but Cade beat him to the punch.

On autopilot, he pushed forward, not stopping until the gun was resting against Alec's forehead.

"Go ahead," Alec murmured. "My career is over, and we'll both be dead soon enough. What's a few days early?"

Behind him, Cade could hear LJ urging Rachel up.

"Save a bullet for yourself." Alec's last words before Cade brought the gun back and bashed him in the temple.

They tied him up—Cade and LJ, as Rachel lay on the pallet with a rain-soaked rag at her throat. Occasionally she coughed, and LJ's attention would be drawn back to her corner, and then his hands would be rough on the unconscious fed at their feet.

"Shoulda killed him," LJ muttered under his breath, a change in tune a shaken Cade didn't dispute. He tried to imagine how he'd feel if Alec had tried to kill Nox, then pushed on in making sure his former friend was firmly bound.

"We need to find out what he knows," Cade said wearily, standing up on rubber legs.

"If there's gonna be a raid or somethin' in the next forty-eight hours, we don't have much time to find your boyfriend." LJ looked up at Cade, a sorrowful line to his mouth. "They light that place up.... I'm just sayin'. Whoever has him, wherever he is—chances are this shit is gonna be in the same place."

"We don't have a fucking clue who has him." Cade paced around the tiny space, the air seeming to have been sucked almost entirely out. On the roof, more torrential rain beat down, echoing his frustration. "The District cops? The drug dealers?" Another player they didn't know about yet?

A chess match indeed, on a board soaked with gasoline and sparks around every turn.

"Alec had to be desperate to come and warn us. Whatever it is, it's going to be big." Cade walked over to Rachel; she gave him one of her patented bitch faces, but her eyes were scared. "We're running out of time."

"So let's move. We leave him here, we take our stuff, and we walk down to the checkpoint," LJ said suddenly.

Cade turned to find LJ rifling through Alec's pockets.

"What the hell are you talking about?"

"We get ourselves arrested by the District police, they give us a free ride over there, we head out to find Nox."

"Okay, sure, that sounds easy," Cade snapped. "Why didn't I think of that?"

"Because you forgot I was with you." LJ pulled his hand out of Alec's pocket, a leather billfold in hand. "You're the only person they're looking for over there. Vigilante's dead, remember? Sam ain't here. Mason ain't here."

"Rachel's here."

"Rachel ain't named by the District police as a person of interest." LJ stood up, flipping through the billfold as he did. "Just you, little brother."

LJ's plan dawned on him slowly.

"Turn myself in, get to the island."

"Break out and there you go."

LJ plucked out a thin plastic card and showed it to Cade with a smirk on his face. "Nice government-issue card—my friends are gonna have a good time with this."

Cade—exhausted and with no hope of finding a rock bottom any time soon—dropped next to Rachel for something very close to cuddling. He didn't want to look at Alec, who, despite being still alive, hadn't woken up from the blow to the head. He left LJ with his laptop, the storm overhead preventing them from venturing out. Given the way the trailer rocked and moaned, they would be lucky not to slide into the water by morning.

Maybe they could float to the island.

Rachel lay quietly, rag still around her throat, tucked under a duvet of canvas. He didn't ask for permission, and she didn't shove him away—proof at least that he wasn't pushing a limit by resting his head against her shoulder.

"Do you think he's dead?" he whispered, pressing his nose against the dank oily smell of her borrowed clothes.

Rachel coughed as she tried to speak, then shook her head.

"Me neither."

LJ's clicking and occasional chortles of delight ran counterpoint to the anger of the storm around them.

"You and LJ, you should leave," he told Rachel in hushed tones. Even with his eyes closed, he'd lost the ability to pretend this wasn't the subbasement of hell.

A sting made him jump—Rachel had pinched the back of his hand.

"Shut. Up," she mouthed when he looked at her.

"You could go somewhere safe."

She rolled her eyes, eloquent even without words.

"LJ's a good guy. He'll make a good husband," he murmured, unable to keep a straight face as Rachel's glare turned murderous. "White picket fence, maybe a dog—ow! Ow!"

He checked to make sure she hadn't torn off the flesh with that pinch.

Cade settled back down against her shoulder, the crunch of the tarp beneath them almost comforting. The windows rattled, and LJ let out a "hot damn" before resuming a stream of muttering under his breath.

A fool's errand, a surefire way to end his damn life. He seemed to be unable to stop touching this burning hot stove with the potential to kill him. Logically he should take LJ and Rachel, get into Alec's car, and drive to his aunt's cabin. The intelligent choice—cut his losses, turn his back on a world of madness and riddles he had no part of.

He could walk away, because this wasn't his mess.

But Nox's face—angry, dangerous, confused, tender—was imprinted behind his eyes, and every time he touched the path that led him away, something pulled him back.

Foolhardy.

The worst decision he could make.

Clearly, it was love.

"Momma and Daddy would be so proud," LJ announced, startling Cade out of his hazy pit of confusion.

"What?" he asked as he sat up.

"I'm a goddamn fed." LJ grinned at Cade and snapped a salute as well. "They're uploadin' the new info to the card's chip, and then once this storm settles, we can set this little passion play in motion."

"So you're a fed, and I'm your prisoner. What about Rachel?"

"She's one of your victims." LJ *tsked* and shook his head. "A hostage, Mr. Creel? You're a fucking dick. I hope they shoot you."

"Don't joke—that's a very good possibility for all of us." Cade crept across the floor toward LJ, sparing a glance for Alec, who was curled up with his eyes closed in the corner. "I'm thinking the District cops don't much like the feds."

"Probably not. Which is why I'm gonna have to act like a douche bag who has information to sell." LJ clicked on his laptop, nodding to himself. "One of my friends suggested that."

"Tell your friends to use their skills to hack the police station mainframe." Cade sat next to LJ, trying to make sense of the stream of data in several different windows. Chats were going on, a rapidly moving conversation in tiny white print on a black background. Another showed a progress bar at 75 percent, while still two more appeared to be satellite maps of the area.

"Already working on it, but that is some complicated shit. Got my buddy Lenny workin' on those money records we found before. Backtracking through the deposits, see if we can't find out exactly who's been stashing money there for so long."

"Jesus Christ—if I wasn't so grateful I'd be terrified of your little anti-American hacker circle."

LJ seemed to take umbrage at the characterization. "Antigovernment—I like America just fine."

Chapter Twenty-Eight

"The storms happened, Nox. I had nothing to do with that," Carson said, his slick, used car salesman tone at odds with his expensive suit and haircut. "Things were moving so quickly."

Nox laughed, bitter and cold. "Moving so—I realize it was seventeen years ago, but I remember it very fucking clearly. You were away for months. You left Mom in that disgusting asylum. You left me at the house." He narrowed his gaze as the memories of those days and the sheer unadulterated terror of meeting Jenny and the men trying to kill them washed over him. "You sent Jenny to kill Mom and me. Don't you try to deny it."

It was a calculated move. His trust of Rachel was tenuous, but the stark reality resonated inside him—he trusted her a thousand times more than his father.

Carson's eyes widened, his body stiffening at the accusation.

"Jenny? My assistant wouldn't do anything like that," he said, recovering quickly. "She died on the ferry, Nox. Poor girl."

"Really? You didn't know?" Nox tipped his head to one side, ignoring his vulnerable position, pinned to the bed by his injuries and at the mercy of a man who hadn't told him a lick of truth in possibly his entire damn life. "She came to Morningside to kill Mom, but she was already dead." His heart fluttered, but his voice stayed calm. "Then she tried to kill me, but I managed to buy her off to leave me there." Nox watched his father with as much focus as he could muster, very aware of every bead of sweat creeping along Carson's hairline. "This was all before her tragic death."

When he finished speaking, the room was utterly silent. He felt every breath controlled in his lungs, the sparks of pain from his wounds mere flickers compared to the growing rage.

"She—I mean, I'm shocked," Carson said faintly. Finally. "Jenny was such a sweet young girl…."

"Who did your dirty work, compiling blackmail material on government officials." Nox finished Carson's sentence and watched him go pale. "I assume she killed for you as well. I saw her in action—getting rid of whatever henchmen were sent along. At least four." In a conversational tone, the words fell out of Nox's mouth. "Did you send them as well? Roy Grimes, the guys at the rendezvous point. I'm just curious. Dad."

Carson's shoulders went back, the first defensive move Nox had seen from him. "So you think you know everything," he said, leaning his hands on the small table at the end of the bed. "You think you have all the answers."

Nox shrugged, a twinge of pain shooting down his spine. He didn't even flinch. "I know enough."

His father's fingers tightened on the edge of the table, going white with tension.

"You don't know anything."

"Is this where you tell me the whole sinister plan? I assume it'll be quite justified, after which you'll blow my head off or dump me in a pit of alligators."

With every poke, Carson's expression grew angrier.

"I kept you and your little brother alive, all this time," Carson exploded. "I let you play fucking superhero on the streets. I let you interrupt my business. You should be dead about a thousand times over, and don't you ever forget that."

Nox couldn't hide his derision. "Fuck you. You should have killed me," he snapped, rage coursing through him.

"Oh really? I should have? Then what would have happened to the kid, huh? You think I was going to waltz in and raise Natalie's bastard?"

Jerking his torso off the bed, Nox reached for his father with both hands, fingers itching to close around his throat, to snap his neck like he had Mr. White's. He bit his tongue as the anger waged war with the ravages of his weakened state.

"I protected you," Carson spat, not even flinching as Nox wrenched his body in a vain attempt to get at him. "I'm protecting you now. The Vigilante is dead, your friends are free, and I scraped you off the fucking pavement. You don't want to be grateful? Fine. I'll dump you on the street and let the District cops throw you in jail. I'm thinking some of the inmates might be interested in learning who you are."

With that, Carson shoved the table to the floor, the clattering sound echoing as he stormed to the door, wrenched it open, and left. In the space of the door going from open to closed, Nox caught sight of Antonio laughing.

Nox fell back against the pillows, furiously twisting against the tangle of the bedclothes.

No one came to check on him, not Kyle, not Antonio or the doctor. His IV dried up, and his head began to pound with the withdrawal from whatever they had been injecting into his line. The pain, exacerbated by his encounter with his father—Jesus, his father—wrecked his ability to think about or deal with what had transpired. Time seemed to drag on until he felt the burning pain of fever, the swollen tongue filling his dry mouth.

In the twilight of his pain and delirium, he sank into his too few memories of Cade, catching and trying to hold on to them as they slipped through his fingers. He felt Cade in his arms, the pressure of his head against Nox's shoulder, the simple peace Nox gained from touching him. Maybe that was the dream and this was purgatory, an endless wheel of paranoia and darkness, where respite came in the form of a tease and a man with blue eyes.

NOX COULDN'T quite grasp what was going on; the rattle of metal and then he was moving, the bed was moving, released from its mooring and banging against doorjambs and walls he could see as his eyes flickered open. In his hazy vision, he could make out Dr. Khanna at his side; when he tried to speak, nothing came out.

"You're being moved," Dr. Khanna said, and that was when Nox became aware of a thudding noise, a growing whine filling the air. Something—machinery perhaps.

Then the smell overwhelmed him.

The white walls and lighting gave way to darkness, the dank smell of rot and decay hitting his nose and irritating his gag reflex.

"Turn on a flashlight," the doctor snapped. Nox heard fumbling, cursing, and then a bright flash of light trained over his head revealed crumbling pink plaster and peeling walls.

Another nightmare. He knew this place.

The wheels of the bed ground through something, their forward movement slowed as the men pushing tried to get it free. The sounds grew louder, forming into a memory for Nox.

Construction equipment.

A shove and the bed came free, and they started moving down the hallway again. At a corner, they pivoted, sending Nox into inky black darkness.

He waited for lights, for Dr. Khanna to issue another terse order, but nothing came. The light moved—away from him, away from the bed. No voices save for one whispered thing before the door slammed shut.

"Don't bother screaming."

Interlude

CARSON BOYET comes home from Harvard for his twenty-first birthday. It's also Christmas, but he could care less. Twenty-one means inheritance, a big fat check delivered into his hand and freedom from beneath his father's thumb.

He can taste the South of France on his tongue and feel the soft, bronzed skin of an eligible model under his fingertips.

So close.

Oh, he'll graduate Harvard. He might even apply to graduate school. An MBA from Wharton sounds about right. But it will be for him, for his résumé and his bragging rights, not his father's.

The grandfather he never knew is his ticket to freedom.

He all but skips through their Upper West Side apartment to his father's study, anxious to get this meeting over with. Once he gets the details settled, there's a party to attend downtown.

Carson knocks twice, then waits for his father's sharp "enter." He pulls his most "devoted son" expression and walks in, a pleasant smile across his face.

His father points to the uncomfortable guest chair in front of his desk, and that's when Carson realizes there's another man in the room.

The suit is Savile Row, the moustache unfortunate, and the accent South American. That's what registers first, as Mr. "Smith," as he's introduced, begins to give a historical overview of the long-standing relationship between his family's business and the Boyets.

Carson doesn't give a flying fuck, but he's been beaten into perfect manners by a long line of nuns, nannies, and his mother. He can pretend he cares.

Then, when Mr. "Smith" has concluded his recitation, Carson's father clears his throat.

It's time, he says, for Carson to know the true nature of the family business. And what happens next for Carson.

Confusion clouds his mind. What happens next? What happens next is he gets drunk in the parentless apartment of his fraternity brother Louis Ravek, fucks a prostitute, and celebrates the fact that he's about to come into money his father cannot touch or control.

That isn't what happens.

None of that happens, and Carson doesn't even get that MBA from Wharton.

Two weeks after he graduates from Harvard, he marries a slender, fragile girl named Natalie von Zandt, whose family controls a solid third of the real estate in Manhattan priced at a minimum of twenty million dollars. The von Zandts welcome a frozen-faced Carson into the family, happily signing over control of their assets to their daughter's new husband, a faint whiff of relief permeating the room.

Carson's father is pleased. So is Mr. Smith.

Two years later, Nox is born. Six weeks afterward, Carson returns home to the posh Ninety-First Street townhouse to find

Natalie barricaded in the basement, screaming about the invading forces while the baby wails from the nursery upstairs.

He suddenly understands why the von Zandts sold him their daughter and their real estate empire.

When his father dies suddenly of a heart attack while on business in Colombia, the business world mourns. And Carson? Carson counts it as the best day of his life so far. The money he wires to the associates of Mr. Smith? Worth every single penny.

CHAPTER TWENTY-NINE

THE RAIN died off in the middle of the night.

Outside, the sky cleared and moonlight hit the trailer like a spotlight.

"Let's go," Cade said quietly.

"What about him?" LJ—now dressed in Alec's nearly dry suit, hair slicked back—kicked at the back of the still unconscious fed's leg.

"Leave him. Let's assume he was telling the truth and he came alone—we have time before anyone realizes he's not where he's supposed to be."

Rachel grunted, leaning against the wall of the trailer. Cade could read her expression clearly—it said *put a bullet in his head and be done with it*—but Cade's stomach for killing might only exist when his life was in immediate danger.

Billy came to mind.

But Alec? He still wore the face of a friend, the body of a lover, and while he was handcuffed, unconscious, Cade couldn't make himself do it.

The gun was holstered under LJ's jacket now, safe.

"Everyone remember the plan," he said, earning an eye roll from Rachel and the finger from LJ. "Jesus Christ, we're dead."

The "plan" was fairly simple. A Trojan horse of sorts, as Federal Agent Alec Allard brought "person of interest" Caden Creel to the District police with a desire to "share some information."

Rachel's damsel in distress role was helped by the fact that her voice was nothing more than a scratch, bruises blooming around her throat. The pulled-together costume of rolled-up jeans, a hoodie and rain slicker, and boots made her look like an abused teenager.

It made Cade a little sick.

They trudged through the muddy mess that was the dozed but unfinished ground—formerly home to high-rise office buildings, expensive condos and hotels, and major congested arteries for commuters and visitors traveling into Manhattan.

Now? Deathly quiet, bathed in moonlight, and oppressively dangerous.

A few hundred yards down toward the water, they spotted the only permanent building for miles: the District checkpoint. A small ferry operated on "District Business" only, tightly controlled by the police. Cade spotted at least fifteen uniformed and heavily armed officers milling around behind the barbed wire-topped fence.

They were spotted easily, a large light from atop the fence sweeping in their direction. Cade tensed, hands already up as his fugitive role kicked in.

"I'm a cop!" LJ yelled, waving his card with one hand as Rachel peered out tentatively behind him. "I got a fugitive and a lady—she needs medical attention."

Guns raised in their direction; the sniper in a crow's nest aimed his rifle at Cade's head. A few officers congregated, as if in counsel with each other, and then slowly the gate creaked open.

"Are you armed?" a voice yelled.

"Yeah, I got my service piece." LJ didn't drop the hand with the ID card in it—it was their only hope of getting through this alive. "You need to see it."

A contingent of five cops approached through the shadows, the bright light cutting in and out of their path. They appeared and disappeared with each pass, coming closer with each flash.

"All three of you, hands in the air and down on your knees. Anyone moves, they get shot," the leader yelled again. "Right now. You have three seconds to comply."

"Right, sure," LJ called out, casual as he could be. "ID in my hand. You can check me out."

Cade dropped to his knees, sinking and squelching in the cold mud. Beside him, Rachel fell, collapsing weakly—he spared her a glance and caught the faintest wink as she began sobbing loudly.

"It's all right, ma'am," LJ said loudly as he joined them in the muck. "Just let the cops do their job, okay? We'll get you to a hospital."

As the cops closed the last few feet between them, Rachel's cries grew louder and more desperate, with LJ playing comforting detective. Cade watched the men's faces—mostly impassive up close—but their eyes kept darting from LJ to Rachel.

She swayed a little, then fell to the ground dramatically.

That jump-started the officers out of their hesitation. Someone grabbed Cade, threw him to the ground, and roughly searched him.

"Clear!" the guy shouted as another said the same from beside him.

"You can take the piece—I don't care," LJ was saying. "I need to talk to someone at the department. A sergeant, a captain, please. It's a matter of life and death."

Cade kept his mouth tightly closed, his head turned slightly to keep the offensive-smelling mud and construction debris from restricting his breathing. Murmurs of conversation—and no one directly answering LJ—increased his concern. This was a ridiculous plan. They were all going to die.

"They're bringing a stretcher!" someone yelled in the distance, and Cade's spiral slowed just a bit.

Rachel's melodramatic cough-sobs amped up as one of the officers yanked Cade off the ground.

"Let's go," he said, barely waiting for Cade to get his footing before pushing him toward the bright lights and more heavily armed men.

They put him in a small windowless cell, still shackled. He slid down to sit on the floor, breathing through a tiny panic attack because, Jesus Christ, what was the next bit of the plan? What was going on with LJ? Where was Rachel? His thoughts raced and rambled, hands and arms going numb in his lap from the weight of the handcuffs.

What if they just shot him? What if the hackers had done a shitty job on the ID and LJ was dead?

He shook under the weight of this madness until light-headedness brought his forehead to his knees.

Breathe. Breathe. He could do this.

The door rattled for a moment, then creaked open to reveal a female guard armed to the teeth and wearing a bulletproof vest. She came into the cell and leaned down to unlock his cuffs.

"Come with me," she said, neutral and banal in tone.

He got to his feet, rubbing his hands together in an attempt to bring some feeling and use back into them; the officer turned to walk out, and that was when Cade realized she didn't have her gun drawn.

In a large white room in the back—with a killer view of the water and District skyline behind wired glass—LJ sat at a long table, a large Styrofoam cup of coffee in his hand and a plate piled high with sandwiches in front of him. Rachel, wrapped in a green blanket, sat next to him.

Cade faltered at the door. Rachel's previous performance of noisy tears was gone; despite the bruises and dirt, she held her head high and her eyes had a calculating look.

He'd be terrified if not for LJ's big smile.

"Come in, come in. I was just telling these officers some interesting information," LJ said, raising his cup in toast.

The officers in the room ranged in age from twenty-five to fifty, judging by the oldest man's military-cut gray hair. They were all wearing the same expression of neutral authority, including the only one allowed a seat.

It was Detective Francis, the man who had arrested Sam and charged him with being the bomber.

The man's smirky grin confused Cade, even as his body rejected any attempts to move it from the doorway. Francis tipped back his chair, gesturing at the empty seat with aplomb. He couldn't have looked more out of place if he had been wearing full Joker makeup.

"How are you doing, Mr. Creel?" he asked.

Someone pushed Cade from behind, and he stumbled into the room. "I...."

"Maybe some coffee would help. How about a blanket?" He snapped his fingers at the youngest of the officers, and the flicker of a snarl alerted Cade to what had been apparent when last they'd met— everyone thought Detective Francis was a piece of shit.

Cade dropped into the chair closest to LJ, shivering a little as the cool air of the room mixed uncomfortably with his wet, dirty clothing.

"Agent Allard was telling me all about your adventures," Francis said, rubbing two fingers on the table in ever-widening circles. "And what you're trying to do."

This didn't sound like the plan; LJ was grinning, Rachel just sitting there with her lips pursed, and Cade had no idea what to say or do. The only things he had at this moment were a host of acting skills and a desperate need to stay alive.

"How lucky you're the person we met today," Cade said coolly. He glanced around, judgment plain on his face. "Interesting promotion."

Francis's smug face fell at that. "Change in leadership at the precinct—you know how it is. Politics."

Someone coughed, another person cleared his throat, and the snarl came back to the policeman's mouth.

"Of course," Cade said graciously, as the young officer returned with another large cup of coffee and a blanket that matched Rachel's. "Maybe this is an even more fortuitous event than I thought."

Detective Francis opened his mouth to speak, then glanced over his shoulder at the silent assemblage.

"Get out, all of you," he snapped. No one refused his order, though the pure contempt thrown his way was impossible to miss.

When the room was cleared and quiet, Cade tucked himself in the blanket and toyed with the steaming cup in his hand.

Rachel made a little gesture, her arm peeking out from behind the blanket. Fingertips together, tipping her head toward Francis.

"You think you can do something with our information, then?" Cade wrapped his hands around the coffee.

Francis laughed—a "ha ha ha" sound, fake and disingenuous. "I think I can turn you all over to the District police and get my money back. Orrrrr—I turn you over to some friends of mine and make a fucking fortune. Maybe enough to retire."

"Or we can arrange a third option—perhaps give everyone what they want in order to get what we want."

LJ pointed at Cade. "Good idea, good idea."

Detective Francis let his gaze linger on each of them, as if trying to determine if they were telling him the truth. Cade suspected that even if he'd once been an actual cop, those skills were long deteriorated, fallen to ruin and overrun by his selfish motivations. Satisfied they were going to help him get what he wanted, Francis nodded.

"So I bring you to the city, but maybe you get lost before you hit Central Booking," he said finally.

Cade tried to control his expression.

"Then we go to the house, we get the money," LJ added, drawing Francis's eyes to him. Dollar signs glowed over Francis's head.

"I want proof it's as much as you say."

LJ lit up like fucking Christmas.

"Bring me a laptop."

EPILOGUE

"LET'S GO," Francis said about two hours later, startling Cade out of a daydream where he wasn't cold and afraid and unable to breathe properly. He blinked himself back to full consciousness to find Rachel curled up in LJ's lap and Francis grinning maniacally from the doorway.

"Okay, sure." Cade got out of the chair with creaky legs and shaking hands, his gaze meeting LJ's.

LJ smiled, a half grin that was probably 40 percent bullshit—Cade matched it with one of his own.

They could both pretend they felt secure about getting on a boat with a crooked cop.

As they walked through the building, the officers who bothered to glance up gave them nasty looks—and a few pitying, which didn't sit well in Cade's stomach. The cops all expected the three of them to be floating in the waves before they touched the shore of the District.

"We're going to the house," Francis muttered when they reached the back door. His beady eyes alighted on Cade, greed dripping from his pores. "I get the money, and then I let you go. If you try anything…." The gun in view on his waist punctuated the threat.

Cade nodded slowly. "We don't have anything to gain by crossing you," he said, allowing a shaking timbre to his tone. The sound made Francis grin. "We need you."

Francis opened the door, waving them through. The wind rattled Cade as he stepped into the darkness.

THE TINY boat bobbing at the docks had clearly seen better days.

LJ—Rachel tucked tightly at his side—went first. The floodlights picked them up as they stumbled down some concrete stairs toward the dock. The cold bit into Cade's face as he watched LJ's broad back a few steps ahead.

Francis came up next to him, shoulder to shoulder in a weird intimacy that made Cade uncomfortable.

"You're a pretty boy," Francis muttered, his voice cutting through the wind. "Maybe you need a daddy when this is over...."

Cade swallowed down a rise of bile.

But he was an actor, a professional whore, and a man who could seduce open the wallet of anyone with a working dick.

"Maybe I do," Cade said, flashing Francis a sideways look, with flirty eyes.

He didn't flinch when Francis licked his lips.

He could do this.

He would do whatever it took to get to Nox.

The Vigilante: Book One

In a dystopian near future, New York City has become the epicenter of decadence—gambling, the flesh trade, a playground for the wealthy. And underneath? Crime, fueled by "Dead Bolt," a destructive designer drug. This New City is where Nox Boyet leads a double life. At night, he is the Vigilante, struggling to keep the streets safe for citizens abandoned by the corrupt government and police. During the day, he works in construction and does his best to raise his adopted teenaged son, Sam.

A mysterious letter addressed to Sam brings Nox in direct contact with "model" Cade Creel, a high-end prostitute working at the Iron Butterfly Casino. Suspicion gives way to an intense attraction as dark figures from Nox's past and the mysterious peddlers of Dead Bolt begin to descend—and put all their lives in danger. When things spin out of control, Cade is the only person Nox can trust to help him save Sam.

www.dreamspinnerpress.com

TERE MICHAELS unofficially began her writing career at the age of four when she learned that people got paid to write stories. It seemed the most perfect and logical job in the world, and after that, her path was never in question.

(The romance writer part was written in the stars—she was born on Valentine's Day.)

It took thirty-six years of "research" and "life experience" and well… life… before her first book was published, but there are no regrets (she doesn't believe in them). Along the way, she had some interesting jobs in television, animation, arts education, PR, and a national magazine—but she never stopped believing she would eventually earn her living writing stories about love.

She is a member of RWA, Rainbow Romance Writers, and Liberty States Fiction Writers. Her home base is a small town in New Jersey, very near NYC, a city she dearly loves. She shares her life with her husband, her teenaged son—who will just not stop growing—and two exceedingly spoiled cats. Her spare time is spent watching way too much sports programming, going to the movies and for long walks/runs in the park, reading her book club's current selection, and volunteering.

Nothing makes her happier than knowing she made a reader laugh or smile or cry. It's the purpose of sharing her work with people. She loves hearing from fans and fellow writers, and is always available for speaking engagements, visits and workshops.

Find her at:

Website: www.teremichaels.com
Twitter: @teremichaels
Facebook: www.facebook.com/tere.michaels.9

When drama threatens to ruin a romance on a reality show, only a true friend can save a groomzilla's wedding.

Daniel Green, an event planner with a neat, quiet, orderly life, reluctantly agrees to plan the wedding of his childhood friend Ander, an outrageous fashion designer soon to marry a wealthy entertainment lawyer named Rafe. To complicate matters, the happy couple have agreed to have their wedding made into a reality show—something that practical Daniel isn't sold on.

Daniel is neither a romantic nor a wedding planner, but he's the only person in the world who can manage Ander. Distracting him from his mission is Owen Grainger, a too-handsome-to-be-true producer whose quiet charm pulls Daniel into his orbit.

When the stress of the show triggers bad behavior from Ander, co-producer Victor Pierce decides it's the key to a ratings bonanza, and he begins to undermine Ander and Rafe's relationship to create more drama. Daniel is determined to protect his friend and his own reputation, but when he finds himself falling hard for Owen, there's much more at stake than ratings.

www.dreamspinnerpress.com

Just a Drive by Tere Michaels

After weeks of flirting, "One Night" Wyatt Walsh spends a fabulous night with his shy coworker, Benji Trammell. As Wyatt tries to sneak out the next morning, he receives a call from his frantic, very pregnant best friend Raven—she needs him immediately. With no other way to get from New York City to the Pennsylvania town where Raven and her husband live, Wyatt accepts Benji's offer to drive him there. Wary and unsure of each other, they start the trip at odds, but as time goes on, the barriers that usually keep people at a distance fail. And what started out as "just a drive" becomes a step toward romance.

www.dreamspinnerpress.com

The holidays are a time for celebration, discovery, coming home, and maybe even miracles for those who are lucky. From the streets of New York City, to the wintery wonderland of the Maine woods, to the quaint, small town charm of Idaho, the men in these stories have different holiday desires. They're looking for familiarity or fresh starts, but they have one thing in common—their happily ever afters might be waiting in the last places they think to look. Come see what they unwrap in these stories by three acclaimed authors of male/male romance.

Holiday Roommates by Tere Michaels

As an actor without prospects, Nate Brandywine needs an emergency roommate for the month of December. During a humiliating gig as a Christmas elf at a NYC department store, he meets Sean Callahan, his producer and a man struggling under the weight of a past-due loan. Sean's desperate for a place to stay in the city for a few weeks. A month of sharing a workplace and an apartment with someone you can't stop flirting with? Maybe the holidays won't be so terrible after all.

www.dreamspinnerpress.com

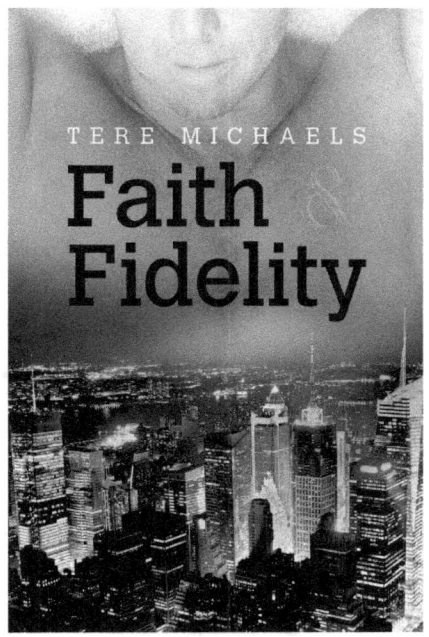

Faith, Love, & Devotion: Book One

Reeling from the recent death of his wife, police officer Evan Cerelli looks at his four children and can only see how he fails them. His loving wife was the caretaker and nurturer, and now the single father feels himself being crushed by the pain of loss and the heavy responsibility of raising his kids.

At the urging of his partner, Evan celebrates a coworker's retirement and meets disgraced former cop turned security consultant Matt Haight. A friendship born out of loneliness and the solace of the bottle turns out to be exactly what they both need.

The past year has been a slow death for Matt Haight. Ostracized from his beloved police force, facing middle age and perpetual loneliness, Matt sees only a black hole where his future should be. When he discovers another lost soul in Evan, some of the pieces he thought he lost start to fall back in place. Their friendship turns into something deeper, but love is the last thing either man expected, and both of them struggle to reconcile their new and overwhelming feelings for one another.

www.dreamspinnerpress.com

Faith, Love, & Devotion: Book Two

Seattle Homicide Detective Jim Shea never takes work home with him—until now. A judge banged his gavel, declared a defendant not guilty, and laid waste to a family. The emotional fallout of the trial leaves Jim vulnerable and duty-bound to the victim's dying father.

It's that man's story that screenwriter Griffin Drake and his best friend, actress Daisy Baylor, see as their ticket out of action blockbusters and into more serious fare. But to get the juicy details, Griffin needs to win over the stoic and protective Detective Shea. Their attraction is immediate, and Daisy encourages Griffin to use it to their advantage: secure the man, secure the story. Neither man has had much luck when it comes to love, and when their one night together evolves into a long weekend of rapidly intensifying feelings, both Griffin's fierce loyalty to Daisy and his very career is put to the test.

Because the more Griffin is drawn into a new life with Jim, the more his Hollywood life falls apart. Secrets and broken trust threaten Griffin's relationships, and he'll have to choose between telling the truth or writing a Hollywood ending.

www.dreamspinnerpress.com

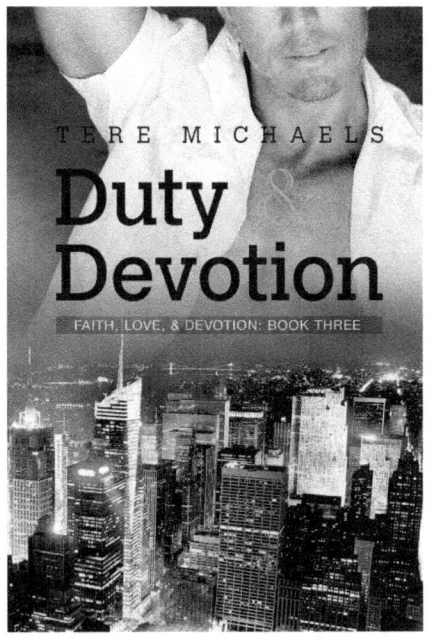

Faith, Love, & Devotion: Book Three

A year after deciding to share their lives, Matt and Evan are working on their happily ever after—which isn't as easy as it looks. As life settles down into a routine, Matt finds happiness in his role as the ideal househusband of Queens, New York, but he worries about Evan's continued workaholic—and emotionally avoidant—ways. Trying to juggle his evolving relationship with Evan and his children, Matt turns to his friend, former Seattle Homicide Detective Jim Shea.

The continued friendship between Matt and Jim is a thorn in Evan's side. Jealous and uncomfortable with imagining their brief affair, Evan struggles to come to terms with what being in a committed relationship with a man means, and the implications about his love for his deceased wife, the impact on his children, and how other people will view him. His turmoil threatens his relationship with Matt, who worries that Evan will once again chose a life without him. But now, the stakes are much higher.

www.dreamspinnerpress.com

Faith, Love, & Devotion: Books Four & Five

Cherish: After several years of happy coupledom, Matt and Evan can relax in the knowledge that their little family has survived the worst of it. The two older girls are away at college, the twins have yet to fully hit teen angst, Matt is doing well with his part time security consulting, and Evan is about to be promoted to captain—it seems like things are calm and bright.

Until they aren't.

As the holidays approach, Evan and Matt get a shock no parent is ever prepared for: feisty Miranda, Evan's eldest, has a new boyfriend, Kent, and they are talking marriage after just three months together. In fact, Miranda wants to bring him to Thanksgiving dinner—along with his parents, Blake and Cornelia.

Blessed: Lives are in transition as everyone gathers at the stunning Hamptons beach home of Daisy and Bennett to celebrate the christening of their new baby. Griffin and Jim—secretly growing tired of their rootless lifestyle—are in a rocky spot in their relationship. And as the godfather, Griffin finds himself yearning for something he's sure Jim won't be interested in.

Fatherhood.

Matt and Evan are looking to reconnect during the long weekend, as their respective careers pull them in separate directions. With less time spent together, Evan grows concerned about what will happen when the last two kids leave the nest.

www.dreamspinnerpress.com

Faith, Love, & Devotion: Book Six

Newly promoted police captain Evan Cerelli takes command of his own precinct as Matt Haight's security business begins to expand at a rapid rate. Both of their careers require more and more of their time—away from home and each other. When his most famous clients, Daisy and Bennett Ames, suffer a traumatic breakup, Matt is drawn into a dangerous and dramatic situation. With attentions diverted, Evan and Matt's tight-knit home life begins to unravel.

As Griffin Drake's movie nears final edit, his thoughts turn toward building a home with his new fiancé, Jim Shea—and maybe even starting a family. Before he can think of a new family, Jim is caught up in his past. The possibility of putting Tripp Ingersoll in jail once and for all beckons, and Jim wants the closure that has long eluded him. As a new lead spurs him on, Jim begins to lose sight of the future by chasing an old ghost.

Both couples struggle to remember that "happily ever after" requires hard work, trust, and tender, open hearts.

ALICIA NORDWELL

ADVERSE EFFECTS

SAVING CAEORLEIA

www.dreamspinnerpress.com

KIM FIELDING

ASTOUNDING!

www.dreamspinnerpress.com

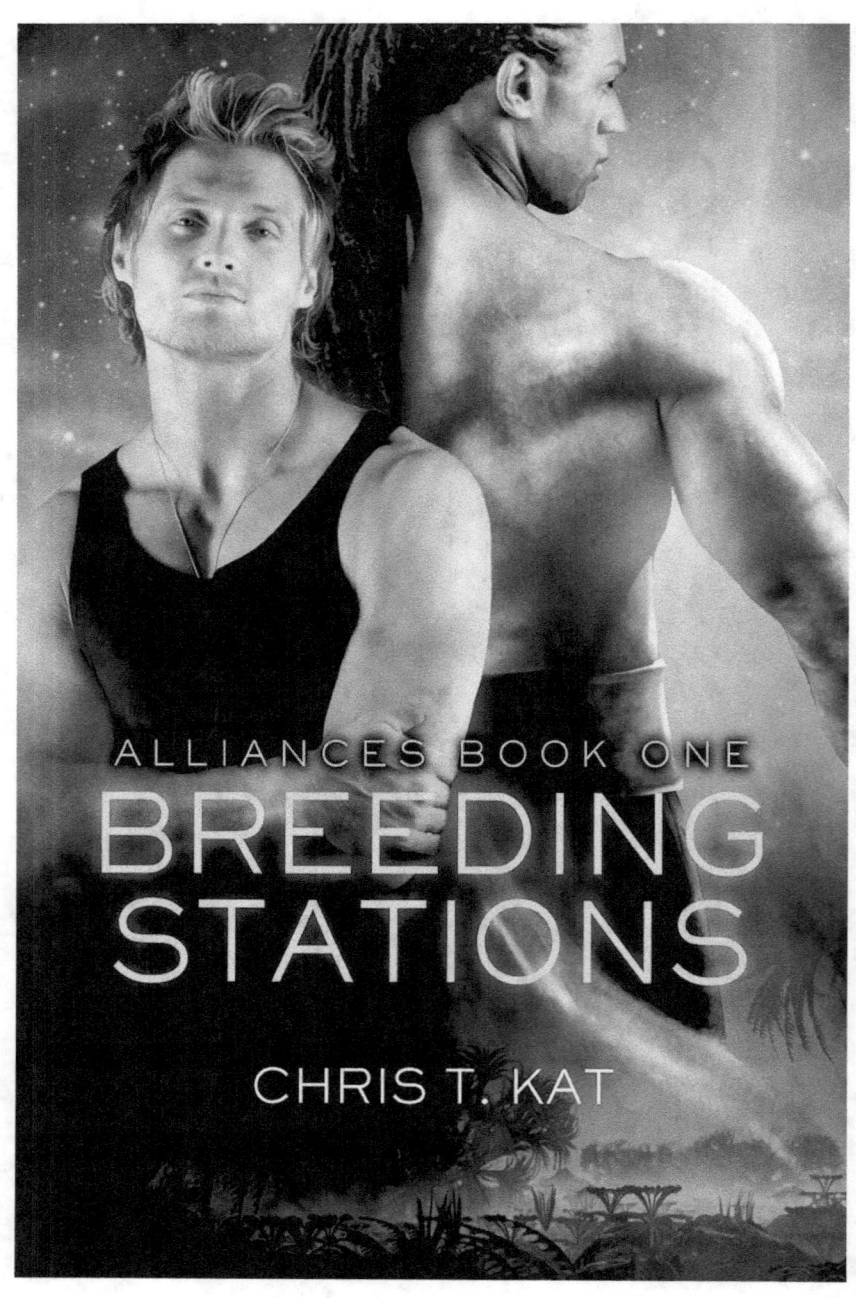

ALLIANCES BOOK ONE

BREEDING STATIONS

CHRIS T. KAT

www.dreamspinnerpress.com

SHORT-CIRCUIT
HIS SOUL

ALANA ANKH

www.dreamspinnerpress.com

www.dreamspinnerpress.com

CAITLIN RICCI

TO THE HIGHEST BIDDER

www.dreamspinnerpress.com

www.ingramcontent.com/pod-product-compliance
Lightning Source LLC
Chambersburg PA
CBHW070108260626
47160CB00004B/1375